Ilona Bannister

When I Ran Away

First published in Great Britain in 2021 by Two Roads
An Imprint of John Murray Press
An Hachette UK company

1

Copyright © Ilona Bannister 2021

A CIP catalogue record for this title is available from the British Library

Hardback ISBN 9781529352658
Trade Paperback ISBN 9781529352665
eBook ISBN 9781529352672
Audio Digital Download 9781529352689

Printed and bound in Great Britain by Clays Ltd, Elcograf S.p.A.

John Murray Press policy is to use papers that are natural, renewable and
recyclable products and made from wood grown in sustainable forests. The
logging and manufacturing processes are expected to conform to the
environmental regulations of the country of origin.

Two Roads
Carmelite House
50 Victoria Embankment
London EC4Y 0DZ

www.tworoadsbooks.com

For my Love, Tim.
For my Life, Leo and Rex.

1

ASH

A Wednesday in August 2016, 7 a.m.
London

Harry's shoes are by the door. Not in the closet, next to the door, but abandoned, right in front of it. Harry leaves them there the way you leave your bed unmade in a hotel room because you know housekeeping will deal with it later. The shoes by the door tell a truth about him. About us.

Back in the beginning, back in New York, when the dimple in his chin and his accent got me every time, there was the day I found him lying on my fire escape, covered in glass with blood on his shirt, wearing his shoes on his hands like two big pot holders. I said, "Harry, what the hell did you do?"

"I heard Johnny screaming and you were gone for bloody ages, I thought he wasn't safe, so I tried to get in, but … it went rather badly," he said to me, and to the super, and to the guy from downstairs who almost called the cops when he saw Harry break the window to my apartment.

I said, "Safe? He was locked in a bathroom in a locked apartment, that's like the safest he could ever be in Brooklyn. You didn't have to climb the fire escape and break the window and knock yourself out—"

"But I wanted you to know you could trust me to do the right thing—"

"Well, you sure fucked that one up, buddy."

And then we all laughed. Because even though Harry put his sneakers over his hands to punch the window he still got cut up on his arm and he fainted and hit his head and that's when I learned that Harry can't handle the sight of blood. And also how much he loved me and Johnny.

What had happened was that the bathroom doorknob fell out of the door, the way it had a thousand times before, and Johnny got locked in. And I was just about to use the screwdriver as a handle to get him out like I always did when Harry walked in with the Chinese food. Except he had dropped a container in the hallway and there was fried rice everywhere. So I went to give him the broom in the hall but then the apartment door shut behind us. Click.

Now Johnny was double-locked in the bathroom and the apartment with me and Harry and the fried rice in the hall with no key. So I said to Harry, "Let me go get the super, he has an extra key, give me five minutes." But if you've ever tried to find a New York super you know that he's never where you think he's going to be and I was gone for a little while and then Johnny started screaming. Harry didn't know, though, that he was just doing that because he liked the sound of his voice bouncing off the bathroom tiles. He didn't know much about kids yet. So Harry took things into his own hands and decided to break in to save Johnny. Of course, all he did was give himself a concussion and ruin his shoes. And break my window.

Anyway, we got Johnny out of the bathroom and wrapped up Harry's arm and put ice on his head and the three of us ate cold Chinese while the super boarded up the window. Then we put Harry in a cab and he left in his socks because one sneaker had glass all stuck in the fabric and the other one was covered in blood. But later when Johnny had gone to bed and I was cleaning up I saw that he had lined up his school shoes next to Harry's messed-up sneakers next to my work shoes in the little closet by the front door. All in a line, like a family. A little family of shoes.

Johnny did that, of course, because he's always known where to put his shoes. I taught him that shoes go in a certain place and that's where he puts them. But Harry – despite our years together, and our life with Johnny, and New York and London, and now the baby – he just leaves them by the door, the way you leave your bed unmade in a hotel room because you know housekeep— I've already said that. It's hard to keep track of your thoughts when you're leaving your husband and you trip over his shoes because he left them by the door again.

We're so far from heroic gestures on fire escapes now. Our beginning was a long time ago. Now there's a patch of my heart that's an open sore, like an ulcer pulsing on the ventricle, or the aorta, or whatever the fuck you call it. And now there's no heart left for the baby. I thought I could make room but I can't. Johnny and Harry took all the heart space I had. And now there's not enough.

The pain is nothing new. The grief and shock and anger, as familiar as my name. But when I became a mother the

3

pain multiplied and grew and stretched my skin and bent my back as far as it would go because the pain a mother feels is not just hers. She feels everyone's pain; she picks it up for her kids, she carries it for the family, she takes it from her parents when they're too old to bear it. She cries when she sees the crying mothers on the news; she tears up when she sees a kid in a wheelchair in the supermarket; she sobs when that Save the Children ad comes on; she has to leave the room when the old man's wife loses the baby in *Up* and that's just a fucking cartoon. Because more than the pain of the person who's hurting she feels the pain of his mother. Of all the mothers. They feel hers too.

But what the fuck do I know?

I know *this*. This is why it's hard to love me and hard for me to love. And why I love so hard when I do. Because this is what I carry. And last night Harry left his shoes by the door again and that's where I found them this morning so I pick them up, I open the door and I hurl them across the street as hard as I can. One lands in the middle of the road and the other one lands on the neighbor's BMW setting off the car alarm. And Harry's yelling at me now, and Johnny's screaming too and the baby's crying and all of them plus the car alarm – they're shattering my skull from the inside and it's time to go.

So I leave them and I start walking.

Manhattan to Staten Island, September 2001

We want to *know* more than we want to survive. We want to know what death looks like before we run away from it. But we don't know that about ourselves until it's happening. Until we see it we don't know that we're the kind of people who run toward death; the kind of people who don't run away even when it's coming for us.

The edge of Manhattan vibrates. Hundreds of people, all of us silent. All of our hearts stop at once. A pause, a moment of quiet, a shared understanding, wordless and bone deep. There is a sound – a drone, long and low, not of our world. We hear it, and then we run. Not toward the terminal doors, to the boat, to safety. We turn around and run to the huge windows, built stories high for the view of lower Manhattan at a time that we would never know again, when our city stood untouchable, piercing the sky. We run to the windows to see the sun blotted out and the City vanish under the smoke and horror, ash and tragedy. We run to the wall of glass, put our hands on the windows, hundreds of pairs of hands reaching for the panes, palms outstretched, like we could stop it. The need to know, the need to put out our hands – so much stronger than the instinct to survive.

On the boat I sit down across from a woman covered in white dust, all over her suit and her hair. She doesn't brush it off. She doesn't know it's there. She's shaking, no shoes, no bag, just wearing a suit and nylon hose. She takes the life jacket from under her seat and puts it on, trembling and silent. Other people do it too because maybe the Staten Island Ferry's the next thing to blow up.

I get up and go to the back of the boat where the doors are open to see if the City's still there but there's nothing except a cloud of gray smoke. It takes a long time to sail out of the cloud. Or maybe it doesn't but that's how it feels. When we pass the Statue of Liberty, sunlight glinting off her torch, somebody starts shouting and people panic because maybe she's the next to blow up. Everyone was relieved to have escaped Manhattan. But now there's a realization seeping through the decks that maybe we're just floating in our graves.

I walk to the steps that go to the next deck up. Keep moving, stay close to the exits, in case, in case …

I focus on one step at a time, one at a time, and then there's his shoes on the landing. Black wingtips but all the decorative holes in the leather are gray, filled in by the falling ash. He must have been caught up in the cloud when he was running for the ferry. I look up at him. The shoulders of his suit are white as if he just came in from a blizzard. His forehead smudged with dust, like Ash Wednesday, except today is Tuesday. He waits for me to reach the landing.

He says, "Hello. Are you alright?" He puts a hand on my elbow.

"No. Are you?"

"No, I don't think I am," he says. A long silence. There's nothing to say. I don't know this man. I mean, I do, he works in the building across from mine and he's British, that's in the accent, but he's talking to me like we know each other. Except we don't.

"Do you need a place to go?" I say, conscious that his hand is still on my elbow, even when we aren't speaking. Under different circumstances it would have been lingering for too long.

"Where am I going now?" he asks.

"Staten Island. Do you know anybody there?" I ask.

"I don't believe so, other than you, if that counts?"

"Sure," I say, but I'm not sure if he answered "yes" or "no." He uses a lot of words.

6

"That's very kind. I'm Harry."

"I'm Gigi."

"That's a nice name."

I don't know what else to say so I say, "My real name is Eugenia Stanislawski."

"I'm sorry to hear that." I get the joke but I don't laugh. Instead I think this guy's a fucking inappropriate asshole because this isn't a time for jokes or flirting but at least I got somebody to talk to so I say, "Is this real?"

He says, "Hold my hand." So I do.

Harry and I go to the same tiny coffee shop across the alley from the back entrance of my office building. I would run over for a break and he'd be in there sometimes. I thought he was cute but he was always in a pink shirt or a three-piece suit and polka-dot socks or something so I figured he was gay. Then I heard him order coffee and I realized he was British. So then I thought, well, too bad he's gay 'cause that accent was sexy. Then last Friday he was two people ahead of me on the line and he turned around with two coffees and handed me one and he said, "I believe it's light and sweet, is that right? Have a lovely day." He walked off before I could say thank you and I thought to myself, *Now that is some classy European shit right there. And that ass ain't too bad either.*

But that was Friday and today is Tuesday and now we're on the Staten Island Ferry. We're looking at the water and holding hands, not because of the coffee but because we need to hold onto something. We're not looking at the City. I feel the tears I haven't cried yet when I suddenly get a picture in my head of all the paper. Office paper, copier paper, reams of paper swirling around outside my office window this morning. I work on the tenth floor so it was strange to see that much paper up so high. I watched it fly past the window when Sharon called my office to tell me she saw the news and that I had better get out of my building. I watched the towers burning from the corner of Wall Street for a minute before I took off my heels to run down Broadway with the wave of people.

I can see it now, the paper flying by the window, and it was theirs, the people who went to work that day – their reports and accounts and files – it fluttered out of their offices like a flock of doves when the planes hit. And the ash. On Harry's shoes, covering that woman, that's not just the tower that fell down, there were people in there. That's the people too. The ash and the paper, they fell like snow. Landed like sledgehammers.

"Gigi, what do we do now?" Harry asks because the boat's docking.

"Follow me," I say. It feels like the decent thing to do, to take him home with me. I take him out through the bottom deck, bypassing the terminal. Staten Islanders know that the bottom level is the fastest way to leave the boat if you don't mind the piss-and-old-beer-salty-swamp smell of New York Harbor. As we leave the boat to cross the parking lot and I see the chaos surrounding the terminal – people in every direction, crying, yelling, laughing, smoking, making calls on cell phones that don't work – it doesn't feel right to leave him there.

The late summer sun is blazing, glorious, oblivious. A girl, early twenties, in her pajamas, twirling around in circles, people leaving a wide berth around her. I tap her on the shoulder and say, "You need help, honey?"

She says, "I moved here last week. I was sleeping. I was sleeping." Before I can say anything else she runs off into the crowd.

Harry and I walk up the hill off Richmond Terrace to my parents' house. There's a clear view of Manhattan from here. But I know the City's burning behind our backs so I don't turn around. I don't want to know what it looks like.

When we get to the house my mom's outside smoking on the steps. My mom and the house both look like they've seen better days except they haven't. That's what they've always looked like – pissed off, shabby, and disappointed. My mother's wearing pink terrycloth bedroom slippers, men's basketball shorts, and her favorite T-shirt. It's fuchsia, XXXL with not much room to give and it says *Livin' la Vida Loca*. My brother, Frankie, gave it to her for Christmas the year the song came out. We all thought it was hysterical because my mother – in her late fifties with a gray buzz cut, a smoker's rasp, and a deep distaste for other people's happiness – was not exactly Ricky Martin's key demographic. But she loved this shirt. It was a good conversation starter. At the deli where she was a regular, Dominic, the meat guy, would always say, "Hey, Donna, how you livin'?"

And she would go, "*La vida loca*, baby!" And they would both laugh until they coughed. Even though that joke didn't make any sense.

She's on better terms with the meat guy than she is with me. Every time I come home since I left when I was seventeen a part of me hopes it will be different and the rest of me knows it won't be. I should've known that a disaster of unprecedented fucking proportions wouldn't suddenly make her Mrs. Cunningham.

I take a deep breath. "Hi, Ma."

"I haven't seen you in, what, a year, and today you drop by?"

"Ma, Manhattan just exploded."

"So it takes some bomb for you to come see us? Hang on, let me roll out the red carpet. Our daughter has returned from the City."

"I'm fine, by the way, thanks for asking."

"Shit hits the fan, you come running home. Life is good, I don't hear a fucking word."

"That's nice, Ma, thanks."

"You should've called first if you were bringing people here." She waves her cigarette at Harry.

"Ma, this is Harry." He puts out his hand but he doesn't know who he's dealing with. She ignores him. "You still could've called."

"Ma, the cell phones aren't working."

"Then what's the point of those things?"

"Can we come inside, please? It's been a rough morning."

Harry tries again. "I'm sorry we aren't meeting under better circumstances. It's been quite a shock for everyone." My mother looks him up and down and I see what she sees: pinstripe suit, slim-cut trousers, pink dress shirt with white cuffs, and he said "quite." Gay and a foreigner. This wasn't going to go well.

"Are you fucking kidding me with this? What the hell is this supposed to be?" Ma fumes from the step.

"Harry, I'm sorry, excuse my mother, she's not a people person. You know what, Ma, I'm glad you're OK, we're going now. We're going to Sharon's. Tell Frankie I'm over there."

"Wait a minute, wait a minute, Gigi, is that you? Donna, I'm waiting for my sandwich!" My dad shuffles up to the screen door in a sleeveless white undershirt and sweat-pants. He's wearing old-man fake-leather slides, with the straps that cross in an X. The kind you buy at the super-market or in the bins outside the 99-cent store. Except for my dad's work shoes, my parents don't buy real shoes anymore. They only go to King of Liquors, Shop Rite and sometimes the Chinese takeout and you don't need real shoes for that.

"Come in, come in, what the hell happened, Gigi, Jesus Christ, are you alright, who's this guy? What happened to you, son, you look terrible. They fell, you know, the towers collapsed. Those sons of bitches. Are you alright, were you there?" He says "collapsed" and I feel it – the sound, the cloud, the ash. Our near miss. I look at my dad. His thinning hair is gelled stiff and combed back from his big face. He's got two homemade tattoos from his army days, one on each arm. They're just blurry blue splotches now – an American eagle on the left arm and a heart on the right. It's been years since you could read "Donna" scrawled inside it.

I force myself to speak to get that sound out of my head: "I don't know, Dad. I just ran. What happened?"

My dad opens the screen door to usher us in but when he looks up into the distance his face goes gray, like his hair. He's looking at what's left of the million-dollar view he used to have. I turn around to see the clouds of smoke pouring out of the skyline. Our view of Manhattan, our American Dream wallpaper. Gone.

My dad says, "Gigi, c'mon, it's over. Don't look."

"They're both gone?"

"Yes, lollipop. Don't look. Are you alright? Donna, where's my sandwich? Jesus Christ, Gigi, get in the house already."

I grab Harry's hand to go inside. My dad goes on: "Kids, come in, come in. Now who is this?" We walk into the living room.

"Dad, this is Harry. I know him from, um, we work together," I say, glancing at Harry so he knows to just go with it. "I found him on the boat and he needed a place to go."

I nudge Harry toward a seat and I look at the living room of my childhood. Brown shag carpeting, olive-green sofas with worn upholstery and Ma's ironic choice of coffee table – "country oak" with hearts carved out on the legs. And, of course, the wood-laminate paneling. It's in every room of the house.

There's a hatch in the wall between the kitchen and the living room. Always handy – an easy way for Ma to pass Dad his sandwiches and yell at us and be sure that we could hear her. Dad moved the TV so she could see it through the hatch from the kitchen. But today there's only the planes crashing over and over. The towers collapsing into dust on repeat.

"'Found him on the boat,' she says, I can't believe you bring perfect strangers here to the house like this," Ma shouts through the hole in the wall.

"Jesus, Ma, Manhattan … I got no fucking shoes on. Please, today can you give me a break?"

"Donna, just make the goddam sandwich! Alright, kids, you OK on that couch? Sorry, what'd you say your name is, son?" I can see the beads of sweat on Dad's top lip. He turns to Harry.

"I'm Harry, it's very kind of you to have me here. It's been quite an ordeal this morning."

"Nice to meet you, I'm Jaroslaw Stanislawski, you can call me Jerry. You met my lovely wife, Donna. What's your name again?"

"Harry."

"Oh, like one of those princes? Right? Prince William and the other one's Harry?"

"Uh, well, I suppose …"

"You know him? Nice guy?"

"No, I don't know any royals, he's still quite young, just a lad really, we just share the name."

"Oh my God, Dad, of course he doesn't know Prince Harry. Do you fucking personally know Giuliani?"

"He's from England. How do you know he doesn't know Prince Harry, you ever aksed him?" Aksed. It took me years to learn to say "ask" with an "s," only after my first boss told me he wouldn't let me on the phone with clients until I could say it right.

"No, I didn't ask him, because not every British person knows the Royal Family, Dad."

"And how do you know I don't know Giuliani? What, you think he's too good for me to know? What, you come around here so much you think you know my associates?"

"No, you're right. I forgot. You're totally a City Hall insider."

"Why're you yelling? We have a guest. Anyway, excuse my daughter, Harry, we tried our best, but what can you do? You know, nature-nurture," and he smacks Harry's knee and laughs his wheezing smoker's laugh and Harry laughs too, out of politeness, or disbelief.

13

"You have a lovely home," Harry says, lying. I don't know him too well but I'm pretty sure he's never seen a completely laminate-paneled living room. "Is this all, um, real wood?" he asks.

"No, laminate. Isn't that amazing how real it looks? So where in England you from, anyway?"

"London."

"Well, well, well. Let's drink to that. Donna, get this man a gin and tonic! That's what you drink over there, right?"

It's clear that my dad's already been at the red wine and Coke. He must have started early, probably after the first plane hit.

"He's British! Donna, pretend you're educated! Get out the good china, the British are coming!" He half laughs and half yells to the kitchen where Ma is putting bologna on white bread and pulling bright yellow cheese slices off plastic sheets. Harry's looking at her through the hatch and I can tell that he's never seen cheese in that format. If he opened the kitchen cabinet, he would've found the spray cheese in a can. But that's only for special occasions. To make rosettes on Ritz crackers as appetizers before Thanksgiving dinner.

"Just a cup of tea would be lovely, thank you." Poor Harry.

"Very fancy, OK, Donna, get this man some tea. Do we have tea?"

"What is this, the fucking United Nations? I got coffee, that's what I got. Oh, wait, I have Sanka. You want a Sanka?"

They're terrified. The sandwiches and the Sanka, the yelling and the jokes. This is too big and all they can do is keep repeating their lines from before it happened. Dad's going to do his stand-up routine and Ma's going to clean the kitchen because if we all keep doing what's normal then everything will be OK. Except that this massive tragedy is unfolding right outside the window and the planes are crashing every ninety seconds on TV. And now I'm here with this guy from the coffee place and my parents are so crazy that even if I wanted to cry, or scream, or just process what happened, I can't. I have to follow the script too so they don't lose their shit. When my hands start to shake I just put them in my lap until they stop.

The news gets worse. The Pentagon, the crash in Pennsylvania, it all blends together. Harry plays cards with my dad. It's strange that he's here but it helps because my parents are trying to act normal. But I shouldn't have brought him. It seemed right in the moment but now all the City's bridges are locked down and the ferry's not taking passengers into Manhattan so he can't get off Staten Island. I don't know what we're going to do with him. I need a drink. I find some jeans and a T-shirt in a box under my teenage bed and I get one of Frankie's old shirts for Harry.

"Ma, have you heard from Frankie yet?" I ask my mother.

"No."

"There probably won't be cell service now for a while. Did he go to work today?"

"How should I know, what am I, friggin' Tom Brokaw with your breaking news?" She brings out more sandwiches and drinks and goes back to the kitchen, keeping herself busy with last night's dishes.

Ma was hurt that Frankie moved out to live with Matty a couple months before. It was time, he was nineteen. He worked at Foot Locker in the mall and delivered pizzas at night. He still came by every day before he went to the pizzeria. Brought Ma her favorite donuts. But he grew up and she wouldn't forgive him.

"He's probably on his way home. I'll try him again." I dial his cell. Still nothing, not even a ring. But he didn't work in the City and he never called anyway. They're probably closing the mall so I bet he left work to go hang out with Michelle, his girlfriend, and smoke a joint and they probably would be here any minute. Right?

Right?

The phone in the kitchen rings. Once, twice, three times. Ma puts one hand on the receiver and waits. She keeps her hand there and doesn't pick up until suddenly she does and answers, "Yeah," not "hello" but "yeah," as if she's in the middle of a conversation. She walks over to the sink, the extra-long phone cord spiralling behind her. She holds the phone against her ear with her shoulder and keeps drying the glass in her hand.

A pause. The silence of held breath just before the exhale into the inevitable. "Yeah," she says again, gasping. She drops the phone and the glass at the same time. Her knees buckle, she falls. The glass shatters into a million diamonds on the linoleum. My father runs to her. Blood and glass. "Donna? Donna!? Donna!!! Donna?" Over and over Dad just keeps yelling her name; first like a question, then a threat, then a plea. Like if he could just get loud enough it would undo this, whatever it is.

My heart stops. I pick the phone up off the floor. "Hello?"

"Gigi ..." Matty, crying. He can't find Frankie. Then there are other words. *Interview. High up, ninety-something floor. Voicemail on Michelle's phone. Did he come home?*

Did he come home?

The phone's attached to the wall in the kitchen and I catch my reflection in the glass of the frame of Frankie's high-school graduation photo. That's how much she loved him. She put his picture in a frame.

Harry at my shoulder, hand on my elbow. "Gigi?"

"Hold on, Matty." My voice is steady. The shrieking in my head isn't coming out of my mouth. I hold the phone to my chest the way you do when you tell someone to hold on. As if this is a normal call, as if I'm going to ask everyone to be quiet in the background and then I'm going to get back on the phone and say, "Sorry about that, anyway ..."

I look at Harry and he looks at me. "My brother," I say. Over Harry's shoulder, through the kitchen doorway, I can see the window and the smoking hole in the skyline. I can't move. Matty's sobs are audible even with the phone pressed to me. I stay still, gripping the receiver, staring at the glass in Frankie's picture frame. I'm not looking at Frankie, though. He's gone. I'm looking at me to check if I'm still here. If now is real.

Broken glass grinding under my mother's weight; my father still yelling her name. If I move, if I take my eyes away from the picture, if I put down the phone, it will be the start of after. Acid burning the back of my throat. My heart beating in my mouth. I don't know if I'm breathing, the air's too hot. Our lives divided now, in this minute, into before and after. If I keep my eyes on his face in the frame can we stay in before?

Everything's moving too fast and everything's moving too slow. I'm under water. I want to ground myself to the earth, into the earth. But there's nothing to hold onto.

Everything spins. The sound of rushing blood fills my ears. Is it mine or Frankie's?

Harry gently takes the phone from me. I think he wants to move me, make me sit down but I keep hold of the wall. Stay focused on the glass in the frame. I find words: "Help my mother."

When I look away from the photo I see Harry with my parents. This morning he was going to work but now he's dusting broken glass off my mother's knees. He helps my dad, unclenches his hand from the edge of the kitchen counter and brings him to a chair. Cleans the cuts on my mother's arm with a dish towel. I keep hold of the wall. Harry finds the whiskey and some coffee mugs and pours my parents a drink. They sob. For a long time. I keep my palms against the wall.

It's a minute later or an hour later when Ma says, screams, "What do we do? We have to do something! What do we do?" She's asking the air; she's asking God.

"We don't know, we don't know that it's true, that he was there. Right? Eugenia, right!" My father pleads with me, shouting; wet, bloodshot eyes searching me for an answer. "Leave a message, tell him to call us," Dad says, once, twice, a hundred times, not understanding that the cell phones aren't working; that I can't leave a message; that if Frankie were alive he would be here with us by now watching this shit on TV; that his son will never answer the phone again because his son is dead. But still, for my dad, I dial Frankie's number again and again from the kitchen phone, knowing that it won't ring and that he won't pick up.

There's nothing to do. There's no hospital to go to, no ambulance to call, no rescue to make, we can't do any of the things that you do in a disaster to make yourself feel useful, less impotent in the face of fate. We can't go to the City, everything's on lock down. This isn't a fire in someone's house where we could stand outside and watch them pull Frankie out on a stretcher, or see him walk out covered in soot and coughing. This isn't a car accident on Hylan Boulevard that we could drive to, or an ER we could meet him at and run alongside his gurney. There's nothing, nothing, there is nothing. Nothing to do but wait for the phone to never ring with his voice on the other end of the line. My dad drinks from the mug with Garfield wearing a Santa hat and my mom holds the one that says Exxon. One was a Christmas gift long ago, the other a freebie for filling the tank. Before.

It's a minute later or an hour later that Harry puts me in a chair at the kitchen table with my back to the hatch so I can't see through it to the window. He shuts off the TV. Sweeps up the glass, cleans the drops of blood off the floor. He says to my parents, "I'm sorry."

Dad says, "I know, son. Do you think maybe you could try to call and leave him a message? Here, I'll give you the number …" and Ma says nothing.

Then Harry goes outside so that me and Ma and Dad can stare at the walls in private. We don't speak. The fridge hums. A bird chirps outside. I hold Dad's hand across the table. I listen to my parents' breathing. Every few minutes, one of us bursts into tears, as though it's the first time we've heard the news, and then we stop. We wait for grief and fear to tell us what to do next.

Finally, Matty and Michelle are at the door. She's high and hysterical, clutching the cell phone that Frankie bought her. Michelle. I'll remember her as she is now, in tight jeans and snakeskin high heels; nails newly done in red; her wavy dark hair straightened; her big Louis Vuitton on one shoulder; her name in gold script hanging from a chain around her neck, a diamond dot over the "i." All done up to see Frankie. Ready to celebrate his interview and everything to come. The plans they made yesterday, before. Now she's cradling the phone, his last words in her hand; her heart broken in her chest.

Harry sees them in. On autopilot Matty shakes Harry's hand, then pulls him in for the one-handed bro hug, ignoring Harry's hesitation. The sight of Matty feels like hands tightening around my neck. Feels like not wanting to live but having to. Matty, in crisp jeans and a white T-shirt with the sleeves tight around his biceps, thick gold chain, Yankees cap on backwards, pristine white Nike's. He smells like a cologne factory. He could be Frankie. They have the same chain. I'm sure Frankie put his on this morning. I'm sure we'll never get it back.

Matty and Michelle go to my parents. They kneel at the feet of their kitchen chairs. Matty holds onto my dad and Michelle cries into my mother's lap while Ma strokes her hair in a way that she has never stroked mine. I take Michelle's phone and try again and again to get to her voicemail but there's still no signal. Michelle said she got his message before the planes hit and the phones went dead so she knew he was there. I throw the phone on the coffee table, and we all stare at it, knowing he's in there, locked in this little plastic box and that we can't reach him.

"What did he say, Mish, tell me again what he said?" my dad asks her, for the fourth, fifth, tenth time.

She croaks, her voice swollen with grief, "He said, 'Mishy, this is gonna be good.' He said the guy was nice and he couldn't believe the view. And that he was gonna take me up there one day. To see the top of the world, he said," she repeats again for him. "'Top of the fuckin' world,' he said," and she sobs. And my dad cocks his head and listens like something in those words will give us a clue to where Frankie is really hiding.

But I just see Frankie slipping his phone in his pocket, turning around, putting out his hand for a strong, firm handshake with some other unnamed faceless man who is also about to die. I see him standing on top of the world minutes before I started running far below him, a few streets away.

Later I sit next to Ma. She holds the phone and I tell her he loves her because it's too soon for the past tense. I put a hand on Matty's shoulder. His white T-shirt, the curve of the muscle under the cotton; I cry out, but it feels like the sound came from someone else's body.

Time keeps moving without us. Everything happens at once. Nothing happens at all. Harry quietly hands each of us a mug without making eye contact, not wanting to intrude on our grief. He puts one in my hand. All I can do is smell the whiskey fumes. I can't swallow. It's too strange to be living. To be breathing, drinking, crying. Involuntary actions are now deliberate. Step One. Breathe in. Step Two. Breathe out. Step Three. Blink.

Harry refills drinks, gets tissues, but the sky is changing now, the day has passed in spite of us and he whispers to me, "Gigi, this is time for your family now, I should go. Unless you need anything? Unless I can do anything else? I've written down the numbers for places you can call for help, they gave them on TV. They said it's quite difficult now, they don't have much information."

"I, I, could …" but I can't speak. I mean to say something but I don't know what. He reaches out to touch me, pat my arm or hold my hand, but then he doesn't. He nods at me, looks down, turns away. Harry says goodbye to my parents and Matty and Michelle, says the right things, I can see by the way they hug him, the way my dad says thank you, the way Ma nods her head, grabs his hand and squeezes it wordlessly.

He walks to the front door and I follow him. Outside I stand on the landing and he stands a step below me. I look only at his face, trying not to see the City still smoking behind him. "I'm sorry, Gigi. I'm so sorry." He means it. He doesn't try to hug me. I would freeze and turn to a pile of dust if anyone touched me. Somehow he knows this.

As he walks down the steps in Frankie's old shirt, hands in his pockets, I stop him. Stand two steps above him. I use the edge of my T-shirt to clean the smudge of dust still on his forehead. "You missed …" I mean to say, *you missed a spot* but that would have been me before, trying to lighten the darkness. Our eyes lock instead. Then I watch him turn and walk away.

As Harry walks down the block, Sharon, Danielle, and Stacy, my oldest friends, run towards Ma's house and brush past him as though he isn't there. Danielle's crying, Stacy's trying not to, saying my name over and over, arms outstretched to me. I'm quickly enfolded in their perfume and big hair and love and sorrow on the steps of my childhood home. Matty must have let them know. They loved Frankie like their own little brother. They hug me and smooth my hair, hold me by the elbow, try to take my weight as their own, but I'm stiff, numb, and they don't know that their embraces are like a steel brush on my skin. I watch Harry walk away as I say to the girls, "Frankie's gone," and this is only the first time of the hundreds of times that I will say the words. *He's gone.*

The girls hold me, arms around my waist as we go up the steps to the front door. I stop before I open it. I don't look back because I don't have to. I know Harry's still there, watching me, sad for me. For all of us.

A couple of days later when we finally get to the City to make the rounds of the hospitals, Manhattan is covered in flyers of the smiling dead. And by then we'll know it's thousands. For days – weeks, months – afterwards, there will be calls to hospitals, hotlines, police. We'll tell them Frankie's missing. And day after day he won't come home. He won't come through the door telling us a crazy story about how he escaped and almost didn't make it. Because he didn't.

But tonight, Ma will hide the phone from a drunk Michelle and keep it for herself, and sleep with it in her hand even though she knows she wasn't the one he called.

Tonight, I'll find Harry's suit jacket, left behind on the arm of the sofa. And I'll keep it and never clean it. Just in case Frankie's still there. In the ash on the shoulders.

2

GOLD

A Wednesday in August 2016, 7:25 a.m.
London

I'm still walking, Harry and Johnny and the baby and the car alarm and the shoes behind me now. I'm not sure where I'm going but it doesn't matter. I see a church, the door unlocked. I slide into a pew, close my eyes and try to feel something.

A strong smell of wood polish. I thought I was alone but the bitter smell is followed by an old lady rubbing circles into the wooden pews with her cloth, taking her time. I wonder what I'll be like when I'm old. I wonder if I'll actually get to be old. Barbra Streisand says that in that movie, right? Remember? That she wishes she was old so that at least she'd know she'd survived all this. My dad loves that movie. He always liked chick flicks.

I leave the lady to her work. I'm intruding on her God time and, anyway, the sharp smell of the polish makes me think of cigarettes. I push open the heavy church door and stand on the stone steps pulling my robe closer, wishing I had changed before I walked out on my family this morning. It's August. I'm in long sleeves and Harry's old track pants, I mean sweatpants, whatever they call them here – tracksuit bottoms? And I should be fine, I should be hot, actually, but not in London. It might as well be autumn this morning. I keep waiting for the heat. Today in New York it's probably hot-hot, spike-in-the-murder-rate hot, steam-rising-off-the-sidewalk-after-the-rain hot. Not here, though. Arms crossed against the chill, keys and wallet and phone in my hands, I walk to the corner shop to buy some smokes.

August. When it's August-hot then I remember the last weekend with Frankie at the Jersey Shore; the Saturday barbeques at Matty's mom's house that we'd been going to since we were kids; the Brooklyn Cyclones game we went to with Dad. When the heat of August pours out of the sun like syrup then I feel the days before we lost him on my skin. And the memories have a place to stick.

The night I left my parents' house Frankie woke up and stood in the doorway of my bedroom in his underwear while I packed. I was seventeen, he was eleven. He looked like Jordan from New Kids on the Block. Curly dark hair, like Johnny's now. Destined to be a heartbreaker. I had to explain to him about how I loved him but me and Ma couldn't live in the same house anymore, so I had to go, but I would still take care of him. I put a dozen Hot Pockets in the freezer and hid a case of mac and cheese under his bed with ten bucks for emergencies. I told him to take Dad's bus with Matty to school and to call Sharon or Stacy or Danielle because I'd stay with one of them.

"What about my games? Who's gonna go to my games?" he said. He was really good at basketball. I said I would be there, even if he couldn't see me I would be there and

I would watch. And I would wait for him after school every day to check in and make sure he was OK.

I looked at him. His little-boy body was lit by the nightlight in the hall and it made a shadow the size of the man he would be one day. I told him I loved him and that he was better than all of us put together and I held him but he squirmed to get out of my grasp and he said, "Iw, Jeej, that's gross," so I had to settle for rumpling his hair. I was already halfway down the block when he came running after me in his underwear and sneakers. He said, "You didn't take any food." He gave me a juice box and bag of Cheetos. "Love you," he said, and ran back home. I waited in the street until I saw him go inside.

I went to every game, I waited for him after school, like I promised, and I gave him half of every pay check from my job at the bagel store to make sure he had everything he needed. I took care of him like I did our whole lives, from when he was a baby. Then he grew up.

That summer before he died was day after day of heat, sudden summer rain that left us just as hot, Technicolor sunsets over New Jersey seen from the deck of the ferry, cold beer and cigarettes on the fire escape of his new apartment. He moved into a building on Victory Boulevard with Matty and they couldn't afford A/C but that didn't take the shine off it being their first place. I came over after work once a week. We'd go up to the roof and look at the disco-ball shimmer of Manhattan against the black sky, and that's when he would talk, lay out his plans, map his future. I was proud of him, the boy I raised. We didn't know that we were looking at his grave.

When August comes around and I feel like I can stand it, I listen to his voice. I kept my old answering machine and re-saved his messages until I figured out how to get them recorded. Two messages: *"Jeej, how you doin', just seeing how you doin' 'cuz you had that thing today at work, love you, bye."* And then: *"Jeej, I'm short this month for Ma's bills, I need $65 if you got it, OK? It's OK if you don't got it, but if you got it. Bye."* His voice in August.

Today I'm like a broken compass. I can't find north. It's never warm here. There's twelve and a half beautiful summer days every year when London is lush and full of light and green and the people rise up and strip down and lay in the sun. But today is gray and misty and my memories are mixed up. I left my kids and I should be home packing Johnny's bag for soccer camp and taking Rocky to baby music but instead I'm buying cigarettes at the corner store.

I buy a little half-pack. Ten cigarettes patiently waiting in a slim box. So European. Like those tiny two-person elevators and eating cheese for dessert. I walk down to the common – it's called a common instead of a park – to sit on a bench. Mist hovers over the grass. It feels like it's rained, but it hasn't. That's just the morning air here, so thick you can see it. So thick you can take a bite out of it. I strike a match and light a cigarette. But the air is so damp and heavy that I can't tell the difference between the mist and the rising smoke. Smoking is one more thing that's not like it is at home.

I've been holding my wallet, keys, and phone in my hands all this time. When I left the house I reached for the diaper bag out of habit. I hate that bag. The main zipper's broken from overstuffing, the shoulder strap's fraying. The front utility pockets always spewing their guts of baby wipes, chewed-up board books, and empty baby-food pouches. I couldn't stand the sight of it. So I just grabbed the essentials and walked out of the house. That's what happens when you escape a burning building or a war. You grab what you can. And run.

That's very fucking dramatic, Gigi, don't you think? Who are you at war with? Who burned down your house?

I stand up from the bench and start walking toward the high street. I don't know why they call it "high" instead of "main." I look over my shoulder as I leave the common to enter the stream of pedestrians on the way to the Tube and I see a woman pushing a stroller walking the opposite direction. Fit, firm, and looking good for thirty-something with a baby in her turquoise Lululemon outfit. I wonder if she's ever felt like me. Probably not. She's not shuffling in the streets in men's sweatpants and a bathrobe so I'd say that alone puts her several levels of functioning above me. You never know, though, I guess.

I walk with the commuters past the common but it's hard to keep pace in my flip-flops. As everyone branches off to the Tube and the Overground and the bus stops I keep walking until I get to the Grand Euro Star Lodge Hotel on the other side of the station.

"Hello, I'd like a room, please," I say to the very pretty, very bored Slavic girl at reception.

"Yes, madam, we have vacancy, how many night you require?" She doesn't look at me, and even if she did, it's clear she wouldn't be concerned about the fact that I'm wearing pajamas and holding all of my possessions in my hands.

How many nights? I hadn't thought about that. How long do you leave a family for? Not knowing what else to tell her I say, "Two, two, please."

"Yes, madam, single room available two nights. Cost is £45 per night, £5 extra for towel."

"Is there a TV in the room?" The TV is critical.

"If you want room with TV is £10 extra, Freeview."

"Yes, yes, please, a room with a TV."

"Is deluxe room, also has half bathtub." I don't know what she means by that and just assume it's a language thing. The important thing is the TV and checking in even though it's 8:45 in the morning.

"Great. Can I check in now, please?"

"No, sorry, check-in half-past three. Leave bag if you like."

"I'll pay fifty per cent extra if you let me in now."

"No, sorry, madam, I cannot make excuse. I have to explain my boss."

I pull out all the cash I have, £25 in bills and two £1 coins, and slide it across the reception desk. I force her to meet my eyes. "I'd like to check in early, please," I say, with a smile. I haven't brushed my teeth today. And the cigarette. A toxic smile from a crazy lady but this girl's seen worse. She doesn't give a shit about me. She slides the money across the counter and under a folder on her desk.

"Room 506. I bring key."

Should I do something different? I got all of London at my feet, should I take this credit card and go to the Dorchester and drink champagne all day and get a massage? Or go to Westfield and buy a new wardrobe? Get a manicure, get a haircut. Put me first. Fuck it all and take a train to Paris? No, that's not what I want.

I get to the room and put my phone, wallet, keys, and cigarettes on the little card table next to a metal folding chair. This place is a shithole. An anonymous place for hippy backpackers and married men who don't want to spend money on their lunchtime lovers and people in business suits engaged in "business." It smells of stale smoke, lemon air-freshener, and prostitution. A shady, cheap, crappy place. Perfect.

I put my head down on the pillow and sleep is instant. Then the phone dings. Another message from Harry. He's been calling and texting since I left the house. I don't read it.

Harry should know it's August. He should know that it's almost Frankie's time. It's been eight months since Rocky was born and seven years since they gave me Johnny and fifteen years since Frankie died and none of them are here in this room with me. And neither is Harry. But he should be.

Staten Island, June 2009

"Sharon, Jesus, slow down!" I shout from the backseat of her Honda Civic, the car she's had since senior year of high school. I'm in the backseat with the baby. He looks so small, and he is, very small for six months. I'm still nervous so I always ride in the back with him, both my hands gripping his car seat, just in case.

Sharon talks to me through the rear-view mirror: "I'm going like, fourteen miles an hour, Jeej. This kid's gonna have an uphill battle with you. You gonna put bars on the baby room windows, maybe? Maybe you could home school him too." I ignore her. I don't say that I've thought about putting bars on the windows. I live in a sketchy part of Brooklyn. And there is no baby room. There's a crib crammed into my tiny bedroom because until a couple weeks ago I didn't know there was going to be a baby.

I adjust the baby's blanket. She's right, of course. I'm overprotective. Obsessive since the baby came. New moms are like that, but this isn't the usual situation, and I'm not his mom, not officially, anyway, not yet. I'm jittery, I don't sleep, and it's not just because he's up every three hours. I'm terrified. Of how I'm going to do this alone. Of hurting him by accident because I don't have the right instincts. Of the day I'm going to have to explain everything to him. Of him growing up and feeling a space in his heart where his mother's supposed to be that I could never fill, no matter how much I love him.

We pull up to Michelle's parents' house. A four-foot-tall statue of Mary greets visitors at the path leading to the front door. Her blue veil is faded, her palms facing out and down, her head cocked to the side with motherly affection, undisturbed by her nose being broken off. She's missing three fingers of her left hand where the metal spokes that held the plaster together poke out, sharp and rusty. Behind her, the grass and weeds are high and chaotic in the spaces between the other statues on the lawn – St. Joseph, St. John, St. Theresa. Jesus on the cross, all of his paint worn off almost down to the plaster, except for the red drops of blood on his forehead from the crown of thorns. And the angels – dozens of angels, wings in various states of neglect, eyes worn away by years of wind and rain and snow but still upturned to God.

Gloria Costello, Michelle's mom, is standing behind the screen door, watching as I pull her grandson from the backseat. She's expecting us. I start to sweat. My skin feels tight, like I'm wearing another woman's life and Mrs. Costello can see it.

Michelle and Frankie were supposed to be together forever. They had been sweethearts since they were twelve years old when the Costellos moved to the neighborhood. Then he died. And part of her died too. Part of all of us died. But it never stopped for Michelle. Pieces of her just kept dying.

We tried, we all tried, to help. But the needles and bottles had gravity on their side in Michelle's downward spiral. I let her stay with me a few times, once for a couple of months. When I'd see her on the block, underdressed for the winter weather, hair pulled back and graying, nails worn down to the sore red nail beds, I would take her to the diner, but she never ate what she ordered. I bought her cigarettes. One time I found her asleep on a bench in the ferry terminal. I gave her my coat and took her to her parents' place. She fought me the whole way. She didn't want anyone's help. She wanted to get high and forget about the life her and Frankie were supposed to have but didn't.

No one saw her for a long time until she showed up at Ma's house with a baby in a broken stroller. Ma said she asked her if she wanted coffee and by the time she'd come back from the kitchen with the milk and sugar Michelle was gone, the baby asleep in the stroller barely standing on its busted wheels in the middle of the living room.

Ma waited to call the cops until I got there so that the baby would have someone to go to the hospital with. Dad was driving the bus, Mrs. Costello wasn't answering the phone, Michelle had left and we had no idea who the father was. So it had to be me. I knew he wasn't mine, but no one else was there, and once I saw him, when I picked him up and held him, I knew I couldn't leave him. He was a part of Michelle and she still had a piece of my brother buried deep.

I stayed in the hospital visitors' lounge that whole weekend. "Excuse me, I'm sorry, can you just tell me if he's OK?" I would ask doctors and social workers but they couldn't do more than nod and say, "He's OK." I wasn't family so they couldn't give me details and I couldn't stay with him. There was a sweet young nurse who would let me know once in a while on the sly how he was – dehydration, a bad cough, infected diaper rash, underweight. He was struggling and scrawny but he was going to be alright.

I went to the hospital every day after work for a couple weeks. I kept calling Mrs. Costello. She never answered, but by then we knew Michelle was dead. The cops found her in a motel off the Jersey Turnpike a few days after she'd left Ma's house. Michelle's funeral was private. I kept calling, though, until finally the Costellos unplugged their answering machine.

Then I went to check on the baby and he was gone, placed with a foster family. They wouldn't tell me where or who. I cried in the hospital lobby, then I cried in my car, and then I forced myself to forget about him. Everyone who should've been there to love him was somewhere else. I wanted to love him. But I had no right to.

I went back to work and law school and life feeling the loss of something I never had, trying to put it behind me until, at work, at 4:15 on a Wednesday, files piled around me, cold coffee sitting on the edge of my desk, there was a woman's voice on the phone: "Miss Stanislawski?"

"Yes," I said, feeling time stop around me.

"This is Sunilda Rosario from OCFS," she said with the staccato punches of a New York Dominican accent, rapid fire Spanish inflections in her words.

"I'm sorry, from the what?" I asked, thinking she might be an expert witness we'd called on a case. "Children and Family Services, Miss Stanislawski."

"Oh, oh, OK," I said, stumbling around, shuffling papers on my desk. She went on: "After investigating all possible options for the placement of Baby Costello it's become clear that there are no immediate relatives on either side of the family prepared to take custody. We wanted to know if you could come in and talk to us about fostering the baby, if you're still interested ..."

"Wait, what?" I meant to put the file in my hand on my desk but I missed the edge and paper cascaded around me. A memory; paper floating by the windows that morning when I stood in an office just like this one. I feel Frankie brush past me. "What about Mrs. Costello? Did you find the father? What about his parents?"

"The father is in prison, the paternal grandparents are deceased, and the Costellos are not in a position to take the baby. I'm calling because Mrs. Costello suggested we call you as a close friend of the family ..."

So on a Wednesday afternoon in my cramped office under the fluorescent lights, a hundred sheets of paper surrounding me, I became his mother. It's not official yet, though. There's a year ahead of us of court dates, home visits, interviews, assessments, background checks. There's the chance that I won't be able to adopt him, not if his father decides to hold onto his rights from prison. There's the chance they'll think that I can't do it on my own when they do the home visits. But there's also the chance that this is exactly how life is supposed to go.

Now we're here, where Michelle grew up, with Mrs. Costello in the doorway, thinner than I remember her, in a pink sweater set, gold crucifix hanging around the soft freckled creases of her neck. I pull the baby from the car seat and walk past the Virgin Mother up to the front door.

"Gigi? Sharon? Hello, girls, come in. I just made a pot of coffee." Mrs. Costello is warm and friendly like she always was and welcomes us in the same way she always did, but she doesn't look at the baby. She doesn't ask to hold him, doesn't pat his back, doesn't do any of the things old ladies do when they see a baby, especially one they're related to. She just notices him on my shoulder and pads to the kitchen to get the coffee; the sound of her nylon knee-highs rubbing against her house slippers gives me chills. Sharon and I sit down on the tweed sofa, its plastic cover crackling under us.

I try not to wake the baby as we sit down. Sharon tugs at my sleeve and mouths, "Oh my God," her eyes directing me to the opposite wall. Above the upright piano the wall is covered in gold-framed photos of Jimmy, the Costellos' son. He died when he was eleven. He was all arms and legs and green eyes that grew bigger and bigger the sicker he got, the thinner his face became. We all remembered Jimmy, how one day he was playing baseball in the street and the next he was waving at all of us from his bedroom window. But when we stood at his window to yell up to him one summer morning, he wasn't there. Just the bedroom curtain swaying slightly; no doe-eyed smiling sick boy waving back.

35

Every time we stopped by with my parents to see how the Costellos were doing after he died, we noticed that Mrs. C had added another framed photo of him to this wall. She kept adding pictures to the wall and she kept teaching sixth grade at St. Ignatius; the constant procession of eleven-year-old boys through her classroom comforting and torturing her every day.

But Sharon isn't looking at Jimmy's wall. She's looking at the three-foot-tall portrait of Michelle, leaning against the top of the piano, no space yet for it among the frames. A full-color rendition of Michelle in oil paint. She's wearing her prom dress – I remember it from Frankie's photos – and sitting on a cloud with huge angel wings behind her, a backdrop of feathers for her face. Around her neck there's a gold locket, opened in thirds, revealing three pictures: Jimmy on the left, Frankie on the right and, although he's still alive in the next room, Mr. Costello in the frame in the middle. I feel sick. I want to fold into myself, to cry, but I do neither. There's no space for my grief in this house. I hold the baby on my lap and clutch Sharon's hand.

"Why is life so fucking hard, Shar?" I whisper.

"I don't know."

"How am I going to do this?"

"Listen, just drink the coffee, say hi to Mr. Costello and then we go. OK? It'll be OK."

Before I can plead with Sharon to get us out of here Mrs. Costello comes in with the coffee. "Here we go, girls, nice and hot. You take milk?" she asks as she pours milk into all three cups before waiting for an answer. Her voice has the same warble I remember, high-pitched and shrill, like Archie Bunker's wife.

"Thanks, Mrs. C. It's good to see you. You look good," I say, trying to avoid eye contact with St. Michelle.

"Oh, thank you, sweetheart. You know, since John got sick I just haven't felt like eating. Weight Watchers should get in on this cancer game, they'd make a fortune, ha!"

She notices us looking at the wall. "Oh, you're looking at the painting. Do you like it? My friend at church did it for me, isn't it beautiful? I just gave her some photos and she painted it from those. Michelle was so beautiful. And I know she'll take care of my Jimmy and Frankie's there taking care of her ... isn't he, Gigi?" Her voice switches from self-comforting to hauntingly desperate, pleading with me for what she said to be true.

"Yes, sure he is, of course, Mrs. C." An uncomfortable silence settles on all of us until the baby wakes up and starts gurgling.

I juggle him as I unwrap his blanket and take off the long-sleeved T-shirt that's over his onesie. I know it's summer but he's so tiny. I keep dressing him in too many layers and then panicking that I'm overheating him and then undressing him in a flurry of incompetence.

I need to say something, Mrs. C's refusal to acknowledge the baby is so awkward, so I force out some words. "Mrs. C, I came over to thank you for writing that letter for me for the social worker. It was really nice, everything you said ..."

"That's alright, Gigi." A shadow falls over her face. "I'm sorry I didn't return your calls. You called a lot of times. I just – I couldn't talk. John's very sick and then—" she's overcome with tears, "and then Michelle. It was too much, just too much." She takes a few moments to compose herself. She's so accustomed to crying it doesn't take her long to dry her tears and then look up at me, smiling weakly. "Thank you for being patient with us, dear."

"That's OK, Mrs. C. So how do you want to do this, you know, how often I should bring him over to visit and stuff? The social worker said it would be good if I could start now with making important people a regular part of his life. I … I mean, I know you didn't want to take him with Mr. C being sick and all, and you had so much going on, I know you weren't ready to see him but now—"

"It's not because John is sick, Gigi," she cuts me off. She sips her coffee, placing the mug on the table carefully, making sure it's in the center of the ceramic coaster of the Last Supper.

"No, no, it's because my kids die, sweetheart." She stirs her coffee and looks into the distance across the room. "They're both dead," she says, to clarify, as if we didn't understand her. Her words hang above me and the baby, hovering, waiting for me to soften them, to contradict or dismiss them. "Oh, Mrs. C—" I reach for her with my free arm, "Mrs. C, don't say that, don't say—" but she stops me, pulling an old tissue from her bra strap, her eyes watery and bleak.

"They died. So I don't want that baby here. It's bad enough he has whatever poison is in our blood. But this is a house of dead children and now John's dying too. Don't bring that baby to this house." Mrs. C dabs at her eyes. I extend my hand to her, place it on her folded arm. She pats my wrist. We listen to the ticking of the clock above the doorway for a long time. An apostle sits in place of each number, the hands of the clock extending from the cross in the middle. Shock and sorrow catch in my throat.

I can't believe that she believes what she's saying, so I try again: "But Mrs. C, you're his grandmother, his nonna, right? I'm sorry about Jimmy and Michelle, you know I am. We're all so sorry. But look, Michelle left you a grandson, she left him here for you." I motion to him in my arms. "I'll take care of him, of course I will, but please, please be his grandmother. He needs you. I need you ..."

Mrs. C looks at me, teary and exhausted. A silent certainty comes over me that after she sees Mr. C through his final passing she'll just go to sleep and never wake up. She's ready for that rest that Jesus promised her.

"I know you think you're doing the right thing. But I wasn't a good mother, Eugenia. Jesus took Jimmy from me because He wanted him back, but Michelle was dying every day and God was testing me and I couldn't save her. Then look what kind of mother she became. Leaving her baby like that. I'll have to answer for it when I get up there, but while I'm still here please don't bring him back again. She chose you – you go be his mother and forget about us."

The baby fusses in my lap. I put him on my shoulder again and get up to walk around with him, keep him moving, but every surface is covered with Jesus and his friends or with the ghosts of Jimmy and Michelle and I want to shield his eyes. I should protest, and argue, and turn around and tell her she's being crazy and selfish and melodramatic. And I would say all of those things if I didn't see so clearly that her losses are so excruciating that even love and joy feel like pain. The happiness of this grandbaby would just make her grief deeper. Because for her, happiness is what happens before sorrow. And sorrow is inevitable when you love. That's why Michelle couldn't live without Frankie. That's why I'm holding her baby now.

If I could shrink myself, sink me and the baby into the ground, evaporate, I would. His soft cheek brushes my face as I move him to my other shoulder. I really am his mother now. I came here thinking that I would take care of him for the family, honor Michelle, that we would collectively raise this kid so we could all recover from the pain of losing the people we loved. But I'm all he's going to have.

"I'm sorry, I'm so sorry." I don't know what I'm apologizing for but it's all I can think of to say to Mrs. C. Or maybe I'm saying it to my baby.

"You girls want more coffee?" Mrs. C's hand shakes on the handle of the Mr. Coffee pot. She speaks to us as though she hasn't just said that she never wants to see my baby again. I don't know what to do next but Sharon, reaching in her bag for some tissues, says, "Hey, Mrs. C, why don't I sit with you for a minute and Gigi can go see Mr. C? Before we go? I think it would be good if she could do that."

Mrs. C, unsure, thinks for a minute. We all have the same thought at the same time that we don't say aloud. This will be the only time Mr. Costello will ever see his grandson. Mrs. C sighs, "OK, dear. He's down the hall. He probably won't recognize you. He's confused, it's the drugs he's on. Just agree with whatever he says. Sharon, sweetheart, can you find me something stronger for this coffee in the kitchen?"

I walk with the baby down the hallway and find the open bedroom door. The room is cornflower blue. The midday sunlight reflects off the walls. Everything glows.

Mr. Costello is lying on a hospital bed, gaunt, but the breadth of his shoulders, the length of him, are evidence that he was once strong as an ox. His milky eyes are open above his oxygen mask, searching the ceiling for something; a few gray hairs lie barely visible where there used to be a full head of lustrous black. Around his neck is a gold crucifix, identical to his wife's. He's so fragile, I'm afraid that the weight of it is crushing his chest.

I lean over and whisper, "Can you hear me, Mr. Costello? John?"

"Who's this?" He turns his head to me with an effort. I'm not sure if he sees me.

"It's me, Gigi."

"Michelle? Is that you?" I stop still for a second, unsure what to say. I don't want to upset him, I don't know if he knows that Michelle's gone, if he forgot, I don't know what the right thing to say is, but he doesn't give me a chance.

"Michelle, where the hell you been? Your mother's been frantic. C'mere, let me see you." I come closer. He moves his mask from his face. His eyes flicker when he sees the baby.

"Oh my God, Michelle! The baby! Oh, honey, I'm sorry, sweetheart, I forgot about the baby. I don't feel too good, you know? C'mere, let me see him." I come closer and sit on the edge of the bed. I lift Mr. C's hand for him and place it on the baby's face so he can feel the perfect skin. The baby babbles at him.

"Ha, ha, he's beautiful, beautiful. Oh, Michelle, you did good, kid. I knew you'd be OK in the end. I always believed that. Your mother, well, you know your mother, but I believed in you, sweetheart. Look at this beautiful baby!"

Everything evaporates – the portrait, the coffee, Jimmy's pictures, my brother in the locket, Mrs. C and the poison in her blood. This is how my baby's life should have started. With his family happy to see him; loving him without having to be asked. All of the tragedy of our circumstances dissipates in Mr. C's eyes, shining with pride for his daughter and his grandchild. I'm not the only one who loves him. Someday I'll tell him that. That his grandfather loved him so much.

"What's his name? It's a boy, right? I don't feel too good, you know? I forgot, I know you told me, but what's his name?" Mr. Costello's eyes sparkle from their hollows.

"Mic …" I start to say Michael, the name his foster mother gave him. On all the papers he was Baby Costello because Michelle didn't give him a name, or if she did then no one knew it. I only used Michael at the doctor's office and I called him Little Guy most of the time. There was so much paperwork to do, so many things to figure out, I wanted his name to be meaningful, to give him strength and purpose after everything he'd survived. It felt so huge, naming a person. But after today I think Michael is his middle name. I look at Mr. C and I say, "John, his name is Johnny. I named him after you."

A tear rolls down the old man's face, his skin as thin as paper. "Oh! Johnny boy! Hey, Johnny! You were always such a good girl, Michelle. Oh my God, Johnny boy, here, Michelle, take this off me, it's for Johnny, you give it to Johnny and you tell him that's from his nonno." He puts his hand to the gold crucifix and limply but frantically tries to take it off. I lift his head from the pillow. I remember a bird skull Frankie found in the park once, long ago on a summer day. How light it was, I think, as I help John get the chain over his head.

I put the baby next to him on the bed, holding him there with my hand as Mr. Costello gives his grandson the cross. Johnny mouths it, interested in the cold metal, how it catches the blue light of the room.

"Oh, is he beautiful! Oh, this kid is somethin' else," Mr. C says, and I see the baby look at him, a glimmer and a question in his little eye, like, *Who are you?* before he decides to smile for Nonno. Mr. C laughs and the baby plays with the cross. We sit together like this until the old man falls asleep, holding his grandson's foot in his wrinkled hand.

3

COFFEE, LIPSTICK

A Wednesday in August 2016, 10 a.m.
London, Grand Euro Star Lodge Hotel,
Room 506

When the receptionist said "half bathtub" I thought she meant a half-bath, like a bathroom with no shower, and that was weird for a hotel but, I figured, this place was more like some Euro hostel thing with a shared one in the hall or something. I didn't mind. Showering wasn't my priority. But when I open the door to the bathroom there it is, an actual half of a bathtub shoved into the corner. In case you want to relax while kneeling in water or just stand and soak your calves for a while. Europe is so weird sometimes.

A text from Harry dings in:
> *Gigi where are you? What are you doing? I'm worried. I've taken Johnny to camp but I don't know what to do with Rocky. Where are you? Please call me*

What should I say? OK, so he's pissed, that's fair. But I don't like his tone.

Me:

I need to take a shit and then there's a Real Housewives marathon. Then I'll come home

Harry:

This isn't funny. What do I do with Rocky? Who do I call? What are you doing!

An exclamation point. An actual exclamation point. He should know better than to exclamation point at me.

Me:

Take Rocky to work with you. He's been following the markets so he'll be good in a meeting

Harry:

Please just tell me where you are. I don't understand what's happening

Me:

I'm fine. I'll let you know when I get there

I set the phone to vibrate and block Harry's number. It's easier than telling him the truth.

For a second I push my thumb down to shut it off but that would be a mistake. Johnny's at a soccer day camp at his school. I've managed to cover well enough in front of every authority figure – the midwives, the GP – but if the school catches on to how fucked up I am then we'll have a problem. If school calls then I need to answer. They never call the dads. Even when the moms work full-time. Even when they make more money than their husbands.

Two weeks ago Johnny was doing Forest Explorers camp. He fell out of a tree and his head ricocheted off the trunk of the tree next to it. I had to take a taxi to Wimbledon Common and run into the woods with the baby to find them because they didn't want to move Johnny until I got there. So I'm sweating, panting, dragging the baby in the car seat through the bushes – and there he is, his whole forehead a purple bruise. He's holding out his Yankees cap to me full of berries. "Look, Jeej, it's all blackberries. I picked them." We spend the next four hours in the emergency room, Rocky crying, Johnny hungry and hurting, but holding that hat like it was filled with gold; the three of us covered in blackberry juice by the time we saw the doctor.

So, anyway, if the school calls I need to answer it.

I look at my watch. Rocky's nap time. I'm sure he's not asleep. I'm sure he's screaming with tiredness because Harry's misread his signs or forgot the sleeping bag he likes or couldn't find his lamb. His face is red, his diaper needs changing, his onesie is soaked with saliva and tears and urine, and I'm waiting for a feeling but I don't have any. Someone else's turn to have feelings today.

I flick on the TV. The *Real Housewives of New Jersey* marathon is on. I exhale, relieved, happy to see the ladies totter across the screen. And here are the enormous houses like you can only get in America; the massive cars; the walk-in closets; the constant bickering; the betrayal; the big hair; the alcohol; the spoiled children; the wealthy husbands; the stream of high-pitched, nonsensical, impassioned chatter that is about nothing and everything all at once – I wrap it around me like a blanket.

I love the vacant beauty of the Housewives of Beverly Hills: their plastic faces and Birkin bags, their house swans and private jets. I love the hilarious, vivacious, Housewives of Atlanta: unapologetically fierce, fabulous defined. I love the Housewives of New York City: their ageing glamor and cabaret dreams, wearing diamonds to drink champagne alone with their tiny dogs. If I could trade lives with any one of these women for a day, I would do it in a heartbeat.

But the Housewives of New Jersey are not aspirational like the others. No one ever wakes up and says, "I hope one day that I'll make it in New Jersey." That's no one's life goal. I only say that, though, because I'm from Staten Island, just across the water, and Jersey, like Brooklyn and Long Island, is a cousin, just your least favorite one. The one you end up moving to anyway because it's actually really nice there and they have great schools and you can get a house with a driveway. But still, it's fucking Jersey.

Teresa appears on the screen, her black hair cascading in glossy extensions over the dark-blue dyed fur of her collar. Her eyeshadow matches the hue of her coat. She's at a liquor store signing bottles of Fabellini, her own line of flavoured sparkling wine. She's gracious with her fans who ask her about Melissa, her sister-in-law, and who are concerned for her because they know about the federal fraud charges she and her husband, Joe, are facing. Oh my God, Victoria Gotti just walked into the store, all fur and black leather and ice-blond hair to her waist. "Excuse me, Miss, do I have to wait on line, with all these people?" she rasps, one finger waving in the air dismissing the mere mortals around her, sending chills down my spine.

I wish I could say I was classy and sophisticated, a housewife of Beverly Hills in the making, but these Jersey girls are really my people – dropping f-bombs every other word, eating Chinese food in the kitchen unless they're having Sunday pasta dinner. Dark brunettes. They don't apologize. They eat dessert. They wear high heels and real furs to drive their Escalades to the mall. Their kids wear Gucci sneakers. They pay in cash. They yell, in joy and in anger. They have meticulous eyebrows, and pride, and loyalty, and real emotions. They say "shtrong" and "shtreet." Maybe they finished school, maybe they didn't. But they're not in the kinds of businesses where education matters. They hug and drink and cry and have each other's backs. They're not rich-lady skinny because they're not trying to be because you can get red leather leggings in any size in Jersey and that's what Spanx and over-the-knee boots are for. And they don't give a fuck anyway.

Of course I never used to watch any of these shows until we moved here, until Rocky came and the world shrank to the size of the living room and everything turned the color of the London sky at 3 a.m., no matter what the time of day.

Now the ladies are discussing a rumor about another girl in the group and her husband and whether he did or did not sleep with his mother-in-law. Amber is so shocked she's about to fall out of her chair, and Teresa reacts because she's in front of the camera but you can tell her heart's not in it. She's got other things to worry about. She's facing prison because of her husband's financial decisions. Papers she signed because she trusted him. It's hard enough dealing with one dick in your life without thinking about the dicks that other women are married to. *Married to Dicks*. That could be a reality show. Every married woman in the world could be on it.

That's not fair. I don't mean it, he's not a dick. Harry is … I was going to say a good man but that's just … that's surface. He's a part of my body, one of my limbs, half my brain. A vital organ I can't live without. He would laugh if he heard me say that about the vital organ. I'm mad at him, I hate him, and I love him. I have no choice, it's involuntary, like breathing.

We don't tell people the real story when they ask how we met. We just say we met in New York. Because how do you explain the tragedy and the loss, the years spent apart, the plans of a God who takes no notice of whether you believe in him and just puts you where you need to be.

I thought Harry would get what's happening to me without having to explain. We used to be like that, we used to have unspoken understanding. One night back in Brooklyn, when we'd been together only two months, Johnny woke up at 1 a.m. with a really high fever. He was shaking and sweating. He was limp in my arms. I was alone and scared to death. I called a taxi for the hospital and when I opened the door of my building to take Johnny outside Harry was standing there, out of breath, like he'd run the whole way.

"What are you doing here?" I said.

"You called, or you didn't know you called," he said. "You must have hit my number by accident, but I heard you talking. I could hear something was wrong so I'm here. I came." Our eyes met. He took Johnny from my aching arms and we got in the cab.

Maybe finding each other after so many years was the best part of our story. Maybe the rest doesn't end well.

Oh, look at this. Gia, about twelve, the oldest of Teresa's four daughters, is crying in the kitchen. She's old enough to understand something serious is happening to her parents. Teresa – in a purple velour tracksuit, her pink acrylic nails as reflective as the shiny marble countertops of her kitchen – wraps her arms around her daughter and says, "I wish I could take your pain and I have it, you know?"

I know you do, Teresa, I know. But who takes your pain for you?

Who's going to take it for me?

Brooklyn and Manhattan, October 2012

I'm being watched. I open one eye, startled to see Johnny at the edge of my bed, his little nose two inches from mine, watching me breathe, like a very small demon in a horror movie. "Oh shhhhhhooooot, Johnny, don't scare me like that, how long you been standing there?" I half-yell, half-whisper.

"Hi, Jeej. Did I do good sleeping?" I look at the clock. 5:42 a.m.

"It's not the worst you've ever done but it's not your best." He climbs into bed, scoots his little backside as far into my stomach as he can, repositions my arms and installs his head under my chin. "OK, buddy, let's try to sleep some more?" And I close my eyes. I haven't slept past 6 a.m. since he was a baby, nearly four years. Seven days a week. Most days, it's 5:00, so I guess we slept in today. I want sleep so much it feels like hunger. I say I resent these early mornings, this need of his to be on top of me. But I know that one morning, not too long from now, it'll be the last time he does this; the last time he's small enough to curl up beside me; the last time he'll need to. I won't know it at the time – that it's the last time – but it will be. I hold him close so he can feel the rhythm of my breathing and be lulled into dreaming and …

Two seconds later: "Jeej, can we go to the playground?"

"Yes, later, go to sleep."

"Jeej, I have pizza?"

"Yes, later, go to sleep."

"Jeej, you are my Jeej. Are you my Jeej?"

"Yes, always. Please let Jeej sleep, OK?"

"Jeej, you need coffee?"

"Yes, always, go to sleep, Johnny."

"I like T-rexes. Oso [he can't say "also"] I like pteradactylyseses, and triceratopses, and oso iguanodons."

"I know. Go to sleep."

Thirty seconds later, a whisper: "Jeej, can we go to the newzzeum and see the dinosaurs?"

This is the point at which other mothers at pre-school drop-off with successful careers and good shoes say, "Then I just give him the iPad and he leaves me alone for an hour." But me and Johnny aren't in the financial position for an iPad so I have to use old-school methods.

"Hey, Johnny, can you put your cars in a line that goes from my bed all the way to the kitchen?" That may sound like a big project unless you understand the tiny dimensions of a one-bedroom apartment in Brooklyn. It's technically a two-bedroom, because they put up two walls and split the kitchen in half to make a windowless space that fits a twin bed and nothing else. It doesn't even fit a small person wanting to walk around the bed. You just have to dive onto it from the doorway. Which has no door. Because, as I pointed out to the real-estate agent, it's not a bedroom. Don't get me started on the bathroom.

I try for ten more minutes of half-sleep but as the sun rises over Brooklyn and comes through the cracks in the blinds the conveyer belt in my mind cranks up. *Student loans, rent, day care. Send Dad a hundred bucks. Don't turn the heat on yet, not till the end of the month. I wish I got that promotion.* You got to let that go, Gigi. *I know but don't they see I do the hours? I just do them when Johnny's asleep?* Next time, Jeej. Don't drive yourself crazy. *I know, but I need the money if we're ever going to get out of this apartment. My tooth hurts. How long can I avoid going to the dentist? Will it just go away?* No, Jeej. You have to go to the dentist. *If I had got that job they would've given me dental cover.* You have to go to the dentist because if your teeth start rotting you'll definitely never meet someone. *Meet someone? Who am I going to meet? Nobody wants a thirty-something toothless para-legal with a kid. And when would I meet this person anyway?* There's never any time. *There's never any time. Johnny needs new shoes.* Dammit. Why are his feet so huge? *I'll stop buying coffee when I'm out. Pack lunch every day for work. Cancel my haircut. Return that dress.* Jeej, it was only twenty bucks. *I know. But he needs a coat and shoes and I need to go to the dentist. Cancel the cable TV.* Really? It's just basic. You're right, though. *I can't meet the girls for drinks. Not if Sharon's having that party for her kid. I can't show up without a present and I can't afford to go to drinks **and** get a present **and** buy coffee because the loan payments are due for the college that I finished and the law school that I didn't to become the lawyer that I'm not. Why didn't I finish?* You would've been finished this year if you stayed with it. *I know. But who would've taken care of Johnny?* You couldn't do it. You couldn't do work and law school and Johnny. *I can't afford everything. I have a good job for one person. I got enough money for one person with huge loans. But I'm not one person. I got this other very small, very expensive person too. I can't do everything and remember everything. I'm everything, I have to be everything ...*

CRASH. THUMP. "Owwww, ouchie ouchie!"

Johnny shouts and I leap out of bed, scoop him up, hug and hug and rock and rock, all of his little body still fitting within the circle of my arms. I start singing our song, 'Like a Prayer.'

"Just breathe, Johnny – *In the midnight hour* – just breathe, you're OK. Did you jump off the couch again?"

"Yes, my wrist," he says, pointing to his elbow. "It's broken."

"Let me check, let me see if these kisses will work, and by the way, this is your elbow," and I cover his elbow with kisses, then I turn into Mama Bear and sniff around him, sniff his shoulder and under his chin which turns his tears into fits of giggles and finally I launch a tickle attack. "You're cured. Now let me brush my teeth. Make me a coffee, please?"

"No, Jeej."

"Why not? Could you learn to do something useful already?"

"NOOOOO, JEEJ. I am a children, coffee is hot."

"OK, you've got a point."

"Jeej, can I have juice?"

"In a minute, baby." I walk to the bathroom rubbing my eyes trying to remember if I bought juice. He looks forward to juice on Saturdays, the only day it's allowed. That's not a limiting sugar thing. That's a budget thing. A small pint of orange juice and a slice once a week. He's happy with cheap and simple things now but it won't always be this way. There'll be video games and sneakers and cell phones and a growing boy who'll need huge quantities of food and I've got to do better than this.

"You can do it," I say to myself over the bathroom sink. Then I read the affirmations on the post-its I put all around the edge of the mirror. I thought it was a stupid idea when I read about it in an *Oprah* magazine that somebody left behind on the subway. But, in a moment of desperation while pressing send to make my student loan payment, I thought it was a worth a try. Cheaper than a therapist. *I am enough. What I do today is good enough. I am strong and I can stand on my own.* Actually, I'm lonely and tired and stressed, but don't tell the mirror.

We get ready for our trip to the playground in Manhattan. We run into Abuela, the old Dominican lady who lives in 3C and tells everyone to call her Grandma, and help her take her groceries upstairs. We wave to Donovan, the Jamaican guy who lives on the ground floor and always sits by his window. He lets Mr. Cat climb out between the window bars so Johnny can pet him. We walk by Mrs. Yang's Chinese herbal medicine shop and today she gives Johnny a pomegranate. Sometimes it's a lychee or a star fruit from a little stash she keeps under the counter from her morning shopping at the fruit stand around the corner. I helped her son years ago when US immigration messed up his wife's visa but still she shares this kindness with me and Johnny every week.

I love this neighborhood. I just wish we could live here without needing four bolts on the door and bars on the windows. Without the ice-cream truck blaring its demented song late into the night when no one could possibly be buying ice cream from the driver. Without the reek of urine down the steps to the subway. I can't do anything about that but I make sure Johnny doesn't see the human feces when it's on the subway steps because it's definitely there sometimes. But this is New York; to be honest, you could see that on Fifth Avenue too.

I have.

We get off the train in Manhattan and go to the playground in Battery Park. I race Johnny, let him win, then trip and fall to his great amusement. I walk toward the coffee cart on autopilot but then I remember my morning's financial planning.

"Coffee, Jeej?" Johnny says.

"No, not today, go play," I say and watch as he runs off.

It's a sunny day. Crystal-blue sky, a cold edge to the air. The first ten days of September are the hardest, counting each one down until the day Frankie died. It gets easier when we're past the yearly reading of the names at the memorial – his just one of thousands. It hits me like a flash of lightning, his name called out by some other grieving relative trying not to let their voice shake into the microphone. But it's October now and my grief takes a different shape in autumn. The sky is a sunny cloudless blue. The change of season pulls me out of memory, but sometimes the sky pushes me back in headfirst.

My boy's running and laughing, screaming with other kids. He's happy. I stand to the side, hands in pockets, sunglasses on so I can check out the other parents. See if I can tell if any of the dads are single. Not that I would ever approach one. I'm just seeing who's around.

"Look, Jeej, it's for you. Coffee!" Johnny runs up to me with sparkling eyes and hands me a discarded Starbucks cup that he found by the trash and filled with soil. A Coors Light bottle cap added on top for presentation. I pretend to drink it. "Thank you, buddy, that's really good," and I hug him, inhale him. He smells like cookies and dirt. He pulls away, anxious to return to his game. I watch him run back to the other kids. Then, a man's voice behind me and everything that might have been suddenly is.

"Light and sweet?" His accent, clear and crisp, like the snap of your fingers, the click of heels on wet pavement.

"Hi ... oh my God ... hi." It's been eleven years and I don't know what to do. A hug? He steps forward to kiss my cheek but I step back abruptly. I'm still holding the cup of dirt. I take my sunglasses off with my other hand and an awkward space opens between us. He looks the same. Tall and slim, nice clothes, collared-shirt-and-V-neck-sweater-not-American-clothes. I'm flustered. I look like shit. What the hell, God? Could I have gotten a little warning? I would've showered. Put on skinny jeans at least.

"I can't, I mean – what are the chances of seeing you here?" I say, finding it hard to swallow.

"Probably none." He smiles, one corner of his mouth turning up at a time. Tiny hints of gray at his temples, that's the only change. They break my heart – the flecks of gray, the time we lost. Another pause.

I say, "Well, it's nice to see you again. I'm sorry ... we never ... a lot happened." What I mean is that I'm sorry I didn't call the number that he left by the phone at my parents' house. I'm sorry that I didn't answer the letters he sent. I kept them all. Life got complicated.

He says, "Yes, it was a terrible time, I'm sure." He's kind. Just like he was then.

Neither of us knows what to say next. I'm terrified there'll be a silence and I'll lose the moment so I say, "I always wondered where you went when you left our house?" I run my hands through my hair nonchalantly to spot-check how bad it is. It's bad. I put my sunglasses on top of my head for a makeshift headband. Can't do anything about the face, though. I don't know what to do with the cup of dirt.

"I went back to the ferry terminal and some very helpful local Staten Islanders directed me to a fantastic little hotel. Very reasonable, they only charged for every hour of your stay, quite an efficient system, really." He's funny, I forgot. Another pause. There's too much to say. He says, "How are your parents?"

"They're OK. Same really. It's still hard for them."

"I'm so sorry about your brother. I can't imagine how awful it was for all of you. I didn't know how to find you again. I wanted to ... I didn't know ... if you had a memorial? Maybe it wasn't my place, but I've never forgotten. You must know that."

"You were there for the worst part. I haven't forgotten that either." I look in his eyes for the first time. I'm embarrassed because I have no makeup on and I'm a decade older and I know how life has written itself across my face but I never thanked him. Trying not to look away I say, "Thank you for everything you did, I never said thank you."

A gust of wind, a seagull cry overhead, I want to touch his face. He says, "Well, I … you're welcome, you would have done the same." Another silence.

Then he says, "When we were allowed back into the building after the lockdown I looked for you. Waited in the lobby of your building too, checked for you in the coffee shop."

"I didn't go back. I couldn't keep coming downtown every day. It was too close to where he died. I got a different job – in Midtown." I don't say that on the day I went to clean out my desk I waited for him in the coffee shop too, hoping he would come down. That one time, maybe five years ago, I thought I saw him on Wall Street walking and talking on his phone, but I was with my boss and we were late for a meeting and I couldn't stop. But when the guy turned around I saw it wasn't him and I was relieved because I don't know what I would have said with my heart in my mouth, unable to catch my breath at the thought of finding him.

"Well, would you …" he starts to say as our eyes meet but then, "Jeej! Look at this!" Johnny runs over, grabs hold of my leg and shows me a red leaf.

"This is Johnny," I say to Harry. "He's the one who made this coffee." I hold up my cup of dirt. Harry hides his surprise. He bends down to meet Johnny's eyes and says, "Hello there, young man. I'm Harry. I saw you running. That was very fast indeed."

Johnny says, "I'm three, then I'm gonna be four," and gives Harry the leaf.

"Thank you very much, I don't have one like this." He stands up and looks at me from under his brow, I forgot his velvet lashes, how they framed his eyes, and he says, "Are you married, then?" *Is he hurt, does it hurt him to think that?*

"Um, no, but ..." I'm about to explain, to tell him where Johnny came from, but behind me there's a rush of perfume and affluence.

"Hello." A tall, thin, gorgeous blond. Prada sunglasses and a Burberry trench. A statement handbag so expensive that I don't know the brand. She's British too. Harry says, "Oh, right ... Gigi, this is Hannah." She looks at me and Johnny, appalled at my leggings and hoodie under my 1995 Gap jean jacket but otherwise indifferent. She's decided that I'm not competition. Her sunglasses would pay half my rent, that coat would pay for a month of day care. I hate her and I want to be her which makes me hate her more. I can tell they don't have kids. She looks at Johnny in a way she must reserve for hotel maids and homeless people and people whose accents she can't understand.

"Mmm, pleasure." She doesn't put out her hand. She turns away. Pretends to have to stand perpendicular to me because of the wind in her hair – her blow dried, highlighted, expensive hair. I wonder if the word for bitch is the same in British.

Harry's embarrassed by her rudeness, or I hope that he is. He says, "We haven't seen each other for ten, eleven years, can you believe that, Hannah, just ran into each other right here."

"Yes," she says. "Well, we have reservations, don't we, mustn't be late." She can't wait to get out of here and away from our cheap clothes and real life so I string it out a little longer.

I say, "You going somewhere nice?"

Harry says, "Brunch at Soho House."

"Oh, that *is* nice," I say.

"Do you know it?" Hannah asks, surprised that the likes of me would know the name of a private members' fancy-ass establishment.

"Yeah, Johnny loves their brunch, especially the Bloody Marys." Harry laughs. Hannah disapproves. I blush and look away, trying not to be melted by his smile.

Johnny, who's been holding onto my leg patiently, is getting restless now so I lift him up to my hip. This is coming to an end. *Shit*. At least when I didn't know where Harry was I had a fantasy that I would find him someday and he would like me and maybe … but that was something I made up to look forward to in a future that I knew would never come. A memory I relied on to ease my loneliness. But he's got this blond chick with the yoga body and the heels on Saturday morning. Of course he does, why wouldn't he.

I watch as Harry bends down and pretends to tie his shoelace but then pulls a quarter from behind Johnny's ear. The three of us smile at each other. I don't know this man at all but there's the feeling that no one knows me better than him. On the worst day of my life he bandaged my bleeding mother and poured whiskey for my trembling father. And now that he's standing here, I know him too. I don't know what he drinks or if he loves his mother; but I know him. And I've missed him.

I'm looking for the words to let him know somehow but then Johnny says, "Jeej, Jeej, I need a piss." He sounds like a very small Al Pacino. Harry smiles and Hannah looks at me like I'm supposed to reprimand Johnny and be embarrassed, but I don't because I'm not.

"Sorry," I say to them. "You know they pick things up everywhere," which is a lie because I know he picked it up from me. I say, "We'd better go."

Harry says, "Gigi, wait, I …" but Hannah's already turned to leave and stops to look at him over her shoulder, pissed off or maybe that's just her face. He's hers. So I defer.

"Um, I got to deal with Johnny. Nice to meet you, Hannah. Have a nice brunch or whatever." Harry stands with his arms crossed and I lean forward to touch the visible bone of his wrist. A small show of gratitude for the past and recognition that his future lies somewhere else. "I'm glad I saw you again," I say, looking at the ground, because the eyes are too much.

I turn to go, Johnny running ahead of me. I know Harry's watching us walk away but my ass isn't what it used to be. Nothing's what it used to be. I regret every step but I don't turn around.

On the subway back to Brooklyn Johnny leans his whole little body into me while he zooms his Matchbox car in the air, pretending it's a rocket, his eyes turned to a galaxy that only he can see on the ceiling of the C train. I watch Johnny play and feel bad about myself. What a loser. That was my chance, a one-in-a-million chance of finding him again and now it's over. *Jesus, Gigi, get a grip. A non-existent boyfriend from a decade ago.* You're right, I know.

I watch Johnny whizz his car-rocket around, tell him to be careful not to bump the lady next to us who's acting like she's not annoyed but clearly is. In Johnny's other hand he's clutching a white business card. I say, "What's this, baby?"

"It's mine from in my pocket." He won't let go of it.

"Let me see. Where did you get …" I wrestle it from his hand, in case it's something dirty he picked up off the floor, expecting an ad for tarot card reading or a taxi service. I flip it over and read: *Harry Harrison, Vice President, European Equity Sales.*

Brooklyn and Manhattan, October 2012–September 2013

"Jeej, c'mon, remember what Tyra says. If you're doing legs, don't do boobs at the same time," Stacy says, reviewing my outfits. She came over to do my makeup and babysit Johnny so I could go meet Harry. She rejects every dress I try on until we finally get to the black one. Tight, bare shoulders but no cleavage and short. Not that I have such great legs but Stacy let me borrow her nice heels so they look alright.

"Should I put some tanner on my legs? I don't know about this, Stace," I ask her through the mirror.

"Absolutely no fake tan. Have you learned nothing from watching *Top Model* for ten years?"

"Belt?"

"No belts! Jesus, what an amateur."

She sits me down to work on my face. "What're we doing here? Big eyes or big lips? One or the other, never both. And are you sure you know what you're doing?"

"What?"

"Jeej, this guy – it's a little crazy."

"I know."

"Turn this way so I can do your foundation," she says, tilting my chin toward her. "I just don't want you to get too wrapped up in it. You haven't been out with anyone for forever, so I don't want you to get too excited, in case he's not what you think. I just want to make sure you know what you're doing."

"Yeah, I do," I say, but I don't. I'm worried all the time. I'm sad and alone. I'm so tired of being alone. I love that kid so much that it's ripping my heart out to leave him tonight. I'm wearing a dress that cost eighteen bucks from one of the stalls on Canal Street and borrowed shoes and I got enough makeup on for three hookers. Like an asshole, I decided to cut my hair yesterday, and now I look like Posh Spice in an outfit from Walmart. I'm meeting a man who gave his business card to my kid so his "friend" wouldn't see. But I think I love him because he bought me coffee once years ago. I have no idea what I'm doing.

But then his hand presses into the small of my back to protect me from the homicidal taxicabs and he slows to my pace and covers me like a shield. Just with the press of his hand on my back to cross the street he's told me what kind of man he is. I've always known.

He takes me to a pulsing-velvet-champagne-lounge with the beautiful people. This part of New York that I've never had enough money to see. His eyes and hands tell me that me and my cheap dress belong here. With him. And I believe him.

Harry finds a place at the bar. I hop up on a stool and he keeps his hand on my waist, stronger, closer, than before, resting on the top of my hip, making it clear that that space belongs to him. He gets the bartender's attention, leans over me more than he has to. He whispers in my ear but I feel it everywhere. He smells like soap, clean-man skin, and aftershave. He has stubble despite the shave and it scrapes my cheek but I like it.

Ice clinks in my vodka tonic when I raise my glass. I bite my straw, cross my legs, and ask him if he likes my shoes. Make sure he gets the full view.

"They're lovely, but I'm not sure how far you'd get in those."

"They're not for walking."

He smiles, a sideways smile, the way men do when they're trying not to show you how much they like you.

We're supposed to go out for dinner after this but I've had a few drinks and I want to pretend that it's ten years ago when I was younger and prettier, when I didn't need so much foundation to hide the lines, because there were none. I tell my mid-thirties body to act like the girl in her twenties is still in there even if things around my middle are softer than they used to be. I wish he could've have touched me back then.

The cab pulls into the circular driveway in front of one of the luxury high-rises in the forties along Tenth Avenue overlooking the Hudson. The lobby has pink marble walls and floors. A glass light sculpture the size of a car hangs suspended two stories above us. Uniformed doormen in navy-blue jackets sit behind the desk drinking coffee in paper cups and reading the *New York Post*.

"Good evening, gentlemen," Harry says as we go past.

"How you doin', Mr. Harrison."

I'm glad that he's nice to the doormen. He's nice to cab drivers and waiters too. He hasn't turned into a dick in the last decade. That's a relief.

The elevator is mirrored on all sides. Emboldened by the alcohol and the rush of being out at night, which I haven't been for a long time, I remind myself that I waxed and I remember my affirmations. I *am* enough, goddammit, and I push him up against one wall, drop my coat and make sure he can see the reflection of my back, my leg wrapped around his waist while he watches himself kiss my shoulders, runs a finger along the tight top of my dress, teasing me, fumbling with the zipper up the back, caught off guard when I slip my hand under his belt. We've got thirty floors to go.

A deep inhale, he shuts his eyes. A light kiss. When we get to his floor he holds the doors open but won't let me out. "I'm afraid I can't let you out without a password, Miss Stanislawski," so I bite his ear, kiss his neck, and when he still won't move I unbuckle his belt, crouch down, and just when he thinks that what he wants to happen is about to happen, I pull his jeans down to his ankles and run. And we laugh, and I get a good head start on him while he's still pulling up his pants by the elevator. We play chase down the halls, I'm running with my shoes in my hand until he catches me, and we're laughing and breathless.

He opens his apartment door. We keep the lights off, but the whole room is lit by the glow from the neon signs and buildings across the street throwing sharp shadows across the room. It's a small apartment, but big for New York, with one window stretching its whole length. I brace myself with one arm against it, the other wrapped around his neck, and that's where it happens, up against the window with the twinkling roof lights blinking at us, visible but unseen, naked but clothed in shadows, thirty-eight stories above the streets of New York City.

But there's more than this. More than the rough, rugged sweat and smell and rocking rawness of skin-on-skin and flesh-in-flesh. There's sleep. Sleep with him curled around my back, the rise and fall of his chest against my shoulder blades. Real sleep. Not semi-consciousness on alert for danger. Not waking up with my hand already on the hammer under the mattress when I hear a noise. Real sleep with Harry's arms tangled around me, his hand still holding mine. I wake up and look at him, jealous of his long lashes, in love with his warm skin.

After that night we have lots more nights like that. Sometimes we have nights eating takeout and drinking wine on the roof of his building where you can see Tenth Avenue laid out like a sparkling runway. Sometimes we have nights in my place in Brooklyn, eating pizza and watching *Toy Story* with Johnny. Johnny jumps off the arm of the sofa and onto Harry's back a hundred times and Harry lets him, pretending that Johnny's knocked him out, or that Johnny's an astronaut and they're landing on the Moon. And my boy laughs and laughs.

There are a thousand moments when we laugh. Harry asked me for a tea towel to clean up something Johnny spilled. I said, "What the hell is a tea towel? You mean a paper towel?"

And I held out the roll and he said, "What's a paper towel? This is kitchen roll."

I said, "What are you talking about?"

"No, a tea towel, this thing."

He held it up and I said, "A dishcloth? Is that what you mean?" and whatever was spilled just sank into the sofa while Harry and Johnny chased me around the apartment waving every dishcloth that we had. We ended up in a pile on the floor, the three of us, out of breath, surveying the apartment wrapped in a whole roll of unwound paper towels, Johnny laughing into the cardboard tube, listening to the sound of his happiness amplified.

Then at bedtime, against my better judgment, we start to act like a couple, like parents, reading to Johnny and putting him to bed together.

"Harry, have you ever drove a race car?" Johnny asks him.

"No, I haven't."

"Where do you work?" Little face cocked sideways, suspicious.

"At a bank. It's quite dull, I'm afraid." Harry smiles, but shows Johnny he takes him seriously.

Johnny's not done. "You been to Central Park?"

"Yes, I have, quite a few times."

"D'you like trucks?" Johnny's got a lot to cover.

"I do indeed."

"What's your favorite animal?" Johnny's rubbing his eyes now. He's tired but the answer is critical.

"The cheetah. It's the fastest."

"Faster than a race car?"

"Almost as fast as a normal car."

"Good, I'm gonna put that in my bemembery."

"In what?" Harry asks.

"Where I keep the fax. Goodnight. I love you." Satisfied that he's settled things, he pulls the covers up to his chin.

Johnny's decided to love him. Harry's taken aback and touched. He doesn't want to say the wrong thing, doesn't want to tell my son he loves him because it's too soon, so instead he says, "And I think you're a splendid little chap," as he rubs Johnny's hair and steals his nose.

Johnny, confused by Harry's accent and the unfamiliar phrase, says, "You need to check, Harry, 'cause I don't think those are real words you just said. G'night."

Then Harry wraps his arms around both of us. I shouldn't have let Johnny get so close so soon but my arms had done all the holding for so long that to have Harry's arms around us both – I had no idea how strong I'd been until he lifted the weight from me.

A year went by, a year of laughing and playing and being together; of happiness; a man in Johnny's life; love in both our lives that we didn't have before. Although me and Johnny said we loved him all the time, Harry could never say it back. But that was OK, it didn't matter because he showed us his love every day.

Then one Saturday morning while we watch Johnny play in the playground there is more than "I love you." There is, "Gigi, come to London. You and Johnny, come and live with me."

This is the part of the movie where Hugh Grant looks up at the woman from under his eyebrows and smiles and his Englishness – his dimple and hint of a laugh under every sentence and puns and understatement and table manners and shirts with real cufflinks – they shoot her through the heart and she leaps into his arms.

But I've got a kid and I'm a real person so I say, "Get the fuck out of here," and shove him.

He takes my hand. "They want me back in London and I'd like you to come with me."

"You're serious?" I pull my hand away, thrilled and terrified. "Because, if you're fucking with me, it's not funny."

He pulls me into him. "They're promoting me, sending me home. I want you to come with me, you and Johnny.

But you need to see it first. See if you're sure. We won't do it if it's not right for you."

How long is a heartbeat? How long is a breath? A fraction of a second to choose a different life. Before I can stop myself, before I can even think of the words, I've said them.

"If it's with you then it's right." Harry pulls me to him. I close my eyes and breathe him in. I'm not sure what I'm doing.

I do it anyway.

4

CHAMPAGNE, SMOKE, DIET COKE

A Wednesday in August 2016, 12 p.m. London, Grand Euro Star Lodge Hotel, Room 506

Luckily, it's impossible to drown in a European half bathtub. I found this out when I woke up in water, shivering and pale. Added bonus, though, the cold water constricted my muscles so my thighs looked, just for a minute, not good, but not horrifying. I fell asleep curled in a ball because that's the only way to sit in half a bathtub and it was painful to stand up, especially around my middle, where my scar's still red and raised. I grabbed my rented towel and, of course, it was half the size it should have been. I pulled on my clothes and got under the covers. It took a long time to stop shivering.

I check the time. Noon. I order a pizza and two bottles of red wine. You can't get wine delivered with your pizza at home. Another check in the pro column for life in the U.K. *Dammit. Shit.* A sudden pang of regret and anxiety.

I forgot to pack Johnny's bag for soccer camp today. I can see the shin guards where I left them, lying at the bottom of the stairs. Of course, Harry wouldn't have remembered. That's fair enough, since his wife just walked out on him. No snack either. Three days in a row that I forgot. An image of Johnny searching through his bag at break time, hungry, tired, knowing that there's nothing in his bag while his friends pull out evenly cut carrot sticks and digestive biscuits. He loves those, kept asking me to buy them and I didn't get why he wanted stomach medicine until he showed them to me in the store. That's got to be, hands down, the worst name ever for a cookie.

I can't do anything about it now. I don't even feel guilty. In these last months I've disappointed Johnny so many times in so many ways that he doesn't get upset anymore. He's just accepted my shitness and hugs me anyway. Like those baby monkeys taken from their mothers in that experiment you learn about in high-school biology. And the baby monkeys, looking for a mother, any mother, kept trying to hug the wire monkey covered in a towel, kept sitting with her, clinging to her, loving her, even though she never responded. Even though a towel could never be fur.

I look down at the phone. There's a red dot over my email app. Harry.

You're not answering my texts. Have you blocked me? I'm so worried, where are you? I'm calling every-where looking for you. Please tell me you're safe. It's been hours. If you don't want to tell me where you are please just tell me you're safe. Please call. I love you. PS: I can't find Rocky's medicine.

71

The TV's still on. The Housewives have left for their Boca Raton weekend getaway. Nicole says, "I want to hear birds chirping, I want to see sunshine all the time, I want to feel the warmth on my face, on my boobs …" It's been a cold, hard winter in Jersey.

I hit reply. Watch the cursor blink.

I'm waiting to feel something. Panic or hysteria, regret, sadness or longing, rage. I thought that's what would happen, some great outpouring of pain that would prove to me how much I love them. Some involuntary impulse to get on a plane and never come back, or to go back to the house and pull my babies close to me and vow to start over. I thought something would happen if I walked out and left.

But I'm calm and my heartbeat is steady.

I watch the ladies order tequila by the pool. Then they go grocery shopping in five-inch heels for that night's dinner. Later they get wasted and compare nipple covers for their strapless tops, a must-have for looks where you can't wear a bra. It gets heated when Dina wants to bring up the rumor to the twins about Rino and his mother-in-law and the fact that Amber knows and that they don't trust her. But Nicole doesn't want to hear it. I wonder if Rocky's screaming with tiredness right now and if Johnny's hungry. I wonder these things and feel nothing.

Not true.

Relief; I feel relief that I'm not there.

And resentment.

Because this email – is this about making sure I'm OK? Or is it about making sure I come home and handle all the shit he doesn't know how – doesn't *want* – to do? Is this insecurity in his messages about me? Or is it about him, having to handle two kids on his own, figure shit out, make shit up, just fucking getting shit done any way it can get done?

It's the P.S., the friggin' P.S. I'm in here having a breakdown and he's asking me where Rocky's medicine is. I bet he's patting himself on the back thinking he's amazing for even remembering that Rocky needs medicine. He can't even, not even now, he can't even open his eyes and fucking LOOK FOR IT. "OK, get it together, Jeej," I have to say out loud when I find myself screaming at the blinking cursor.

I start typing:

It's in the fridge asshole that's where you keep liquid antibiotics and our kids have needed antibiotics at least four times in the past year and every time they have been in the fridge and they have not been camouflaged as lunch meat or apples every single time they have been there in a translucent bottle full of fluorescent yellow liquid and you live in our house and you are the father of these children and you should know that and the fridge is a discrete area it's not hard to find something in a fridge especially not ours since it's empty most of the time because you never help me because you are incapable of entering a supermarket or maybe that's just what you expect the help to do oh wait WE DON'T HAVE ANY HELP ITS JUST ME YOU MOTHERFUC—

I delete it. The intimate management of shit and dirt and food and children is of little interest to him. Of so little interest that he doesn't even know it exists for him to have no interest in.

73

When I was pregnant and still working I would set my alarm to get up early so I could vomit twice and still get to work on time. One morning, while I was lying on the bathroom floor, just to feel the cold tiles on my face before I puked again, Johnny poked his head around the door.

"Jeej, are you alright?" he said, head tilted upside down to see me better. Sweet boy.

"Yes, baby, go get ready for school, I'll be OK."

"OK, but Jeej, do you have a shoebox? Remember I need a shoebox today."

Oh, fuck. The fucking shoebox. "Um, go ask Harry to find one, OK?" I croak from the floor. Johnny needs a shoebox, a glass jar, a cardboard tube, or a historical costume every week. The school seems to think that we have a huge surplus of shoeboxes and jam jars that we keep on a magical shelf with our bottomless box of cardboard tubes next to the closet full of child-sized Roman emperor's capes and pharaoh's headdresses because God forbid they learn anything without appearing in full costume and dragging a bag of garbage to school.

The point was I had done everything the night before. Packed the waterproofs with the rain boots in a named plastic bag for forest school; signed the homework diary; checked the spelling sheet; packed karate uniform and after-school pre-karate snack; labeled the water bottle; tested him on his five-times table. I did a nit check with a metal comb because somebody in the class has friggin' lice again. After he went to bed I finished three client letters and emailed a brief to counsel. I knew I'd be throwing up in the morning so I did everything the night before. Everything except finding the fucking shoebox.

While I washed my face between rounds of vomiting, Harry came into the bathroom, in boxer shorts and dress shirt, tying his tie and checking his shave in the mirror. "Pukes, Johnny needs a shoebox," he said. Pukes was his new nickname for me. I vomited on his business socks.

"My God, are you alright, darling?" Harry says, alarmed.

"I'm fine. Find him a box. And change your socks."

Twenty minutes later I pulled on a black dress, put on my sneakers and put my work shoes in my bag. I did the best I could with my makeup but it was hard to cover the spray of red dots from the broken blood vessels left around my eyes from the vomiting. Harry had left for work and Johnny was standing at the door waiting for me. His shoes were on the wrong feet and he skipped a button so his shirt was crooked. His teeth were brushed but his hair wasn't, but I had to let that go. He had his school bag with all his stuff; I had my work bag with my plastic bags for emergency puking on the train, water, foundation and a bag of Cool Ranch Doritos, the only thing I could keep down.

"OK, baby, where'd Harry put the shoebox?" I asked Johnny, ready to walk us out the door. He pointed to the table: "It's there, Jeej. I'm not sure it's right though."

On the table was the extra-large cardboard box that we used to move our bedding from the States. I knew because it was written in marker on the side: *Bedding*. It was fifty times the size of a shoebox. The presence of the box on the table meant that upstairs in the loft, everything that was stored in this box was now in a huge pile on the floor.

Johnny, already skilled in British understatement, said, "I think that's a bit too big, Jeej." I would've screamed if my throat wasn't so raw. Instead I sighed, opened a kitchen cabinet, took out a box of cannelloni shells and emptied them into a bowl.

"Jeej, what're you doing?" Johnny asked, peering over the counter.

"Gettin' shit done, Johnny."

"Language, Jeej, £1 in the jar, please."

"Sorry, remind me later, will this be OK?" and I held the empty pasta box up, an acceptable substitute.

"That's good, thank you, Jeej."

I wasn't angry about the box. Or the mess in the loft. Or the insanity of waking up early to vomit and dealing with every last tiny detail of Johnny's life and then working ten hours every day in a haze of nausea and Doritos and Coke. I wasn't angry at how unfair it was – I was angry because I knew a woman would never hand me a half-ton of cardboard when I asked for a shoebox. I was angry that Harry wasn't a woman.

That's still the problem. He hasn't been trained since before he could speak to intuit the needs of others. He hasn't been shown how to push against the pulsing muscle of his heart to make room for everyone who needs a space in it. When he does try I say his attempts are inadequate. I don't accept his limitations. But he doesn't admit he has them. He doesn't do what I would do. He doesn't apologize for his presence, take up as little room as possible. Every time he pretends to step up but doesn't and every time I'm disappointed. But neither of us explains and neither of us changes.

We used to say thank you and please. We used to try to be what the other one needed and wanted. I thought we were special. I thought we wouldn't take each other for granted like all the other couples I knew because we'd lost each other for so long.

I used to love him, I used to think he saved my life, I used to think he took care of me, I used to ... lots of things.

I hit reply.

I am terrified of the pain I feel. It's paralyzing me. I'm afraid that I'll hurt them. I won't mean to but I will. That I already have. I'm afraid that I can't get better, that I will always be like this, brittle and cracked and empty. I used to love you but I don't remember how to now. You used to love me too but I'm sick and I know you're afraid of me and you can't look at me anymore. I need your help, I need your hel—

Delete, delete, delete, delete. I delete that. If I say that then he'll have to do something. And what if the something he does is leave me. Because I'm not who he thought I was. Because the kids are better off without me. Or what if he says he'll stay if I promise to get better but I can't. And I don't, ever, and I'm always like this. Or what if I tell him and he decides to ... what if I tell him and he knows but then he does nothing at all?

I start typing.

Amoxicillin in the fridge. Yellow bottle. If he missed the breakfast dose don't double up just make sure you give it to him on time at lunch and at 4.

Press send.

London, October 2013

The tub is huge, deep, with claw feet. The floors and walls are white marble tile. Gold taps. Gold-frame mirror. This bathroom is nicer than any apartment I've ever lived in. I slip into the hot water and try to remember how this feels in case I never stay somewhere this nice again. The wedding floats around in my head.

There were chandeliers and champagne. Just like the weddings you see in the movies about English people. Every other guy looked like Benedict Cumberbatch. And I was doing OK. I didn't understand seventy per cent of what anyone said to me and I did a lot of fake laughing but everyone was nice, said nice things about New York; complimented my dress even though a banana yellow mini wasn't right for a black tie wedding, I now knew. But everybody drank so much so fast that it didn't matter. And Harry held my hand the whole time, explained the references I didn't get, gave me all the gossip about the people I had met and I thought, *OK, we can do this.*

Then, a loud booming voice and a big hand on Harry's shoulder and we were face to face with Hannah and one of the beefier Benedicts, more like a Daniel Craig, who gave Harry a huge bear hug. Hannah stood there being beautiful. Her dress was long-sleeved, fitted black lace over a nude slip. Racy and restrained. I looked like Tweety Bird next to her.

"Hannah, Rupert, this is Gigi," Harry said as Rupert lunged toward me for two violent cheek kisses, unsteady on his feet. Hannah put out her hand and only let the fingertips touch slightly when we shook. Clearly still a bitch.

I was about to say, "Yes, we met once, that time in New York," but she cut me off and said, "Lovely to meet you, are you enjoying London?" and stared straight into my eyes, telling me to play along.

"I, um ..." and before I could answer, Rupert slurred, "Yes, I've heard about you, Jenny, Harry doesn't stop talking about you, lovely to meet you. Anyway, I know this is a wedding but we're also celebrating ourselves tonight, aren't we, Hannah?"

"Oh, Rupert, honestly, don't make a fuss, it's not the right place," she said with a smile and an eye roll, covering up something he was close to revealing.

"We're expecting! She's up the duff! What do you think of that, Hazza, I finally did it! Where's the champagne – ah! Thank you, sir," Rupert said, accosting a waiter and taking his whole tray of champagne flutes.

"Expecting ... expecting." Harry said it twice. He was looking at her when he said it, only for a few seconds, but I saw it. Something unfinished between them. Something unresolved in his voice.

"Well, aren't you going to congratulate us?" Hannah said with a sparkling smile as she touched his arm, which is OK if you're friends, which is what he told me they were. Except that then her hand ran down the length of his forearm. All the way down to the wrist. It only took a second. A second for me to know he loved her. And that he lied to me.

"Sorry, I ... well done, you two, fantastic, great news, great news," and Harry's voice trailed off. He managed to smile, to look like this was alright. But I could see that it wasn't. Then he said, "Yes, well, have you seen the bride and groom? We should be getting on and saying hello, shouldn't we, terribly rude of us, Gigi hasn't met them yet," Harry's hand on my back trying to move me away from Hannah and Rupert, but there was no way to make a quick getaway in the crowded room, not with Rupert forcing glasses into our hands.

"Not yet, don't go, a toast is in order, don't you think? Let me sort everyone out." Another look passed between Hannah and Harry as Rupert handed each of them a glass. Then Rupert drained his drink and fumbled his reach for the next one, spilling champagne on my dress while I watched the man I thought was mine try not to drown in some old regret.

I missed Johnny suddenly and painfully, wished that I was at home in our little apartment, in our little world, the way it was before I let Harry through the door. I looked around the room, felt the cold champagne soaking through the fabric into my skin, watched a drunk couple try to reenact the lift from *Dirty Dancing* in the middle of the floor. I didn't belong here. We came to this wedding so I could meet Harry's friends and see London and fall in love with it, but I didn't belong here. I don't know why I thought I did.

"I'm so sorry," Rupert spluttered at me as I backed away to avoid the spray and keep myself from stumbling into Hannah and Harry's affair. Or whatever it was that was sitting there between them. I said, "That's OK, would you excuse me a sec ... I'm just going to the ladies." I broke out of Harry's grip and pushed my way through the crowd with him calling my name and me refusing to hear it.

I fixed my makeup in the bathroom because I didn't know what else to do. I blotted at the dark patch of champagne on my dress to look busy. He didn't pull his arm away as fast as he should have. He should have pulled his arm away when she ran her fingers down to his wrist. He should have lifted his hand to have a sip of champagne and shrugged her off. But he didn't. He looked down at her fingertips on the fabric of his suit. He said ... what did he say? I asked him, when I called him, before our first date, I asked him, was he ...

Are you with her?

Who, Hannah? No, not at all.

Because I don't want to get involved, you know, if you're taken.

No, Hannah's a friend, an old friend from university, that's all.

Because if you're with her, even a little bit, it's kind of shady, to give me your number like that. How'd you know I didn't have a boyfriend?

I didn't. I looked for a ring, but didn't see one. I thought that if you had a boyfriend then I would have to take the risk. You could explain me away. A friend from long ago.

Yeah, it was long ago.

Yes, and I'd waited for you for a long time.

Me too. I was waiting too.

Maybe he was waiting for me, but I could see by the way the air was knocked out of him when Rupert said "expecting," that while he was waiting for me he had been passing the time with her. The champagne buzz lifted from my head. The clarity was harsh, like summer sun through a window, showing up all the dirt.

"Oh, Gigi, thank goodness you're in here, I thought I'd lost you. Thank you so much. That could have all been very ugly," Hannah said from the bathroom door before opening her clutch to take out her lipstick. I glanced at it. Laura Mercier. The bag, YSL. I watched her for a minute, reapplying makeup, combing through her hair, spritzing perfume. Her eyes focused entirely on herself as she talked to me.

"You're really a star, I'm sorry you had to be in the middle of that, I tried to keep Rupert away from you both, but you see what he's like. He was drunk before we even got to the first course. I'd be so grateful to you if you just wouldn't mention this to anyone else tonight and preferably wouldn't speak to Rupert again, you understand, don't you."

"No, I don't, not really," I said to her reflection. She had everything: looks, money, friends, my boyfriend. She got away with things because she was pretty. She talked to people like they worked for her.

"You know, don't you, Harry told you, of course, at least, I assumed he had. No? Well, alright, the short story is that Rupert and I got together after uni and we were on and off for six years. Things would be so good for a while and then they just, wouldn't. He always managed to get me back. But we were off when I was seeing Harry, so it could hardly be described as cheating, *not really*. Rupert just never knew about us. When he decided to really *be* on and finally propose to me, well, everything moved very quickly. I think poor Harry was quite put out but he knew it could never work between us."

"You were on a break when you were seeing Harry?" I said, just to say something, wondering if Monica, Phoebe, and Chandler would be joining us in the bathroom too.

"Yes, and we agreed it would be better for Rupert to never know. Rupert loves Harry and always has, so, it was easier all around for everyone, kinder really, even though we didn't *really* do anything wrong, just easier never to tell him or anyone, don't you think?"

She brushed her hair as she told me this, her eyes casting glances at me through the mirror, a very light smile at the corner of her lips because she was secretly pleased to know that I didn't know; and that Harry loved her once, and maybe he still did.

"And when we saw you and your son that day, well, things were still … delicate. I thought it was just better not to mention it tonight. Better to stay on message."

I watched her bend sideways so that the cascade of her shiny long hair was easier to comb through while she explained her plan for lying to her husband for the rest of her life. "Really, I really do appreciate your discretion."

I looked at her reflection above the sinks. She was pretty, but in that light I could see the crow's feet, some dark spots from too much sun. I picked up my bag and said, "I didn't do anything for you. And I think you sat on something. There's a snag in the lace on your ass crack. Also, you're a real bitch." Then I walked out of the bathroom, past the bar, out of the lobby, and into a cab.

Halfway to the airport I asked the driver to turn around. I came back to the hotel room, opened the door, got in the bath. I came back instead of leaving. But he's not here.

And the fancy bubble bath in the claw-foot tub and the tiny little vodka bottles from the mini-bar don't make him appear, and they don't take away the sting of wanting to believe that whoever came before me didn't matter. Because I know she still does.

I sink into the water and try to put it all together:

So what if he was sleeping with his friend's girl? I mean, he shouldn't have done that, but that shit happens. I can't be mad about that, that's got nothing to do with me.

It had something to do with you tonight.

OK, but she said she was on a break with Rupert, so maybe it's not that bad.

Oh, well, if she said it then it must be true.

Alright, OK. He said he wasn't with her. They were friends. People are friends with their exes, right?

Yeah, of course. That always works.

Shit, OK. Why did he lie about her? There was more to it, is that why?

Yes. He has a penis.

I slide my head under the water. Feel the hot silence.

You love him. You have to take all of him.

But what about Johnny? What about Johnny?

That's your fault. You let him get too close. But that's because you love him. Both of them.

Shit. I know.

When I come up for air I hear the key in the lock. Harry opens the door to the room, sees the bathroom door ajar, and surprised he says, "Gigi, your dress is on the floor. I mean – you're here." He's somber and sober.

"It's your lucky day," I answer from the bath.

"I thought you'd left. Hannah said … she saw you … it doesn't matter. I came up here to look for you before but …"

I put my arms up on either side of the tub, stare straight ahead. I hope my wet hair is doing something sexy even though I'm furious. "Well, I didn't and I'm not. Where've you been so late?"

He puts his hand on the bathroom doorknob, unsure where to stand. He says, "I was just down in the bar, after the reception finished. I didn't want to be alone."

I wave him into the bathroom. "You're not alone now. Pull up a seat."

He goes to sit on the edge of the bath but I point him to the toilet. I turn on the tap to heat up the water. He starts talking. I can't hear him while the water's running but I look at him, his elbows on his knees, head in hands, talking to the floor. I'm mad at him, I feel bad for him, I'm nervous, I hate him and I love him and I can't deal with his face, the big brown eyes and the stubble. I look at my watch on the chair by the bath: 2 a.m. I want to punch him. I want to hug him. I want this part to be over. I want to know what happens to us next.

"There'd better be more to it than just fucking around," I say, turning off the tap.

"Gigi, please. Don't make it sound like that. I loved her." He looks at me like I've wronged him.

"Yeah, I can see that, she's really lovable. What did you love about her the most? Was it her great personality or just the regular blow jobs from a supermodel?"

"Why did you come back here? Just to eviscerate me?" Harry asks, defensive.

I say, through my teeth, "That's a big word for this time of night."

He takes his jacket off. He must have changed after the wedding. I recognise that T-shirt. The one he wore when we took Johnny to the Bronx Zoo and Harry carried him on his back half the day. When we were happy. Before the past woke up and met us in this bathroom.

I say, "I came back because it's fucking stupid to sit in an airport all night, no matter how mad I am at you. And I'm here now so you might as well explain yourself."

85

Harry gets up and starts pacing the bathroom. The space shrinks around his height.

He rubs his forehead, raises his face to the ceiling hoping I won't notice that his eyes have gotten glassy, like he might cry. I saw him do that once before. We were watching *School of Rock* with Johnny and it was the part when Tomika, the little Black girl, takes Jack Black aside and says she's afraid to sing. But then she sings 'Chain of Fools' with a hundred-year-old soul like a baby Aretha. I looked over and I said, "Are you crying?" and he rubbed his forehead and smiled and said, "Don't be ridiculous," which meant yes, so Johnny went over and patted his face.

Fuck. That's why I love him. That's why I'll love him even if he did something wrong and stupid. I'll love him even if he lied to me. And even if he lies to me again.

Harry puts his forehead on the towel rail. Talks to the floor. "We were a circle of friends in uni, me, Hannah, a few others, Rupert was my housemate. When we graduated they stayed in London, I left for New York, and they kept breaking up and getting back together. I never went near her, never, when they were together, or at least, when I knew they were together, in all these years."

He paces the bathroom floor, looking at the tiles, the bathmat, the door, anything but me. "Rupert went to work in Hong Kong and they broke up. Hannah got promoted and it meant business trips to New York. We've known each other since we were eighteen. It would have been strange for her not to call when she was in town."

He stops pacing, leans against the vanity, half-sitting on the edge of the sink. "I was lonely. I worked eighteen-hour days. I started work at 5 most mornings on the European desk. I went to work in a box in a building and went to bed at night in a box in a building. It was all very empty. I made money. Bantered at the office. Talked to girls in bars who just wanted me to say inane things with a British accent. It was awful. But then Hannah would appear and I didn't have to explain anything. She was lonely too. She'd given up on Rupert. She was lost and so was I and—" he looks away from me, "we fell in love. I knew at some point we'd have to tell him, I broke the code, I should never have touched her, but I thought we could all be adults about it. Maybe it should have been me and her all along."

I try not to flinch at that last sentence. I say, "Why didn't you tell me, when I asked you about her? Why did I have to stand there tonight and look at you looking at her?"

"I feel awful, I ..." he mumbles. I wish I was dressed. I keep hold of my knees to cover myself, goose bumps rising up on my arms. My skin is tight, itchy. I stare at the taps and he slides down the vanity to the floor, hands to his face. We're silent for a while until he finally says, "Gigi, she was pregnant. I was going to marry her."

I'm overcome with jealousy. It didn't happen but I'm jealous that it could have. I'm trying to remember that I'm angry. I'm angry and jealous and in love all at once. I make him turn around so I can climb out of the bath. I put on the fluffy hotel robe, devastated and furious. And afraid.

He leans his head against the cupboard under the sink. He tells me about the future he didn't have as I sit on the edge of the tub. "She told me about the baby and we decided that I would move back to London and we'd get married. She flew home and I sublet my apartment, got a job transfer, sold my furniture on Craigslist. Made enquiries about houses in Clapham. Found out about registry weddings in Chelsea. I was going to push the pram on the common. I was going to get one of those carriers so that on Sunday mornings I could strap the baby on and get coffees and the paper for us while she slept in."

I can see him doing it, flashes of him as a father and husband. I dig my feet into the bathmat. I look at my toes, candy-apple red polish like drops of blood. A cheap-looking red against the Egyptian cotton or whatever fancy stuff this mat is made of. I want it to be me, me in the picture of that life he wanted.

He keeps going: "I wanted her and school plays and rugby matches and Christmas morning." His eyes are shining. "It was stupid of me, turning my whole life upside down like that. I just wanted it. She said she had to tell Rupert, alone, in person. We owed him that much. But then one week became two and all my calls went to voicemail. I had to move into a hotel until she got round to telling me what was happening to my life."

From his spot on the bathroom floor Harry tells me about how she emailed him a month later from Thailand. She never told Rupert about Harry or the baby. She just made a discreet visit to a clinic and a few weeks later accepted Rupert's proposal on a moonlit beach.

These are his secrets, the pieces of his life that broke. But there's more, there always is, so I say, "But when I saw you in the park, it was over between you?"

He sighs. "She made me promise not to tell him. She thought it would ruin their engagement, destroy our whole circle. But I was going to tell him anyway, except that then he asked me to be in the wedding. We were at a bar, we'd had a few drinks, there was no way to say no. I was about to tell him but then he said he wanted to be with her so much, he loved her, had loved her for years. I wasn't brave enough to do it. And she had already ruined my life, I didn't see why she should ruin his as well. God, I sound like such an arse." Harry shakes his head, looks ahead at the bathroom radiator, embarrassed and ashamed.

This is all of him. He betrayed his friend, had his heart broken, thought he was a dad and then he wasn't. He didn't tell the truth when he should have. He's still entwined with her lies. But he also swept the glass off the floor when my brother died. He reads stories to Johnny. He's taken away my loneliness. He's flawed. He's made mistakes. I soften, the anger dissipates ...

Um, Gigi, you're getting carried away here, I know you love him but he lied to you, can you get to that part please—

Shit, right, OK. "OK, so, why didn't you tell me any of this before? It was so obvious when you saw her tonight."

"You're right. But you and I had just started dating, it felt like such a lot to explain and I'm not a hero in this story. That day, when you saw us, I was taking her to a surprise brunch with all their New York friends, her first-anniversary present, and Rupert wanted as many people from the wedding there as possible. He asked me to take her. It was humiliating but we were in too deep by then. When you saw us we had just met up to go. I should have refused; I was so spineless. And what would you have thought of me? I thought I'd lost you forever and suddenly there you were, and I just didn't want ... I thought you'd leave."

"Come here," I say, and put my arms out for him to join me at the edge of the tub. I close my eyes for a minute and ask myself if this is OK. I put my hand on his knee, he puts his hand over mine. I ask myself if this will be good for my boy. If I'm doing the right thing.

He interrupts the silence: "I'm sorry, I'm … it was a mistake. What a cock. But if it cost me you too—"

I stop him. "You loved her. Love's fucked up sometimes." He looks at our hands, fingers interlaced. I don't say that men are fucked up sometimes too. How they would do anything – anything – for a beautiful woman. How a man will reach for that beauty and tell lies for her even when a real woman – the right woman, not beautiful but loyal and full of heart – is standing right next to him. I know Harry doesn't love her, but he will always know he had her; he will always secretly hang on to that fact, that he had a beautiful woman once. He doesn't love her but all it took was her hand running down his sleeve to put her between us tonight. And she did it because she's beautiful and she knew that she could.

I tighten my grip on his hand. "Don't lie to me again."

"I won't," he says, clutching me to him, wanting me to feel how much he means it.

"You're asking me and Johnny to move our whole lives here. You have to give us your whole life too. Even this stuff, this shitty stuff."

"I promise," he says.

"OK," I say, pulling away from him up to standing.

"OK?" he asks, unsure.

"OK already, you're right, it's a really nice tub." And as I push him into the bath he pulls me in with him, and we're a tangle of clothes and robes and bubbles and water. We sit there for a while like that in the tub, laughing, water flowing over the sides, sloshing through the leftover bubbles.

He picks up my left hand and says, "I was going to prop—"

"No. Don't say it."

"But, this weekend, it's all been ruined now but I brought you here to—"

"Don't talk about it. Just do it right."

"But I ... do you want—"

"No. Just do it right. You'll know when."

He pulls me out of the bath, picks me up, sits me on the edge of the sink, presses me against him, carries me, kisses me in the doorway of the bathroom, one arm up on the frame to brace himself. We stumble and laugh, tearing off wet clothes, pushing up against the walls, falling to the floor. The air of the room is cold on wet skin, but it makes everything better, heightened. I run my hands through his wet hair. We find the space we fit in together.

Staten Island, March 2014

"So, what, you're really doing this?" Ma barks at me from her usual position: sitting in her vinyl armchair, cigarette in one hand, other hand resting on her beer in the built-in cup holder. Her belly resting on her thighs, forcing her legs apart, filling the whole chair with her flesh and disappointment. It's only ten in the morning so she's trying not to drink the beer too obviously in front of Johnny and Harry.

"Yeah, Ma, we are." I come into the living room from the kitchen and stand to the side of the TV because getting in the way of *Wheel of Fortune* will only make this more difficult.

Harry stands behind me, grabs my hand, speaks to the back of her chair, "Donna, we wanted to invite you to the ceremony tomorrow."

"How romantic." She takes a drag of her cigarette, staring straight ahead while Vanna turns the letters.

"Do you want to come to City Hall?" I ask her even though I don't want her there and she doesn't want to be there. But we go through the motions of this conversation. Harry said he didn't feel right doing it unless we asked her. He's not related to her, though.

"Granma, will you please come? Did you know Jeej is getting married? I have a suit," Johnny says to her, sitting on the floor by her chair, his little hand absent-mindedly rubbing the terrycloth top of her slipper. He's learned that that's the closest he can get to her. He doesn't, can't, understand that he's too much for her. Just the fact of him, a little boy, is too hard, too close to the deepest part of her heart, even though Frankie was a grown man when she lost him. This is the most love that she'll allow and the only memory he's going to have of her; sitting on the floor next to her feet, rubbing the top of her slipper and watching *Wheel of Fortune*. Or sometimes *The Price is Right*.

She puts out her cigarette in the Niagara Falls ashtray, white ceramic with the gold edging long since worn away. A souvenir from my parents' honeymoon. I remember a picture of them from that trip. Sitting in some tourist restaurant, young and tan, each holding a lit cigarette. Almost smiling.

Johnny gets on his knees for a minute to trace the spirals of smoke rising up from the ashtray. "Yeah, Granma, please come. I have a bow-tie and oso shiny shoes."

She puts another Newport in her mouth, talks to me and ignores Harry while she lights it. "So what, you think this is your happily ever after? Good luck with that." She inhales deeply and sips her beer. Vanna turns two more letters. "That's a 'J' like my name," Johnny says, returning to his spot by her feet.

"OK, Ma, fine. Fine you don't want to go. But I don't want to hear for the next ten years about how you weren't invited. We asked and you said no."

Silence. Harry puts his hand in mine. We all watch as Pat Sajak jokes with the audience. He's gray now but still handsome, trim. I check the time. Might as well set it up now so she can take me down. I know what her response will be but I say, "You could do it for Johnny, you know? It's a big deal for him."

"Why, because you think Johnny has any idea what's happening? He's friggin' three years old. You think he's gonna remember this?"

I look down and Johnny is still petting her slipper, not watching the TV but listening to us talk, his eyes focused on the carpeting. "Granma, I'm five now, five and then six is next. I'll remember. I'll remember you."

"OK, Ma." And I walk back to the kitchen, lean against the counter. Through the hatch I watch her ignoring Johnny, filling the room with smoke. Harry leans against the wall near her chair, careful not to block her view.

"You're so dramatic, Gigi," she says to the TV.

"Donna, we just thought you might like to be there and that we should ask you in person," Harry says.

"You're getting married in City Hall. Big whoop. You couldn't spring for something nicer than that, Harry? That's a red flag right there, Eugenia, if you ask me. Why don't you stop by the DMV while you're at it, renew your driver's license real quick." She waits. But I stay quiet. Let her keep going.

"There's no telling you anything, Eugenia. You have to fall on your own fucking face to learn. So go. Get married. But don't come crying to me when it hits Shit City." Johnny's little shoulders flinch as she talks. He tries to rescue the situation, the way an adult tries to distract a crying child, and he says, pointing at the TV, "Granma, look. 'P' for Pop-Pop." That's what he calls my dad.

"I assure you, Donna, I mean to take care of them. That's all I want to do. I love Gigi and Johnny. I know that a City Hall wedding is perhaps not your ideal, but in the interest of time and getting the necessary visas and other—" I stand next to Harry and put my hand on his chest to stop him. I know he's trying but there's no point.

"Ma, you understand we're leaving, right? We get married, we wait for the visas and then we're gone. You get that, right?" Tears come on suddenly when I say "gone" but I have to save them for when she won't see. Tears because I hate being here and because I don't want to leave.

"Yeah, I get that, Princess Di. I get that you got a rich boyfriend and you think you're better than everything and everyone that you grew up with. Yes, you've made that very clear," she says over her shoulder, still focused on the spinning wheel, sipping beer.

"What're you talking about? When did I ever say that, Ma?" I have to get her to the end, let her say what she needs to say.

"It's what you didn't say, Eugenia. Have you ever thanked me for everything I did for you? Did you ever say, 'Thank you, Ma'? No. And now look at you. Picking up and going, like you got nothing tying you down here. You think you belong with him? You think you're going to take this kid over there and what, fit right in? Go ahead. But I see through you, Eugenia, and you're not doing right by your family. An ungrateful bitch by any other name is still a heifer. Look that up. I think Shakespeare said that."

"Ma … Ma, I swear to God!" I tremble in anger, itemizing in my head all the bills I've paid for them: the car insurance, the heat, the electricity. For years. Years and years since before Frankie died, when I was still a kid, when I didn't even live here, I gave Frankie whatever money I could because I knew that if the choice was between beer and food that week then the beer would win and Frankie wouldn't have enough to eat. And Johnny, wheezing in that stroller where Michelle left him, Ma just sitting there smoking cigarettes waiting for me to figure it out. Never once saying I had done a good thing.

I want to hit something, throw something, scream. I fly toward the back of her chair, to kick it, to punch it, to yell at it, but Harry catches my wrist and braces me. He looks in my eyes and whispers, "You don't have to any more."

He puts himself between me and Ma's chair. In a tone I've never heard before he says, "Donna, it must be very taxing, always begrudging your daughter her happiness. I'm sorry you don't feel that you can attend tomorrow, but if that's the case then that's entirely down to you. Gigi and Johnny and I are going to be a family whether you wish us well or not. Out of respect, Donna, as Gigi's mother, we're inviting you to attend. The day will proceed – with or without you."

Vanna turns another letter. Me and Ma weren't expecting that. We're not sure how to respond. We're not used to arguing where someone says so much without yelling. No one speaks for a minute. Ma, surprised by Harry's boldness but pretending not to be, rasps, "Alright, alright, gay boy, don't get your panties in a bunch. You'll need 'em for your big day." She takes another drag, another sip, pretending, like always, that she's won.

Harry puts his arms around me. We breathe in unison. I let the back of my head fall to his chest. He sighs into my hair. I know he didn't want to do that. He was there for the worst day of Ma's life too. He's never forgotten that. But he's put me first and maybe that's what's so hard for her. She's never been first for anyone.

I say, "Alright, Ma, we're leaving. Johnny, let's go, Granma's busy and we need to get ready for tomorrow. OK, buddy?"

I pull Johnny up off the floor. "Jeej, where's Shit City?"

"Don't say that, baby, that's just a pretend place Granma made up." She doesn't look when Johnny gets up, her eyes focused on Pat and Vanna as she takes a last drag. She crushes the empty beer can and leans forward in her chair with a grunt to put out her cigarette in Niagara Falls.

I get our stuff together and notice the laminate paneling, see how the boards have warped and cracked with age and the pressure of all the dysfunction they've had to contain. Harry takes Johnny to the bathroom and I wait for them in the kitchen. I put my hand on Frankie's framed high-school graduation photo still hanging by the phone on the wall. I whisper to my brother's smiling face, "Keep us safe."

"Jeej, who you talking to?" Johnny comes out of the bathroom, his jeans all twisted. I kneel down to straighten him out and I say, "I'm just talking to your uncle, up in heaven."

"Can he hear us?"

"I hope so."

"Hi, Uncle Frankie!" Johnny shouts and waves at the photo, smiling. "Can I take him with us? When we go to London?"

Ma's standing in the doorframe of the kitchen. I catch her eye and I know she heard that so before she can say anything that'll hurt Johnny I quickly lie, "You know what, baby, I have a copy of that picture, I'll put it in a frame for you, OK? Let's go or we'll miss the ferry."

"Bye, Granma! I love you!" Johnny shouts, as Harry helps him with his jacket. He knows she won't hug him so he just waves.

Then Harry says, "Goodbye, Donna. I'm sorry if I spoke out of turn. I care very deeply for your daughter. I hope you know that. If you change your mind about attending tomorrow you'll be very welcome."

"Yeah, sure, whatever," she says as she walks past him into the kitchen. Harry nods and waits in the doorway with his hands on Johnny's shoulders, keeping him still. Ma says to me over her shoulder, "I don't know how you listen to this guy. Does he ever talk like a regular person?"

I try to move past her to get to the doorway and I say, "Bye, Ma."

She says, "Wait, Eugenia."

"Ma, we got to catch the ferry."

"I know," she says. The air is thick with smoke and all the words we aren't saying. The ancient olive-green fridge clicks on, hums in the corner.

She moves past me to the kitchen table and picks up her denim purse with the fringe and gold studs. It's faded now and ragged, the denim brown on the bottom, almost black with dirt and age. I remember when she bought it on a back-to-school shopping trip at Kmart when we were kids. It was two bucks from the last-chance bin. My mother was never a denim-fringe-and-gold-studs kind of woman. But maybe that's why she bought it, to feel like someone else, some sassy stylish lady of the eighties with a different kind of life. My father lost his shit when he looked at the receipt and saw that she bought something for herself when money was so tight. They argued all night but she still kept it. She still uses it.

She rifles through the bag, looking for something. Harry's not sure whether to leave us alone but my eyes tell him to stay. Johnny shifts his weight from one foot to the other but stays quiet. In a movie this would be our last chance to say something so that this scene isn't added to her lifetime of regrets. I'm supposed to bear the weight of this time for her but I don't know how. I've never known how to do anything but love and hate her at the same time. Watching her search through that sad, old, dirty bag, I feel sorry for her too. So I reach forward to touch her hand: "Ma?"

She pulls a $5 bill out of her bag and says, "Here, take this for the kid. Buy him a donut or somethin'."

I take the bill and look at her hand. Swollen with thick fingers, stiff and arthritic. Our hands brush each other in the exchange. Her skin is like wax. It feels old. Her life wasn't easy.

I put the five bucks in my pocket. I swallow hard so I don't cry and whisper, "Thanks, Ma," and I walk to the door, to my family, and Ma watches me from the kitchen.

Manhattan, March 2014

Harry's hungover, unshaven, wearing yesterday's suit. He's chugging a Snapple Iced Tea, the last one he'll have for a long time because he's flying to London tonight and there's no Snapple there. Or iced tea. Before he goes, he has to prove to the British government that he really loves me and that I didn't just marry him for a visa. That's hard to do, though, because I look pretty suspicious, standing barefoot in a dirty white dress, swigging a warm Diet Coke in the Staples on 50th Street the morning after our City Hall wedding.

The wedding my father was the only witness to and which he almost missed because he got caught by the metal detectors bringing a pocketknife into the building. And his pat down and search took a while because he wore his dressy tracksuit, the one with lots of pockets. I'm also not sure if we actually were legally married because the officiant mispronounced my name and I'm pretty sure she called me Gonorrhea instead of Eugenia. Story of my friggin' life. She said, "And do you, Gonorrhea Andrea Stanislawski ..." so I don't know if my vows actually counted.

Harry leans against the copy machine and reads his statement from a crumpled sheet:

... we are prepared to face life's hurdles together, drawing strength from each other, but perhaps more importantly, stepping forward to catch one another

when our individual weaknesses cause us to falter.
Where I waver in the face of decision, Gigi forges
ahead with certainty. Where she is plagued by
self-doubt, I give her my steadfast faith in her. Gigi
and Johnny have brought a happiness to my life that
I did not know possible. I cannot imagine a future
without them ...

"OK, Captain My Captain, let's just take it down a notch. Can you stick to facts, please? Date and time we met, then go chronologically through the important stuff: first date, Christmas, Valentine's, Johnny's birthday etc. They don't need the whole fucking *Odyssey* and shit," I say, pressing start on the copy machine and wishing my Coke was still cold.

Harry turns to me and says, "I'm sorry but I believe those are two *quite* different literary references and not *really* comparable, Gonorrhea." I laugh so hard I start to cry.

It's the third time since we got married fifteen hours ago that I've cried hysterically. The first time was when Dad wrapped Harry in a huge bear hug after the ceremony and said, with tears in his eyes, "Take care of my girl." I lost it. Not just because of that but – Ma is Ma, and I knew she wouldn't be there, but still. It hurt. I told Johnny I was crying because I was so happy but he knew. He knows a lot.

The second time was at the bar. We went to meet Sharon and Stacy and Danielle and their husbands and boyfriends and they had filled the whole back of the bar with white balloons and got us a cake, it was all a surprise, and I couldn't help the tears. The girls got three matching pink halter-top gowns, sequined on top and satin to the floor. They got dressed up so I could still have wedding photos with bridesmaids standing behind me. We did them outside. One with some firemen in front of their truck and one on the subway steps in front of the bar. They brought four bouquets of pink roses, one for me to throw, which I did, to a whole bar of New Yorkers having their after-work drinks. They barely looked up at me because, you know, it's New York, there's always some crazy drunk woman throwing something at somebody and you just learn to ignore it. The bartender caught it, though, and we got a free round.

Later, Sharon, four drinks in, came up to Harry, put her hands on his face and said what she had said to every groom who had married one of her best friends: "I will hunt your ass down and fucking kill you with my bare hands if you ever hurt her."

Harry, slightly traumatized for a second before he understood that this tradition of hers had made him one of us, said, "Sharon, I would expect nothing less," and they hugged. Then Harry toasted my girls: "To the beautiful bridesmaids and their love for the bride; may we all be spared their wrath." Then they all did a shot and laughed. I grabbed my phone and took their picture when they weren't looking, to freeze this moment, the three of them laughing with my Harry, him loving them and them loving him back, in those ridiculous pink dresses. And all of them doing it for me.

But that was last night and now it's this morning and this is the third time that I'm crying in public. Of course, it wouldn't be so bad if we had slept. Or not drunk all the alcohol in the West Village, or if I took the bag with the passports and every document for my marriage visa with me, instead of leaving it in the back of the cab we took from City Hall to the bar. I only realized when I got a voicemail at 10:30 last night, several bottles of champagne into my new marriage:

> "*I'm lookin' for Miss … Miss or Mr.? I don't know, Eugene? I can't see this without my glasses. Yeah, anyway, I found some papers in a taxi, they look important, this is Robert in Ridgewood. I'm off Myrtle Avenue.*"

Robert in Ridgewood had our passports; Johnny's birth certificate; photos of the three of us; letters from our friends saying they knew us as a couple; bank statements Harry had to get from England; pay slips from his job; proof of his new job; a mortgage statement for his house in London. Robert in Ridgewood was holding a thousand irreplaceable pieces of paper that we had collected for weeks to submit with this application. Papers that had to have the right dates, in the right format, signed and verified by the right people. If any of it was missing the whole application would be rejected and we'd have to start all over again, and lose the hundreds of dollars we'd already paid in application fees.

I had planned everything to make this part as easy as possible. I made sure that every piece of paper was there, every box checked. All we would have to do the day after the wedding was put the marriage certificate in the package and let the lawyer do the rest. Then we'd pick up Johnny, have pizza at our favorite place and take Harry to the airport. But instead the stack of papers that our new life hinged on ended up in tatters in some guy's apartment on the fifth floor of a walk-up in Queens. And now I was standing next to a broken copier and crying in Staples.

The copier jams again. I kick the machine through angry tears and shout, "Motherfucking-fuck-shit-ass-fucking-machine!" The copy guy behind the counter looks up blankly, hoping he doesn't have to come over. Harry pulls me gently away from the copier and takes out his pocket square for my sobs. I look at the purple silk edged in navy blue. I realize that I've just married a man who owns a pocket square.

"Darling, don't do that, don't cry. It's alright. Let me get us some help." I try to calm down and watch Harry approach the counter. "Excuse me, sir, so sorry to bother you, would you mind helping us, please," and the copy guy gives him that look that New Yorkers often give Harry, like, they're not sure but he might be a time traveler who's just arrived from the 1800s.

"We'll be OK," I whisper to myself. Despite its reputation, New York is full of good people who do the right thing, and Robert was one of them. When we got to Myrtle Avenue it was it was almost midnight but he didn't mind and he gave us everything he found. Harry offered him $100 in thanks but he waved us off and said, looking at our wrinkled, sweaty wedding clothes, "Get outta here with your money. Good luck."

We needed it. Almost everything had been mangled, torn, covered in footprints or coffee-stained in some way after an evening on the floor of a taxi. First we went to my place in Brooklyn. We reprinted my statement and the photos and used a pencil eraser to get the footprints off the bank statements. I ironed the letters from our friends.

Then we went to Harry's place in Manhattan to find the duplicate mortgage statement. That took a couple hours because Harry's whole apartment was in boxes, ready for the movers. When we finally found it, the hotel reservation for our wedding night long forgotten, we did a quick stop at a deli for a sunrise breakfast of cold caffeine and Doritos so we could get to Staples when it opened to make copies, put everything together, print the form and get to the appointment with the lawyer on time. The last thing was Harry's personal statement. We couldn't find the USB stick he saved it on and there was no choice now but to write the whole thing again.

The copy guy comes over to fix the machine. He resets it, trying not to make eye contact. Harry strokes my hair, hugs me. I calm down for a minute. Then, panicked, I say, "Shit, I just remembered, you know what we haven't done yet?"

"Anal?" Harry says, innocently. I laugh so hard my laughs are silent, until I start crying again. Harry hugs me. "I'm sorry, darling, I wanted to make you laugh, don't cry."

"Be serious. This is really hard," I say, sniffling, wiping my nose, and then we both say, without missing a beat, "That's what she said," and even the copy guy had to laugh.

Then Harry says, "You mean calling Sharon's mum about picking up Johnny? I've already done that. Now should I go and collect him? My statement's done and you've almost finished here." He runs his hand down my arm gently, holds my hand, pushes my hair behind my ear.

"Yeah, you'd better go," I say.

"Are you sure you'll be alright?" Harry asks. No. I need him. There's so much I want to say, so much I'm worried about. But we have to get Johnny, we have to finish this application, he has to catch his flight, he has to start his new job. Whatever I feel has to wait.

"No, it's fine. You go, let me finish this. Call me when you've got him."

I wait for Harry to leave before I start welling up again. Hot stress tears. The copy guy looks up at me from the machine. "You OK, miss?"

He realizes too late that he shouldn't have given me an opening. I take off: "No, this is such bullshit. This was my wedding night, I said I didn't care about not having a real wedding and going to City Hall because we had to, because his job, and finding a school for Johnny over there, and so many things, we just didn't have time. But look at me! Look at my dress!"

The copy guy glances at my white mini-dress, blackened by a night of subways and taxis, but quickly looks away because he knows he's not supposed to look at customers' dresses, even if they ask him to. "I mean, I know it's not a real wedding dress but it's *my* wedding dress, you know?"

The copy guy is so young he still has acne and he doesn't know. "Um, would you like some water or somethin'?" he asks, trying to remember if he got any training about managing the copying needs of crazy brides.

"Sorry, no, that's OK. Thank you, though." He begins to creep away from me but I start up again: "It's just, it's a lot, you know, I'm going all the way to London. We have to say bye to everybody and pack everything, my kid's only five, I mean, what if it doesn't work out? And look at this, do you know what this is called? A fuckin' pocket square. He has, like, four of these. What the fuck?" I show the copy guy the purple handkerchief in my fist.

"Um, do you want to call somebody maybe?" he asks. I notice his name tag.

Johnny.

I can see my Johnny, nineteen years old, skinny and sweet at his first job. I remember Frankie, this one time I watched him at Foot Locker, when an old lady made him get ten boxes of sneakers and then didn't buy any. How he laughed when she left instead of getting mad.

I turn to the copy guy. "I'm sorry. You didn't want to hear all that. It's been a rough night. I'm gonna get outta your hair in a minute." The young man backs away, relieved that I've released him. I hope he doesn't remember this encounter ten years from now and then decide not to propose.

I rub my eyes. I sit down on the floor, lean my head against the copier, try to finish this paperwork, not surprised that this is how my wedding turned out. I knew it was going to be a quick City Hall job but I hoped that some small part of it would be memorable and not because of the, "And then she called me Gonorrhea," way that we'll always laugh about whenever we tell the story. I mean the bar – I'll never forget that, even though we had to leave before the end. But for my wedding night I wanted a beautiful moment, something pure to keep for when we're old that's just for us. Instead I have Robert in Ridgewood, standing in his boxer shorts with a cat on his shoulder holding my baby's passport. That's alright. At least I got a new last name out of it that people can pronounce.

All I have left to do is go through Harry's statement, line by line, and look for any mistakes, replace the pages if he messed up.

I turn the page. Stop short.

One day in Battery Park I saw a young woman and a small boy on the path ahead of me. The little boy fell over and cried and the young woman quickly scooped him up and covered him with kisses. In a flash he took off running as she gave chase. It was a lovely scene; very ordinary but very happy. But then she suddenly tripped and fell over quite spectacularly, landing face down upon the pavement. I wanted to go to her aid but then I recognised her and stopped where I stood.

It was Gigi lying on the ground laughing. She did not try to get up quickly to recover, or to pretend that nothing had happened. I watched as she laughed and the little boy laughed too as he tried with all his might to help her off the ground. Realising that she had become a spectacle, she stood up, lifted her head high and said to the passers-by, 'New York, thank you, you've been great,' and she took several bows as her little boy applauded. The stony-faced New Yorkers softened as they passed and could not help but smile.

It was the Gigi I had left more than ten years before, grief-stricken on the steps of her family home. And I was humbled, for like the city, she too was still standing and had begun to live again. I did not know if she would remember me, or if the sight of me, so tied as it would be to the memory of that worst of days, would upset her. But I knew that if I did not approach her then I would spend the rest of my life in a purgatory of 'what if'. For, truly, how could I not love her? A woman who had gone to the edge of life and back, and who could still laugh, or, at least, who laughed so that her child would laugh freely, unaware of the pain she carried.

He saw me fall. He never told me. He was too polite to mention it that day. Too kind to draw attention to my lack of grace. Too possessive of this memory to ever share it until he thought he had to write it on this piece of paper to keep me with him. I hold the paper to my chest. Copy guy Johnny rolls a desk chair over to me. He hands me a cold Diet Coke.

"I found this in the back and I thought maybe you needed it. Um, congratulations on getting married, I mean, the guy seems alright."

I take the can gratefully, wishing I could tell this boy's mother what a nice kid she raised.

"Yeah, he is," I say. "He's beautiful."

5

GLUE

A Wednesday in August 2016, 12:30 p.m.
London, Grand Euro Star Lodge Hotel,
Room 506

I light a cigarette and open the window. There's a scraggly city pigeon on the ledge. Not a fat, middle-class, wood pigeon who only pecks respectably around the back gardens of houses with newly renovated extensions. She's the kind of pigeon I used to ride the Staten Island Ferry with. She hangs out on building ledges, by the Tube station, on the tracks of the Overground – where the action is. A badass city pigeon with a missing foot. You know how that happens? Human hair. Urban pigeons build their nests with shit they find in the street and sometimes they use human hair which gets caught around their feet like a tourniquet so that while the pigeons sit on their eggs they feel their feet rotting off their bodies from lack of circulation. Then the chicks hatch and grow up and leave. And the mother pigeon just limps and hops and crash lands for the rest of her life. So, I guess things could be worse.

I take another drag and exhale. The last time I smoked was the night before my custody of Johnny was finalized. He was eighteen months old. I smoked my last two Camel Lights on the fire escape of my apartment in Brooklyn, looking down at St. John's Place: the bodega and the laundromat; the old trees and wide sidewalks; the brownstone spectrum from derelict to gentrified. I'd already quit by then because I didn't want to be that lady pushing the stroller with a cigarette in her hand. I didn't want Johnny to have the kind of baby blanket that I used to carry around when I was little, with its two perfect burn holes where the ash had fallen from my parents' cigarettes. There were parts of me that were Ma's that I couldn't change – my laugh, the way my weight settled on my hips – but I didn't have to be a mother like her. So I quit, but I saved the last two cigarettes in case of something big and I smoked them the night before they made me his mother. Tonight will be the night before something too but I'm not sure what.

I put the cigarette out on the ledge and the pigeon coos at me. She doesn't like smokers. She has high standards. Just like Rebecca. Rebecca who's just sent me a text:

Eugenia, Harry said that you were called away urgently. Rest assured that the children are being suitably supervised. Do let us know how you're getting on. Best, Rebecca

"Called away urgently." Wow. Now is she really saying, "I know you disappeared to get drunk and watch TV in a hotel room alone you crazy bitch," or did he tell her something to make it sound classy and important? Well, whatever he told her, now she's helping with the kids, and, if we get through this, I will hear about how she rescued my children today every time I see her. Reason enough not to ever go home. If you asked me to describe Rebecca I would say, *She ends text messages with "Best,"* and I feel like this would tell you all you need to know.

I pound on the ledge to scare the pigeon and light another cigarette. I don't need her avian judgment. I check my email compulsively for Harry's response. *Response to what? You didn't tell him anything.*

It took a long time for Harry to tell me about his parents. One night, Johnny had one of his Michelle dreams. "But Jeej, I don't remember her, I don't remember!" he said, wailing, half-awake. Holding him I said, "It's OK. She loves you. She gave you to me and I'm not going anywhere." He had no memory of her but her presence through her absence was very real for him. I tried to do what the social workers said. Tell him that he was always loved and wanted whenever it came up. And it came up every time the mother died in a cartoon movie; every time there was an orphan in a fairy tale or a widower starting to date again in a family sitcom. I showed him photos, I gave him the chain with her name plate and his grandfather's gold crucifix. He kept them under his pillow in a special box. But each time she visited him this way I was eaten up inside, worried that I wasn't – hadn't been, couldn't be – enough for him. It's hard to compete with a ghost.

That night, when he could hear my voice breaking, Johnny's raw semi-conscious love for her just too hard for me, Harry took Johnny from me. He put him back in bed and stroked his hair until his breathing slowed and steadied. Harry had never done that before, but it was so natural to him, like a muscle memory. Closing Johnny's bedroom door he said, "Poor lad. It's different but it's the same."

Later, just before we went to sleep, Harry said to the ceiling, "I was lucky. I had time with him. Mum hadn't sent me away to school yet so I spent every minute by his side." And he told me, lying in the dark while I held his hand, about the last months with his father. Doing his homework by his bedside, reading to him, eating dinner with him, sleeping on the sofa next to his bed. The months that shaped the man that he became.

You don't forget watching someone die. The gradual frailty that creeps through him until one day the protrusion of his clavicle catches your eye in a certain, devastating light. The long hours of his daytime sleeping, his slow breathing that suddenly stops and then starts again, giving you a glimpse of the inevitable moment when the next breath will be the last one. The delightful waves of lucidity that come when you most need them to, when the old self sparkles in his eyes again and he makes you laugh like he used to and you say to yourself, "Remember this, remember this." Because soon he will sleep again and when he wakes it won't be the same. Harry was a boy when he saw all that.

But Rebecca saw all of that too and probably much more. And we're mothers, so I know that she shielded Harry from the worst indignities of his father's disintegration. I know she made sure his memories weren't tainted with his father's dependence and helplessness, that she took care of all the intimate hardships that come with caring for the dying when Harry was at school, or asleep, or doing homework so that he wouldn't see. That's why he can talk about that time like that; love his father like that.

I check my phone again. Nothing. I know things were hard for Rebecca too. I know that, in her way, she was a good mother; in all the ways that she thinks that I'm not. Well, I've proven her right today. And I know she didn't say it out loud when she saw Harry and he handed over the kids, but she didn't have to. He already knows.

Ascot, January 2015

The terrine is going to be a problem. Every time we come here for lunch there's some kind of food I've never seen before and out of politeness I put it on my plate. So Rebecca called this thing a terrine. What's it made of? Lamb liver, calf hearts, strawberry ice cream – all three? Because that's what it looks like – liver ice-cream cake.

I shift in my chair and I hear the plastic crinkle underneath me. Rebecca covered Johnny's seat in a clear plastic tarp. Fair enough, it's an antique chair and he's six and I get it. She also covered the floor under his chair with a piece of plastic, because OK, it's light carpeting, overkill maybe, but I understand. Interesting, though, that the plastic under his seat was extended to include the carpeting under my chair as well.

"Jeej, Jeej – what *is* that?"

Johnny's whisper is as a subtle as a bulldozer, but I just say quietly, "It's a terrine, buddy. It's a … French. Keep coloring, that's a great picture." Johnny had already eaten his ham sandwich and was coloring at the table. At least

Rebecca understood what children ate and the coloring was a small concession that I appreciated.

Johnny whispered whenever he was here. The house, with its high ceilings and antiques, signaled to him that it was like a library or a church. But it was also Damon. Johnny stayed close and very quiet whenever he was around.

Damon is Rebecca's third husband. He's 6'5", as big as a moving van and wears an eye patch which no one has explained and which we're not allowed to ask about. He played rugby for Gloucester in his youth which is impressive for some reason but I don't understand enough about it to know why and when I asked he didn't answer. He's semi-retired, in his seventies, and he has an encyclopedic knowledge of racehorses. He watches rugby. He drinks whiskey. This is all I know about him. He's said about eleven words to me since we met because a) I'm a woman and b) I'm not a horse.

Despite his surliness he's sweet with Rebecca. She has rules about where people sit for meals but he never observes them. Rebecca sits at the head and he always sits next to her instead of at the other end of the table. She loves this because when we come over Harry sits on her other side and then she's flanked by her two faithful men. This leaves me and Johnny on the periphery on Damon's other side and he always sits at an angle with his back to me to give more of himself to her. I can't see past him to Rebecca's end so I don't participate in the conversation directly. But maybe that's best for everyone.

Rebecca gets up to put a water jug on the table. She's slender and taut. Her hair is chic and short, a honey-blond meticulous bob. She's dressed in a tight ivory cashmere sweater set with a tailored gray wool pencil skirt and a string of real pearls, black stilettos, and nude fishnet stockings. Like what a seventy-year-old Claire Underwood might wear to a casual family lunch before she murders someone.

"How was the traffic? Was it *awful*?" Rebecca begins as I choke down the terrine. From the *awful* traffic, she moves on to the *ghastly* British weather and then the *dreadful* people in the papers.

Then Harry says, "The house looks marvellous, Mummy, really, and this terrine is lovely, really lovely," trying to get her onto another topic, while I gulp wine and look away to stop the involuntary rolling of my eyes.

"Well, thank goodness for that. It was all very stressful, because I planned an *entirely* different menu that I had found in the *Sunday Telegraph* but when I went to Waitrose for the ingredients they had almost none in stock. Can you *imagine*? I had a word with the store manager. Surely Waitrose know that most of their customers are *Telegraph* readers? *Shocking*."

I think about how, "I planned an entirely different menu," is a sentence I have never said. I check out for a while, try not to taste anything and pretend to be occupied with Johnny. I run my fingers through his hair, pretty sure that I can see lice. Rebecca might have to be hospitalized if she finds out so I'll just keep that to myself.

"... now Eugenia, you must do *something* about your phone line. I called and it rang and rang the other day with no answer," Rebecca huffs at me and so I snap back to attention.

I consider what she's just said. *You're the only one who calls that number so I didn't pick it up because I knew that in thirty seconds you would call my cell phone from your cell phone while calling my landline from your landline at the same time, which is exactly what you did. And it was ten o'clock at night. And why are you saying this to me when we both know it's only Harry that you want to talk to. And stop calling me Eugenia,* is not the right answer, so I just say, "OK, I'll look into it," from behind the mass of Damon's giant shoulder.

"You do look *awfully* thin and pale, Harry, darling, really you do. And Johnny has dark circles under his eyes. Is *no one* looking after you?" Rebecca asks Harry, the *no one* obviously, being me.

"I don't need to be looked after, Mummy, I'm a grown man," Harry says, sighing, looking at me for approval. But I wonder if there are many grown men who call their mothers 'Mummy'. He adds, "And Johnny has no such thing, he's perfectly fine."

"Well, this is the curse of modern life, isn't it, the family falls to pieces with *no one* there to look after it properly," Rebecca says, very pointedly not looking at me.

"We look after each other, Mum, and we're doing just fine. And Gigi is doing very well at work, aren't you, darling?" He smiles at me, but he should know that this nod to gender equality will be too much for his mother.

Desperate to change the subject, I start to say, "So when's the big horse race? It's here in Ascot, right ..." But it's too late. It's Rebecca's Correct Opinion Time:

"Surely it must be better for Johnny to have his mother at home, given his ... *history*. It's very nice for Eugenia that she has something to do, but, especially once you have another child, that will *have* to change. *Certainly* the children come first, ahead of the mother's … *interests?*" Rebecca sips water from a cut-crystal glass.

Jesus, Harry, why did you have to take her here? Working mothers. A No-Go Area with Rebecca along with women playing sports (undignified); Princess Diana (didn't deserve all the fuss); immigrants (should stay where they belong); American actors playing British roles (inappropriate); "the gays" (meaning lesbians in particular, but rich gay men were OK as long as they were quiet about it); "the Blacks" (not white); "the Poles" (not *really* white); anything organic (idiotic); female, Indian or Russian doctors (can't be trusted); astroturf in back gardens (disgraceful); civil and human rights (an excuse for criminals and immigrants to take advantage of Britain); and finally, the European Union (full of Europeans).

I listen to Rebecca say that I'm not around enough for Johnny while I sit there and don't say how the hell would she know anything about it since she sent Harry to boarding school at age nine and only saw him once every four months which is why they talk to each other like they're in a 1940s radio play.

My cheeks flush and the room gets hot. I lean forward to try to say something that will get us off the subject of what a selfish mother I am, but Damon turns to me. He points a massive sausage finger at Johnny and puts his bear-paw hand on my shoulder. He says, "Have you put the boy down for rugby yet?" I brace myself. Damon's moved us onto one of his three topics and I wish he chose horses or whiskey instead.

"Well, Johnny tried it and it wasn't a good fit, not right now, anyway," I stammer, looking at Harry for help. The rugby trial class was a disaster. It was cold, Johnny fell in the mud, it started raining and the coach, who was as big as Damon and just as personable, yelled at him because he confused his left and right and started crying. "Sort yourself out, lad, *c'mon*," he said, and for Johnny, who tries so hard to please, that kind of disapproval was like a punch in the face.

And then I made it worse. When I saw his tears I couldn't help it and I said, "Hey, why don't you lighten up, big guy. He's just a kid," but me getting angry just made Johnny cry harder. We had to leave. It was a scene. He's finally gotten over it but now …

"A good fit?" Rebecca scoffs, her Dior-coated lips pursed in a little matte-rose knot.

"I don't want to, Jeej, I don't want to do rugby," Johnny whispers to me, clutching my sleeve, and I can feel his little panic rising.

"It's OK, you don't have to," I say to him and squeeze his knee under the table.

Damon says, "He's scrawny. He needs it. You're too soft on him."

"I don't want to, Jeej, I don't want to!" Johnny's little voice gets louder.

"It's OK, baby, you don't have to."

I try to reassure him but Rebecca says, "Of course he *has* to. He *has* to do whatever you tell him to do."

"No, no, I don't want to! I don't want to! I hate it, I hate it!" and he gives the high-pitched cry of a much younger child, embarrassing and unsettling. He struggles to get out of his chair but the legs are getting caught on the plastic tarp on the carpet.

"Johnny, what on *earth* do you think you're …"

Rebecca stands and her voice goes up an octave, then Harry comes in: "Mum, just leave it, it's been quite a tough transition for him, he's been through a lot."

And as Harry gets up to come to us, Johnny, in his fight with the chair legs, bumps against the table, tipping over my wine glass, red wine seeping into the tablecloth where the plastic cover hadn't reached.

"The *salt*, go and get the *salt*, Damon, for *God's* sake!" Rebecca shouts, more concerned about her table linen than my son. "I *cannot* understand why you *cannot* keep him under control," she snaps at me, but I can't think about her now.

"Johnny, it's OK, it's OK." I try to put my arms around him but he elbows me in the chin as he struggles out of my grasp.

"Gigi, let me take him."

Harry tries to help but Johnny screams, "Noooo! You're hurting me! I said no!" I'm not hurting him and he knows that. He knows it's a defense to say that, a way to get grown-up hands off of him. But I have no choice now and I pick him up with my whole body, pin his arms and try to carry him while he kicks at my shins, hard, and screams.

"Baby boy, you've got to stop, you've got to stop now." I try to keep my voice level as Harry helps me get Johnny out of the dining room and upstairs. But I know that he can't hear me. Just like the time outside Pizza Express where he thrashed around on the sidewalk for half an hour because I tried to tie his loose shoelace. And the time in Sainsbury's when I said we weren't buying the chocolate milk because we already had some at home and he tipped over the shopping cart and store security had to come over.

I can handle the stares and judgments of strangers. But Rebecca's eyes burning a hole in my back while Damon pretends nothing is happening as he pours salt on the wine stain – fuck, I really wish Johnny hadn't done this in front of her. I wish that coach hadn't been such an asshole. I wish I knew how to help him when his screams burst my eardrums, when his face gets red and when I can hear in his voice the anguish of the small and powerless; that pain he doesn't have the words for.

Johnny pulls away from me, out of breath and exhausted as he throws himself on the bed in Harry's room, face first. He cries into the duvet, his shoulders shaking with every intake of breath. I hold in my tears and rub his back until his sobs slow down. Harry quietly pulls out the old trunk of his toys that Rebecca saved and lays them out on the floor. After a while, Johnny looks up and sniffles, "What's that?"

"Oh," Harry says, "these are just some of my old things, I thought you might like them. This one's called *Crossbows and Catapults*. Do you want to see how it works? There are toy soldiers and some Lego too," and Johnny slowly peels himself off the bed, wipes his nose on his sleeve and joins Harry on the floor, crisis over as abruptly as it began. Harry and I look at each other knowing we have a lot to talk about later.

I lay back on the bed while Harry and Johnny play, making my way through a box of Entenmann's chocolate-chip cookies that Danielle sent me from home. I always bring a stash of comfort food to Rebecca's. I look around the imposing bedroom of burgundy embossed wallpaper and gilded mirrors, bedside tables with ornately carved legs. I feel a longing, almost a craving, for our old apartment in Brooklyn.

"Jeej, I won, I won," Johnny says, and crawls up on the bed to me; his face is still tear-stained and swollen, but the hurt look has gone away.

"I'd better go down now and smooth things over," Harry says, kissing me on the forehead.

"Yeah, you better make sure her tablecloth's alright," I say.

"Look, I know she's not easy to deal with," he says, sitting on the bed.

"No, she's not. And could you tell her to stop calling me Eugenia?"

"She's just formal, you know that. At least she didn't call you fat this time," he said, elbowing me, trying to make me laugh, remembering the time that she had said I looked "well" three times in five minutes; "well" being the middle-class code word for fat. But I didn't find it funny today.

Harry's going to go down there and she's going to drink sherry and Damon's going to drink port and Harry's going to nod and agree with all her criticisms and find the words to appease her. He'll validate her concerns about the wine stain and notice that she won't ask whether Johnny's OK but he won't point that out. He'll assure her that she's right about everything and that her constant phone calls are no bother. Mothers and sons. I wonder what I'll be like when Johnny brings someone home. I wonder if refusing to share your son and hating his partner are an inevitable part of aging, like cataracts and cellulite. Well, there's no way I'm going down there. Wish I could sneak some wine up here.

I turn to Johnny to say, "Are you alright, baby boy?" but he's fallen asleep. I pull the covers around him, kiss his closed eyes and find myself exhausted and wired at the same time. I snoop around the room. I open the desk drawers, the closet, I examine the shelves, "looking for something to read," but also because I'm hoping I find some secret shit that I can judge Rebecca for. Like a drawer full of expired psych meds or proof she kept of her second husband's affair.

Instead, on the bottom shelf of the bookcase, wedged next to an ancient encyclopedia, I find the photo album, the old photos stuck in with black corners. Harry as a two-year-old covered in mud. Rebecca and Richard, Harry's dad, young and gorgeous in their wedding photo. Rebecca in an all-white tennis outfit looking like a British Jane Fonda. Richard, in a lab coat, with baby Harry on his knee holding a fat science book upside down, pretending to read. Rebecca, holding Harry on a smooth, slim hip, all big sunglasses and *Charlie's Angels* waves.

Richard was a scientist who made a lot of money from inventing a special lens for telescopes. He didn't inherit his money, he earned it, which at that time was rare for a rich man in England. Harry told me that he worked constantly and wasn't interested in any of the stuff that came with the money – cars, holidays abroad, tailored clothes, black tie dinners, the races, the theatre. Nothing, that is, except Rebecca. You could see in the photos that she was the kind of rich and beautiful girl who knew that rich men wanted to possess her and so she made herself easy to possess; it was probably her best, maybe only, option. And she was good at it. She still is. She did it today as she served the family lunch in stilettos and full makeup. She does it when she calls on a Sunday morning or Friday night when we just sat down to dinner, when she knows that it's our time with Harry. Appearing delicate and frail, knowing how to look like she needs protection because in her world men don't stick around unless you make them feel like they can rescue you.

There's a photo of Harry with Richard wrapped in big coats, cheeks flushed, holding a toboggan. The tree behind them weighed down with snow. He was Harry's best friend, I can see it.

Johnny stirs in his sleep. I turn to the last page of the album and pull out a loose photo tucked in the back cover. Rebecca, looking serious and unamused at someone to her right. Someone we can't see because they've been cut out of her photo. Or maybe, she's been cut out of theirs. There's a crisp white cotton man's shirt and a slip of forearm; a lock of unruly curly hair in the corner. And I feel a sudden stab of sadness when I realize what this is.

One night in Harry's apartment in New York, I opened the drawer of his bedside table looking for a pen and I found a picture of Harry with Richard. It had the blue-green tinge that old pictures get as they fade. They were sitting on a wall with the beach behind them. The wind was whipping Richard's unruly hair that was kept short on the sides but that curled and waved all over the top of his head. He was in a white shirt with the top two buttons undone, the sleeves rolled up. His forearms and chest were those of a lean but chiseled man; that slim sculpted look that everyone's parents had in the eighties from cigarettes and coffee.

Richard had a sideways smile that I recognized from my husband's face. He was looking down at his son, little Harry, about eight years old, in super-short swimming trunks. Harry was laughing, a wide, happy, toothy laugh. Neither one was looking at the camera, immersed in some secret joke. A moment of happiness so true on both their faces I found myself grieving for the father that Harry had lost and the child that he once was.

I bought Harry a silver frame for his birthday. I thought that picture deserved a home. He took the photo out of the drawer and told me about his dad. Harry was thirty-six that day, the same age Richard was when he died. He took the back off the frame to slide the picture in and we looked at it for a long time, me holding onto his arm while he sat there feeling the age of the man in the photo and feeling sadness for the boy who didn't know he'd lose him soon after this last trip to the seaside. Then he put the picture in its frame back in the drawer. That's where he keeps it, even now.

Rebecca looks like she knows where the rest of this photo is, so beloved that Harry can barely look at it. Her arms crossed, a lit cigarette held near the crook of her elbow. A strapless sundress, tan shoulders, a tiny gold chain glinting on her collar bone. She isn't laughing like Harry and Richard on their side of the photo. She was left out of the joke. She has the look of a mother who's been taken for granted; needed by her child, but never preferred over Daddy.

Did she get up early and spend all morning packing for the trip, taking care of the details Richard never thought of? Did he make a joke about her, her cross expression, that had Harry in stitches and only confirmed that her new sundress went unnoticed? Did she dress up for lunch at a beach-side hotel only for Richard to make her look humorless when he took them to the boardwalk for fish and chips wrapped in newspaper instead?

I wonder if she cut herself out of this picture because she didn't like how she looked. Or she cut herself out of this picture, not thinking of herself at all, but so that her son could have a pure memory of his father. Or she cut herself out of this picture because it's hard to be the mother, the one who does all the mundane things that children need to have done – making sandwiches, packing raincoats, washing socks – but don't notice because they're infatuated with their father, his frivolity and laughter. Then Richard died young and everything about him was forever wonderful. But Rebecca had to keep doing the work that he never did, noticed even less now that his shadow was so much larger in death.

Johnny wakes up and as I go to put the album down, the cover comes loose, the bound pages falling to the floor. I dig some school glue out of Johnny's pencil case and, as I squeeze it onto the binding, I realize that I've never seen Rebecca laugh. I've only ever seen her the way she looks in that picture – beautiful and distant. Wanting to be closer, but not knowing how.

6

SPECIAL SAUCE

A Wednesday in August 2016, 3:25 p.m. London, Grand Euro Star Lodge Hotel, Room 506

I wake up, surprised I fell asleep, surprised another few hours have passed. My phone vibrates. A text from Stacy. What time is it in New York? About 9 a.m.? 10? Melissa and Amber are on the TV, tan and glossy after the Florida trip, having cocktails and a heart-to-heart. They're being filmed from behind the bar and I feel like I'm their bartender. I pour another glass of wine for myself as I listen in on their conversation, and when they get their bar food I look over at my pizza, congealed now on the little table, untouched. The phone vibrates again.

Stacy:
> *Jeej it's the worst I'm so upset, I missed it, he took a step and I missed it*

Do I answer her? How do I answer her? It's a crisis and she needs an answer. She knows it's the middle of the day here, that's why she chose me because Danielle and Sharon will be at work and won't be able to talk. I need to answer her but it feels like she's communicating from a parallel planet, one where I'm still normal and not flipping out. It's hard to type with shaking fingers. I check to make sure the words seem casual, like this would be the right thing to say if I wasn't locked in this room, losing my mind.

Me:

What happened? Did day care call you?

Stacy:

Yes, right in the middle of a meeting I thought it was an emergency because they're calling and not just sending a text or whatever, and she just said he took a step just wanted to let you know because the last time when he rolled over I made such a big deal out of them not telling me. I went back to my meeting crying. I missed another thing

Me:

You didn't miss it

Stacy:

Of course I missed it

Me:

No Stace you forgot the rule

Stacy:

What rule?

Me:

It's only the first time when the mother's seen it for the first time. Everything else is rehearsal. It doesn't count as a first until the first time you see it

So normal. Such a me thing to say. I'm still in here somewhere.

Stacy:

Really? Oh my god you're right

Me:

Yes

Stacy:

Do those f'ing girls at the day care care if it's his first time? They don't care. I CARE

Me:

Exactly. They don't get his firsts

Stacy:

OMG I'm going to do a bunch of videos at home and say it's the first time like I'll make him roll and say look it's the first roll! And then we'll do one for his steps and be like hey it's the first steps!

Me:

OK you don't have to lie on camera to the child just don't feel guilty. You work hard for that kid

Stacy:

My parents lied to me my whole life

Me:

See how that turned out though

Stacy:

Ha ha. Love you

Me:

Love you

I should tell her. If Stacy knew I was here, in this hotel, what I did this morning, she'd help. I know she would. I just have to tell her and Danielle and Sharon, *Hey, I'm struggling.* But it's hard to find the right time. They got jobs and kids and there's the time difference and there's only so much you can say in a text. You can't say in a text, *I think I'm too sick to go back to work. I think I'm too sick to take care of these kids.* That's not a texting conversation. You don't drop that on your friends when they're thousands of miles away.

I got Johnny when he was six months old. I took four weeks off and then I went back full-time. There was no adoption leave and I didn't give birth so no maternity leave. I took my vacation and some unpaid family leave. But without a husband with an income, with no support from Mrs. Costello and my parents always short on cash, unpaid time wasn't an option with a baby to raise and bills to pay. And I did it, alone. Where is that woman who worked her ass off all day and took care of a screaming baby all night and then got up at dawn and did it all over again? And so what if I quit law school, so what if my job was just a job and never a career, look at that kid. What a beautiful kid he is.

Of course, I'm not alone now. Like this mother said to me at the school gates once, "You don't *need* to work, though, do you?" As if it was any of her business. As if having a purpose to every day isn't a need. Yes, Harry takes care of us. But people die, marriages fail, banks collapse, shit gets bombed, babies show up in your kitchen and I needed to know that I could rescue us. That, if it came down to it, all me and Johnny needed was me.

Because I was a mother before I was a wife. But now – I keep waiting for the switch to flip so I'll be me again. On, off, on, off. I keep switching it but the room stays dark. And we're dependent. The one thing I swore I'd never be.

I light another cigarette, take a drag holding my hand out the window, scroll through my emails. School, more from Harry, you can guess what they're like, and then there's the one from Aneela, my boss, that I haven't opened yet because I can't handle the disappointment, hers and my own. She sent it two days ago. ashah@gillianmc-carthy.co.uk. *Catching up.* That's the subject, *Catching up,* except that the subject really is, *Are you fucking coming back to work it's been almost nine months and you said you'd be back at six and I thought you were American and don't you guys go back to work three days after you have your babies?*

Just before I left Aneela said that the firm would pay for my law courses and they'd give me a training contract so in a few years I could be a solicitor. She said I was good. But I knew I was good. I've always been good, I've just never had the chance or the money to get the piece of paper to prove that I could be just as good as any lawyer I ever worked for. And here she was, giving me a stepladder; finally, someone saw in me what I knew I could be or – could have been. Past tense.

I should have written back sooner. Let's try.

Dear Aneela,
It's so nice to hear from you. I've just left my children and my husband today so now I find that I have a lot more time to devote to working. I'm ready to start on Monday, does that suit you?

How about this:

Dear Aneela,
Unfortunately, due to an unforeseen mental break-down I've had to return to America. Thank you and I really enjoyed working with you.

Or this:

Dear Aneela,
I just finished reading Lean In. *Thank you so much for sending it to me along with the beautiful baby blanket. Sheryl Sandberg is so wise. Unfortunately, I've done the math and leaning in with my full-time salary is less than the cost of the childcare we would need for two kids so there's actually no financial point in me working. That makes me feel worthless and powerless because my professional contribution to the world amounts to an economic loss for my family. But I'm grateful for the opportunity. I really enjoyed all the times I got home too late to see Johnny awake and wasn't paid for it.*

Too harsh. That's too harsh. Let's try this:

Dear Aneela,
I don't know why you can do it but I can't. You have kids too and you're really successful and nice and you believed in me but I'm sorry, I have no explanation for why I used to be a competent, smart, hardworking, ambitious person but now I stand in the pasta aisle of the supermarket too overwhelmed

by all the different shapes to pick one. I always seem to manage alright in the wine aisle, though.

I put the phone down, put out my cigarette. On the TV, they show the news footage of Teresa and Joe's federal fraud sentencing in between scenes of their crying family members following the news on their phones. Teresa will serve a year while Joe takes care of their little girls, then he'll 'go away' and do four years when she gets out. It's devastating. Some asshole reporter shouts at Teresa, "Have you been watching *Orange is the New Black*?" as she walks with her husband, head down. They cut to Rosie, Teresa's cousin, in the kitchen with her family reading a prayer off her phone: "God, my family needs your help today. Give us strength and compassion to help one another …"

"Help me too," I say while she prays, reaching for my wine bottle, crying for Teresa.

Crying for myself.

London, September 2015

I put my tray with the Big Mac and large fries down on the table of the two-person booth in the back corner of McDonald's. It's a small, out of the way McDonald's, with counter space for some stools and a few booths near the registers within earshot of the fryer.

Charlotte's on the other side of the table with her usual black coffee and today it's one – no, two – apple pies. Something's up.

"Charlie, you OK?" I ask her, sliding my way into the booth.

"No." That was the answer I expected. That's how we always opened our proceedings at McDonald's.

"Bad night last night?" I ask, knowing what the answer will be as I unwrap my burger with morning sickness rolling over me. Looks like I have the kind that's going to last the whole pregnancy and persecute me every day. Just like the Duchess. I try to draw strength from the Duchess.

"I was up every hour from twelve till four, and then the baby was up for the day at five-thirty."

"Fuck. Didn't Pete help?" I say, taking a sip of my lukewarm Coke.

"Oh, please. Fuck Pete." She bites off half an apple pie, smearing the cinnamon sauce off her face with the back of her hand. "You look terrible," she says.

"Threw up three times already today, and it's only eleven," I said, stuffing fries in my mouth.

"Fuck. Did Harry not do the school run for you today?"

"Oh, please. Fuck Harry."

And now that we had gotten our reasons for being there out of the way and did our usual fuck-Pete/fuck-Harry routine, we sat there quietly, eating shitty food, each knowing how precious a moment of quiet here was for the other woman.

Even before I discovered that McDonald's was the only food that I inexplicably didn't throw up with my morning sickness, I would come here whenever I got tired of being the foreigner in the office and I couldn't keep up with the banter and the references anymore. I just wanted to sit somewhere familiar and American where I understood how shit worked. Except for the warm soda without ice. No ice in your drinks in England. It's not like I loved McDonald's in America. It's just one of those things I do sometimes, like wearing a Yankees cap even though I never owned a baseball hat before or standing over the Oreos in the cookie aisle just to look at the logo.

About a year ago, when I was still new in the office, I had a whole conversation about how nice Scotland was with a client whose Liverpool accent I mistook for Scottish – and sidebar, if we could just be honest here, neither one of them can speak English in any kind of way that the outside world can understand so what the fuck's the difference – and everyone in the office had a huge laugh at my expense. After performing my self-deprecating, wise-cracking New Yorker routine and shrugging my shoulders good-naturedly to re-affirm everyone's opinion that Americans are lovable but ignorant, I came here, to my usual booth. And there was Charlie. One of the brightest young associates at the firm.

I said, "Hey, are you OK?" She was sitting with two apple-pie wrappers on her tray and a chocolate-chip cookie on standby.

"No," she said, not looking at me, sipping her coffee.

"Neither am I," I said.

"Sit down, then," she said, so I did. And we sat there, in silence, sharing our understanding of the sacredness of this place. The noise of the kitchen. The click of cups pressed against the soda dispenser. The smell of French fries. The bright lighting. We were here because we knew no one else from the office would ever find us. We worked in a liberal-leftie-Whole-Foods-Oxbridge-vegan-*Guardian*-reader kind of office. Everyone was friendly, kind and socially conscious but their deep concern for the problems of the proletariat meant that they could never lower them-selves to actually crossing the threshold of a McDonald's. But not me and Charlie because we're both mothers. And we know what all mothers know, which is that – unlike husbands or your family or even your friends – McDonald's is always there for you when you need it.

Charlie is five years younger than me. She has a three-year-old boy and a little baby. Unusually for a British woman she went back to work after only three months of mat leave because she's ambitious and driven. She's also the only associate at the firm who isn't white and I wonder how much that had to do with it too. Charlie's half Jamaican, half French, tall, beautiful, smart and serious. She married the very English and very white Peter who loves her very deeply, although, like everyone else's husband, he never does enough and doesn't know it.

I asked her once if she felt pressure to come back sooner because she was the only Black associate. Actually, first I said, "Uh, mixed race," and then I said, "Uh, um, I mean bi-racial?" with a question in my voice and she said, defensively, "What do you mean by *racial*?" My face dropped and I went red before I got the joke and she laughed and said, with a smile, "Relax, darling, I'm Black. My mum's white, she taught me French. My dad's Jamaican, I look like him. My husband's white, my kids are mixed like me, people think they're Black. We're all OK. You should be too, so stop being so American talking about race all the time. This is the UK, you know, we're not all racists like your lot." She was only half-joking, sliding past an uncomfortable conversation that she didn't want to have, using humour to disarm in that way that British people are so good at.

Still, in the office, I knew it was visible but unspoken: her skin color, the extra scrutiny it brought, both unconscious and very conscious; expectations others had of her and she of herself; assumptions made about her in the office, or barristers' chambers, or the courtroom; worries about her children and what they would face and how it would be different and how it would be the same. Hoping things would move forward and knowing they wouldn't move forward enough. It was all there in the crumpled up wrappers of her apple pie.

She and I don't get to socialize much in the office because we both have our heads down, working as fast as possible so that we can leave at five on the dot to pick up the kids. We understand what it's like when you're trying to do a good job and your children are constantly lighting up the background of your mind. We see what other people don't notice about us. The blouse turned inside out and then covered with a jacket to hide the stain before the client shows up. The skirt that used to fit that still almost does if you don't button it at the top but instead hold the waist together with a safety pin. The massive crack in the screen of the phone because your kid dropped it. She always has an emergency cardigan on hand and a Sharpie for coloring in scuffs on our heels. I always have a few spare tubes of mascara in my desk for brushing into my roots before big meetings. We're both just making it work, every day, like most moms.

When I saw her at McDonald's the first time, because she also knew that no one from the office would ever be seen there, our friendship was sealed.

I break our usual code of silence and I say, "Is it just the bad night?"

Charlie, staring at the lid of her coffee cup, chipped manicure toying with the pie wrappers, says, "This is hard. Much harder than I thought it would be."

"Yeah," I said.

"Sometimes I don't know why I'm doing it."

"Yeah, I know."

"It's much harder with two than it was with just Noah."

"Sure it is," I said, looking up at her, involuntarily putting my hand to my belly.

Without looking up from her coffee lid she said, "I don't know if this is worth it, you know? I did it, I'm successful, but I feel like shit. You know what happened yesterday? They shut down the nursery. A water main broke and they shut the water off for the whole street. So I'm standing there with the baby and Noah, their bags, my files and nowhere to go. I had twenty minutes to get to court, counsel wasn't picking up his phone, Pete had a board meeting and couldn't get out."

"Your parents weren't around?" I asked, already knowing the answer but giving her a chance to get the frustration about them out.

"Fuck no. I didn't even call because I knew they had my sister's kid, who needs the undivided attention of *two* adults. So there I was, in the middle of the high street, and then Noah stepped in dog shit and I just gave up. I mean, why do people have dogs if they don't want to *fucking* look after them? Don't they realise that they are putting *actual shit* on my children's shoes? It's so *fucking* offensive." Charlie leaned back with a thump, shaking her head, infuriated, exhausted, exasperated by humanity.

I said, "Oh, sweetie, I know, people are monsters. So what happened?"

"I went home and put them in front of CBeebies and fell asleep on the sofa during *Waybuloo*. And now Aneela wants to meet with me because she said I lacked professionalism. Can you believe that? Granted, I didn't call the office until ten-thirty because that goddam *Waybuloo* gets me every time but I have never, never put a foot wrong until yesterday. I have left my children in all kinds of shady childcare establishments, left them at nursery until they were the last ones there at night, I have … so many things I've done and I had one bad day, one crisis, and I'm lacking – *lacking?* – professionalism …"

"Wait, that can't be right, I'm sure she's just going to give you a pep talk. She has kids, she knows," I say, trying to make her feel better.

Charlie looks at me, pushes her tray away. "Aneela knows *fuck all*. She knows about her parents living next door, and her live-in nanny, and her cleaner who comes three times a week. She's going to say I can't use childcare as an excuse, that I'm supposed to have it sorted, that associates without children are expected to be here and I can't expect special treatment, that there are plenty of parents in the office and maybe I can't handle being on this track …"

I don't know what to say to make it better, so I say, "Shit, I'm sorry, hun. Here, you've got apple pie in your eyebrow," and I pass her a napkin.

"*Fuck*," she says, in that way Londoners do, with the extended "f," practically spitting out the hard "k."

I pull back. "I'm sorry, it's not easy."

"It's just … I'm grabbing at sand and it's running through my fingers. What am I doing this for? Why I am doing everything alone?" Charlie looks up at me and I wish I had an answer for her other than all women do it alone. I don't know when it started but that's what everyone expects of us. Even other women who know how hard it is. Especially them.

I look at my tired friend. "OK, well, we've got some time," I said. "That spot by the office threads eyebrows in, like, five minutes. Let's go to New Look across the street and get you a clean shirt too."

"Why? Do I look crazy?"

"A little. Let's get you ready for this meeting. And listen, you can fix this. You tell Aneela that you're working your ass off to build a career and you had a bad day because you don't have enough support. And that your dedication to your career means you've left your screaming, crying children in substandard care many times for your job and you're prepared to do it again, this was just a one time crisis, and she should know you by now and how hard you work."

Charlie cracks a sad smile. "That just makes me sound like a bad mother."

"Yeah. It does. But we're all bad mothers, Charlie. Kids wouldn't be such assholes if there were any good mothers. Do you know any kids who aren't assholes?"

"Aneela's?" she says, eyebrows raised.

"Good point. They're amazing. Well, if it makes you feel any better, I know for sure that this baby's an asshole based on the amount he makes me puke alone, but I'm just a paralegal so ..."

Laughing now, Charlie says, "Gigi, what the fuck are you talking about? And you have special sauce on your face."

"Yeah? Let me tell you, I would take a bath in this shit right now if I could," I say. Then we both laugh and make our way arm in arm down the street, two bad mothers.

7

BLOOD, MILK, SHIT

*A Wednesday in August 2016, 4:30 p.m.
London, Grand Euro Star Lodge Hotel,
Room 506*

I stare at the wall. I stare at the wall because this room has ceiling tiles like the hospital. So I keep my eyes on the wall, on the TV, on the floor, anywhere else but up.

Trigger warning. That's a thing. Trigger warnings for documentaries and podcasts and articles in women's magazines. They do it to be kind. They do it to make sure you're not ambushed by your pain when you're just trying to take the bus to work. But like most good intentions, they're obvious and misguided. Because there's no trigger warning for ceiling tiles. For the color blue. For the sound a sheet makes when it's whipped off a mattress. I can handle people talking about birth. But please warn me if we'll be getting into an elevator with bright fluorescent panel lights. Please warn me if there will be ceiling tiles. The kind with little holes.

People say that you don't remember the pain. You don't remember the pain of having a baby because if you remembered it, then no one would have more than one child. They say that and then they laugh and sometimes they touch your arm and wink. It's true – you don't remember the pain. But you don't need to. There are so many other things to remember. There is so much more than the pain.

Shit. More wine. Another cigarette, please. As I light up I see the red dot over my emails change again. From 32 to 33. Guess who. It says:

Johnny's home now from camp. He's upset because you're not here. I don't know what to say. I'm really worried now, panicked actually. Why won't you speak to me? Please tell me what to do. Anything. Anything you need, anything you want. We'll sort all of this out later, just please come home …

I don't read the rest. *Anything you want,* he says.

I want to sit in a chair and drink coffee that's hot. I want to cut my toenails. I want to go to the post office and stand on line, alone. I want to go to the supermarket and not worry that in the moment that I look away to find my wallet my children will be stolen. I want to shower for longer than three minutes, sleep for more than three hours. I want to go back to my job just so I can eat lunch at my desk.

I want to go to TK Maxx, and not even a nice one, like Covent Garden, I mean the regular, standard, over-stuffed one over here on the high street, and try on the clothes in the dressing room, instead of rummaging through the racks with one hand and rocking the stroller with the other and picking up last season's ill-fitting batwing tops off the floor and buying them out of desperation to wear something other than your old work shirts. Or just leaving them in a heap somewhere because Johnny's going to piss himself and we have to leave the store.

I want to have something to say to the mothers at the school gates after 'hello.'

I want to not need a drink by eleven and another one by four and another one at seven and another one at eleven.

I want them to stop calling for me, clawing at me, walking on me, sitting on me, leaning on me, punching me, throwing things that I have to pick up, crying for me, dropping shit, spilling shit, needing to be carried, wiped, washed, lifted, moved until my muscles feel like they're coming off my bones, my scar pulsing, breasts heaving, back breaking and then, Harry, you grasping for me, pawing for me in the bed at night, looking for sex and wanting my body too. And how could you, how could anyone, want this body.

I want to stop screaming at Johnny in the street because I can't handle my shit. I want to love our baby.

I want to talk to someone besides baristas and supermarket cashiers and the postman. I want someone to say they feel like I do.

I want you to not look at me like that. I want to stop dreaming about my scar tearing open, blood erupting from me and me dying under the operating-room ceiling tiles. You're not supposed to be able to see yourself die in a dream, but I have. And I want Frankie back.

Got all that, Harry?

I know I'm ranting. That I seem ungrateful. I can't explain the anger. How exhaustion and anger are the same feeling. I'm angry about being so tired, and the more tired I get, the more enraged. I wonder if I would've been different if things had gone right. If Rocky had been born the regular way and I could have pushed all of this out of me. Pushed out the hormones and the blood and the water. Instead I carry it all with me, swirling around inside, trapped. Liquid rage pushing against my organs, covering my heart, filling my ears. I hear the rush of the blood in my veins. All the extra blood I made for him, displaced, unneeded now that he lives outside of me.

Harry, do you remember when we found out about him? When I ran out of the cab and into the house and pushed you out of the way of the door so hard that the tea in your hand went flying against the wall and the cup broke? But despite my speed I didn't make it to the bathroom in time and in the space of fifteen seconds we had a pool of vomit on the antique floor tiles, a huge tea stain on the wall, shattered ceramics everywhere and you said, "Gigi, my God, how much have you had to drink?" and you got all pissy because it was Saturday and you thought I had been out getting wasted when I told you I was working on a case with Charlie but I just sat down and cried and cried and cried. "I'm not drunk, I'm not drunk," I kept wailing.

"Then what is this?" you said, and you pulled out a half-drunk bottle of white wine from my bag.

"It's Charlie's, it was Charlie's," and I couldn't explain through my tears that I couldn't drink my half at dinner so she insisted I take it home.

And you started laughing, "And you expect me to believe that? It's alright if you've had a few, Gigi, let's get you to bed."

And I said, "I'm pregnant. I'mpregnantI'mpregnantI'm pregnantI'mpregnant."

And you stopped and looked at me, and left me there, with the vomit and the broken mug and the tea dripping down the wall and you ran out of the house and you came back ten minutes later with three kinds of tests and every ginger product you could find in the store. And we did the tests and you read them and you were so happy. And I was too. And you took care of me that whole night. And in the morning, you and Johnny made me breakfast in bed which was so sweet but impossible for me to eat and when I asked you to go to the gas station and get me some Cheetos instead you said, "Anything you want," and you kissed me on the forehead. And you made sure there were always Cheetos in the snack cabinet, and then Cool Ranch Doritos when I switched to those at twelve weeks.

Anything you want. I scroll through the rest of the emails: the PTA president about next term's events; invoice for soccer camp; Pizza Express voucher; refunds from Gap and H&M for all the cheap clothes I bought that didn't fit; British Airways autumn offers. Fly to New York for £200.

I put out my cigarette and hit reply, stare at the blinking cursor for a while. Tears want to come. I consider another half-bath. I consider a slice of pizza. I consider another cigarette. I consider my boy, how I miss being the kind of mother I was when it was just him and me. I consider my baby, his blue eyes and dark curls, how his knuckles are still only dimples in his hands, how he reaches out to be held ... but I consider him only for a second, because ... because ... trigger warning.

London, January 2016; Baby, 8 days old

I hold my stomach with both hands. It's huge and round, as if the baby's still in there. A big skin-bag stuffed with rubber-fat and flesh and water and blood. My post-baby body. Quick, take a picture and post it. Show everyone my baby bliss, how blessed I am, my Kardashian curves, my Blake Lively-breastfeeding-in-a-bikini body, my Jessica Alba after-the-baby abs in *People* ...

Oh, wait. Not me. That's not me.

The midwives told me that luckily the doctors make the incision on the bikini line. So the good news is that I don't have to worry about a scar adding to the post-partum, post-natal, post-apocalyptic, post-modern, post-war, post-all-my-hopes-and-dreams stretched-out wasteland of stomach that's sitting on top of where my body used to be.

Everyone loves a pregnant woman. "Oh, you're glowing," they say, until that shit comes out and you're left like this. And then everyone's like, "Whoa, dude, well, at least the baby's cute. Did you always have that beard?"

Ding. A text from home, Sharon:
> *G you ok? You can't call people? What happened? How's the baby?*

Me:
> *Sorry, I'm a f'ing wreck. I'm out of the hospital. This shit is like Afghanistan right now. I'll call you later. Baby's OK*

Sharon:

OK well luv u. You'll be OK. Send a picture soon

Me:

OK

But OK is far away.

Where's Johnny? I can't remember.

I can't see my feet if I look down, my stomach's in the way, so I shuffle over to the mirror to look for the incision. I open my robe and hold my stomach up with one hand, peel off the bandages with the other and there it is, my flesh sewn together with black thread, a freaky smile stitched between my hips.

I catch my eyes in the mirror. Brown and bloodshot. My hair is black with grease. Neglected and unwashed for days, it looks like I cut it myself with a steak knife. Like the heroine always does in movies about crazy women. Then the beautiful actress walks the red carpet with a pixie cut ready to get her Oscar for gaining twenty pounds for the role. *So brave.*

I keep looking in the mirror. My knees are fat. Did you know you can gain weight in your knees? That shit's just bone. It's a bad day when you find out your knees are fat. My tits are terrifying, blue veins under transparent, taut, pale skin, veering off in opposite directions. East-Westers. That's what Harry would call them. My thighs are giant, formless. Don't even talk to me about my ass right now. I stopped at full frontal today so I don't kill myself.

Ding. Danielle's texting.

What's your problem, you can't answer the phone?

Me:

I'm fine. We're OK

Danielle:

How's the baby? Is the baby OK?

Me:

He's fine, he's good

Danielle:

OK then tell me if you like this dress

Look at this. She texted a picture of her in her wedding dress. She's getting married at the end of the year. Soon she's going to start sending ideas for bridesmaid dresses. God help me. The thought of stuffing all of this body into some floor-length satin number makes me cringe. The thought of getting on a plane to get there for her wedding; the thought of getting anywhere beyond the end of today – not for nothin', Dan, but now is really not the time for this. Whatever, let's see.

Me:

I love it, you look great

Danielle:

What about my chicken nuggets? Are they bad?

Me:

Your what?

Danielle:

You know, the skin by your armpit, you know when you wear strapless? I like how my cleavage looks but I'm worried about the nuggets in the photos

This girl's brain's a nugget.

Me:

If you got chicken nuggets, then I'm a whole f'ing bucket of KFC right now. OK? You look beautiful

Danielle:

LMFAO. K, I love you, talk to you soon. Send a picture already?

Me:

K, luv u

But there's no pictures. Or maybe Harry took some, proud daddy, but I don't have any. I can't tell her what happened. I can't tell her or Stacy or Sharon because they'll just feel bad and talk about me and worry and call me every day and they're too far away to do anything and I can't right now. I can't – don't want to – talk about how it was or tell them now, how this feels; what it's like. If I use my old voice, then no one has to know.

I go back to bed to sit down and there's another gush of blood and water between my legs. In the hospital they act like this is no big deal, sitting in bed in a pool of my own blood and piss and pieces of uterus and fuck knows what else. The midwives just look at you like, *It's time to pull your socks up, dear,* or one of those phrases they say here when the going gets tough. They work hard, I'm not saying they don't work their asses off, I'm not saying they didn't save my life, NHS-universal-health-for-all-isn't-it-amazing-blah-blah-blah. What I'm saying is that I really need Oprah right now and all they got here is that short lady from the *Weakest Link*.

Goodbye.

The woman in the bed across from me, her baby was screaming too, but she just held it to her breast, whispered to it, smiled a tired smile. Fell asleep content, baby on her chest, tiny hand wrapped around her finger. The circle of life spinning round and fucking round. I couldn't stand up to close my curtain and hers was open so I had to sit there and look at her with the love dripping off her like honey.

Seven women in the ward and five of them were at the pinnacle of womanhood and then there was me and the girl next to me. I never saw her face, curtain pulled between us, but I heard what was going on. The man threatening her in whispers; her sister asking if she was safe; her crying because he'd kicked her out of bed and made her sit in pain in a chair while he took a nap. I called the midwife over after a few hours and pointed silently to the curtain so she would intervene. They asked him to leave. When he was gone I heard the girl say, "Thank you," through the curtain. But I think she was saying that to God. If I knew God like that I might have asked him for help too.

Harry had to leave because dads couldn't stay at night on the ward. That was better for Johnny anyhow, to wake up and have Harry at home. But that meant it was just me and the baby. Harry left and I hadn't held the baby yet. It was all him till then. No one noticed that I couldn't touch my baby; that I couldn't reach him to hold him if he cried.

And I didn't want to.

My labor was three days long. I bounced on a ball, held onto a bar, sat in a bath, inhaled frankincense, whatever they wanted me to do, all of it over and over for days. Harry did everything he could which was almost nothing. He'd stroke my hair, tell me that it would all be alright although I knew he didn't know if that was true and I could feel the anxiety pulse through his hands. It was the first time he'd ever been powerless, vulnerable, physically afraid. The first time he'd felt what women feel all the time. There we were, scared, in the hands of strangers and the baby wouldn't come.

Finally, an epidural. The pain stopped. Just for a minute, though, just a minute of relief. Because then it travelled up my spine and collided with some of the other shit they gave me before and then I was fucked up. Really fucked up, outside my body fucked up. Thinking I was dying but unable to say any last words, looking for Johnny, hoping that the last thing I told him was that I loved him.

Then the baby's heart rate dropped. Then the blood. The terror in Harry's face. Shaking hands, blurred vision, when the me-outside-myself heard what they were about to do to me. Papers shoved in my hands to sign. They wanted me to write my name on the paper and I couldn't remember how. Harry's hand on mine to quickly make the letters. My last moment and all I could think was that, if the baby got out that would be good and maybe if there was just a little time then I could get to see his face. Just once.

Flat on my back, I was trying to tell the doctor, please, I can't breathe, I can't breathe, but I didn't have the breath to say it. The half of me behind the blue curtain was being pulled and pushed around the table. Prodded like a tough piece of meat that wouldn't yield to the knife.

Harry brought him over, and his face – his face, his happiness. Harry thought that now that it was over I must be OK. He said, "You did it!" But I was counting ceiling tiles to keep breathing. I had to keep count and I couldn't speak because I had no voice. They cut it out when they cut out the baby. Harry kept trying to show him to me, near my head at my left shoulder. I turned to the right. So that I didn't have to see all the blue. Blue scrubs, blue rubber gloves, blue walls, blue for a baby boy, wrapped in white? Was he? I don't remember what he looked like. The ceiling tiles were all I could manage. 52.

Later we're in a room smashed into a corner. Harry wedged into a chair holding the baby. Midwives coming in and out, looking, checking, asking questions that only Harry answered. I heard myself talking sometimes, words coming from somewhere, echoes in the back of my throat. I stopped rocking by then but if I closed my eyes I still felt the motion. No one noticed; my body was emptied out now and the baby was more important.

Harry was gone before I could say, *Don't leave me.* On the ward everyone was in love except for me and that poor girl behind the curtain next to me. Milk and swollen breasts and whispered phone calls to new grand-parents – the sounds of happiness everywhere. But I was drowning. The waves had taken me under and no one had seen.

The baby didn't know that I couldn't reach him in the little cot by my bed because of the catheter digging in, my mountain stomach and paralyzed legs pinning me to the bed. My arms couldn't reach to pick him up and then over the side of his cot. I had to try to shift myself closer to him, pushing up on my fists to move over, but there were too many tubes and wires, and the hole in my mid-dle – all my strength had fallen through it. There was also the terror of what I would find under the long rectangular bandages. Some future agony waiting for me.

He had a wild monkey cry, not the sweet hiccup sound of newborn babies. His screeching wail, his angry animal call, conveyed his rage that he had ended up with such a useless mother. I gave him a pacifier to stop the screaming. A midwife scolded me: 'That'll interfere with the feeding, you should know that.' There are lots of things I should have known.

They made me express colostrum by hand. They watched me squeeze the gold out of my breasts into a syringe to feed it to him. Because I hadn't done enough, hadn't been through enough. *Please, I'm soaking wet, please could I have a different gown? Please can you change the sheets? I can't move with the catheter, please, please can you help me. In a minute, dear, fill the syringe, Baby needs it.*

I tried to sleep but when I closed my eyes there was just the rocking and my own screams, the room swinging like a pendulum. Finally, when the sun came up the midwife put him in my arms. I thought, maybe, it's a new day, I'll love him now, I'll hold him and I'll love him and yesterday is over and now there is today. But – nothing. He could have been a loaf of bread.

The doorbell's ringing. "Babe, the midwife's here." Harry's calling from downstairs. He calls me Babe, always has, since New York. I thought it was cute back then with his accent and everything.

That was a long time ago.

"Babe?" I cover up as much as I can so Harry doesn't see Jabba-belly in its full glory. "Are you alright, darling?" He's standing in the doorway holding the baby, looking at me, worrying. He's so good, this man, such a goddam good man. And when I see him being so good I just want to stab him in his worried face. "The midwife's here, can I help you get dressed?" *God, I wish I had a knife.*

"No, I'm fine. Where's Johnny?" I say, trying to roll onto my side.

"He's with my mother, remember? Let me help you, the midwife's waiting downstairs." He puts the baby down in the mini crib next to the bed and reaches for the covers but I stop him.

"Nah, just give me that nightgown from last night." He picks the nightgown up off the floor, and in the daylight I can see the huge pink stain.

"You can't wear this, Babe."

"I don't give a shit, give it to me."

"Well, I do. You can't see the midwife like this, let me help you."

"Don't look at me. Just deal with the baby. I'll be ready in a minute."

"I want to look at you. Please ..." He tries to hug me. I swear to God, if I had the strength, I would tear his balls off. "Get off me. Deal with the baby. I'll be ready in a minute."

Harry's getting angry now in his subtle English way. I don't think he knew that anger was an actual emotion until he lived in New York. It was one of those things he only ever saw in American movies when he was growing up, like basketball and cheerleaders and frat parties.

"He needs you. Do you want to try to take him?" He holds the baby out to me.

He needs you. If he would just get mad and yell back, then I wouldn't want to punch him so much. I know it's irrational, unfair, to be mad at Harry. It's not his fault. But it's not my fault either and he's the one's who's here so …

So anyway, *fucking Harry*, you think I don't know what the baby needs? When I was on the table and they cut me open I saw him go up, up above us, lit by the fluorescent lights up against the ceiling tiles, before he started breathing. I saw him hovering in the lights, deciding whether to stay or go. Whether to take his chances with me. I know what he needs, I'm the only one who knows, but I also can't walk or shit or sleep. I know he needs me, and Johnny and Harry, they all need me.

"Mr. and Mrs. Harrison, can I be of any assistance at all?" The midwife's voice carries up the stairs. Fuck. It's show time.

"Get dressed, I'll go and get her." Harry looks at me with his hurt face and goes off to pretend that we're OK and give some excuses about why I didn't answer the door with my hair done in my pre-baby jeans, a cake baking in the oven. I pull on the stained nightgown. I slide over on the bed to the side of the crib. He's lying there, sleeping, swaddled up, like Baby Jesus. He's a quiet breather. Scares the shit out of me.

She's at the bedroom door now. "Hello, Mrs. Harrison, I'm Katie/Kate/Sarah/Sara, I'm the Community Midwife." She stands at the door of the bedroom holding her bag. Community Midwife. They send one to your house. Maybe, if they had let me see a doctor or something, or maybe the same midwife instead of twelve different ones in nine months, maybe all this wouldn't have happened. And now there are health visitors and community whatever-the-hells walking through my house every other day asking me my name for the twentieth time, asking me to repeat my history again and again. I tried to go with it and do what they do here. I tried not to be that American one who complained. But look at me now.

"And how are Mum and Baby today?" She bounces into the room ready to save the day. I look to see who I'm dealing with. White, young, bosomy, stuffed into a floral dress that she tells everyone is "vintage" but really is just cheap and too tight. She's never had a baby, probably never had a real boyfriend yet. An accent from some other part of England with words that end on a higher note than they started. Definitely not middle-class but it had the small town kicked out of it by years spent in London and a university degree.

"Uh, Mrs. Harrison? How are you today?" Katie/Sarah asks again, moving herself into my line of vision.

"Oh. We're OK. He's sleeping now. Can you check me first before you do him?"

"Of course. Let's have a look at you, then, while we have a few minutes of quiet before Baby wakes. Please lie down on your back."

"That's how I got into this mess."

"Yes. Now lie down if you will, please." Not even a smile.

"Sure," I say, trying to shift onto my back. The numbness is starting to go in places. I feel things, but they're muffled. Almost sound more than feeling. Like listening to the neighbors talking through the walls in my old apartment.

"Now, Mum, how are you feeling in yourself?" she asks. Doctors, midwives, nurses, they always ask this but I don't know what it means. "In myself." *Am I angry?*

Alcoholic? Obese? Paranoid? Check, check, check, check. Thanks for asking.

"I'm OK, I guess."

She looks at me, head to one side, "Are you feeling unwell?"

Oh, I don't know, it's so hard to say. I thought I was dying a week ago when they tore this kid out of me and I kind of hate this baby, but I'm considering a change of career and cutting out sugar. "No, I'm fine. I'm just very tired," *and I can't hold the baby.*

"Alright, if you could pull down the waistband of your knickers and let me have a look at the incision. Do you have any pain?" I pull the nightgown up, conscious that my stomach is exposed. Knickers – I always liked that word. Naughty but nice.

"Yeah, there's pain. It's coming through." She peels the bandage off. "Now, hmm, I can't quite see the incision clearly. Would you mind if I just move your apron so I can get a better view?"

My what?

Apron.

Did she just say 'Apron'?

Yes, Apron.

Apron.

An apron. A skin-and-fat apron. Rolls of fat and dead flesh, rubber, jelly, fat, fat-apron.

She picks Jabba the Apron up off the incision. I hear the fat peeling off the raw cut and the stiches. The slurp of skin pulled off the wound. Velcro made of skin.

"That looks fine. Just keep taking everything as prescribed and the pain should subside. Feeling will come back over the next few weeks."

I say, "OK, great," wanting to cry but not having the energy, wondering if I could use my Apron to wipe my tears if I did cry, and then an old memory of my grandma putting her kitchen scissors in her apron pocket.

She asks me some other questions and the bandages go back on but all I can think about is my Apron. "Shall we have a look at Baby?" They always call him "Baby." As if the only name I could come up with for him was "Baby."

"He has a name," I say. But I can't remember it. I can only remember Johnny. Where is Johnny? I can't remember and I can't remember the baby's name. I'm about to say Paul but Harry says, "Alistair."

When-did-Dickhead-come-back-in-the-room-and-now-he's-speaking-for-me-and-sorry-if-I-can't-remember-the-baby's-name-for-a-minute-and-excuse-me-but-what-the-hell-is-Alistair is what my eyes are saying to Harry.

He sees my look and corrects, quickly, "But we're calling him, um … Rocky. My wife insisted because he was such a fighter on his way out. Alistair is just a family name, my middle name, in fact."

Now I remember. When they were wheeling me to the operating room I said, "Call him Rocky."

But every time Harry says his name he says, "Um … Rocky." With that British "um …" that means he's embarrassed about it but pretending he isn't.

I don't care how British he's going to be about it, we're sticking with Rocky because Alistair is not an option. I know, I get it, it's a nice name here, it's an old name. It's cute in this context of sweet little kids with British accents who all think they're going to Hogwarts when they turn eleven. But I can't take *Alistair* home. *Alistair* wouldn't survive a day in New York City. They're not even going

157

to let *Alistair* off the plane at JFK. They're going to be like, "Sorry, dude, you got to take that shit back to England, you're not gonna make it here." And what do I say when I go home to Staten Island? I might as well be saying, *Hi, guys, this is my son, his name is Kick-my-ass.* C'mon now, obviously I can't call him *Alistair.* I can't even say it right.

The midwife brings me back to the moment. "Rocky, is it? What a strong name," she says, but she's too young to even know it's a movie so whatever, Sara/Katie/Kate, just get out of my house.

She has to weigh him, prick his foot and check the cord. Harry reaches for him in the little cot and takes him out because he knows better than to expect me to do it. He tries to cover for me. He holds the baby and takes the swaddle off, comforting him, like he's father of the year. *Dick.*

There's forms and questions, the red book with the carbon pages for keeping his notes for the rest of his childhood because it's 1965 here in the UK. I'm trying to look like I'm paying attention but I don't hear a word. The baby's screaming his howler-monkey yell. He's looking for me. I'm sorry, buddy.

"Is Baby feeding well?" the midwife asks and Harry has to answer because I don't know.

"His name's Rocky," I mutter under my breath.

"Yes, he's doing fine," Harry says.

"Mum, are you breastfeeding?" Here we go.

"No, I'm not."

"Are you finding it difficult? Sometimes when a birth has been traumatic both Mum and Baby can take great comfort from skin-to-skin contact and establishing a bond through breastfeeding. We can support you if—"

"No, thanks."

"It can be difficult for mums to establish feeding at first, especially after an emergency C-section, but we do encourage you to try because—"

I cut her off: "I said no."

She sits down on the bed to get closer to me and I think about picking up Apron and throwing it at her. "Can I ask why you don't want to try the breast?"

Try the breast. Makes me think of sitting in a restaurant, two breasts on a plate, parsley garnish on the side.

I don't want to try, Sara, because I don't want to touch him. Because I don't want anyone to touch me. Because I got him out alive and that was all I could do. And no one thinks that's enough. Now you want me to get my tits out and feed him too? With what? What's my milk made of? Anesthetic? Paracetamol, stool softener, Clexane for blood clots, iron supplements, adrenaline, cortisol. Caffeine to wake up and alcohol to sleep. Pure mother's milk. There's not much I can do for him but I can at least not make him drink poison.

I don't say any of that because the tears have started. My rage melting into water and when I close my eyes there are the ceiling tiles and the fluorescent lights blistering under my eyelids.

"My wife has tried, Katie," Harry intervenes. "She's been through a great deal and she's done the best she can. She managed to give him colostrum in hospital. Didn't you, darling? And she is, quite frankly, exhausted. I'm sure you've seen that many times before in your [pause] experience. So we're using formula for now. We've written down all his feeding times and how much he's taken. There's been a bit of spitting up but um ... Rocky seems happy enough." Harry picks up a notebook and taps the cover.

"We shall certainly seek professional help should we need to. You've no need to worry about us but we are [pause] very grateful for your concern and all your help and support today."

I look at him and she looks at him and she looks at me and I look at her. We all know Lord Grantham just said the opposite of everything he means. In the politest way possible he just told her to back the fuck off and lied to her face because there's nothing in that notebook. Part of her knows he's lying but she's not going to call him on it because she and Harry understand each other. They're British and this is how they do confrontation. By not doing it, really politely.

He's defending me and protecting her because he sees I'm about to lose it and this girl, she doesn't deserve it. He's trying his best, standing up for me, but it's how he's done it that makes me worry. When he channels his inner middle-class-private-school-impeccably-mannered-Tory-voter and his accent goes aristocrat, I get it – I know he's just using it to control the situation. He doesn't do it often, it's not who he is. But it still makes me wonder if Harry ever would've married me if I was from my family but we were from here. Would he have ever married me if I was the daughter of a bus driver from Croydon and I talked like Eliza Doolittle and he had met me here instead of New York where no one cares what his accent means or where he went to school?

I get a free pass because I'm American and I'm white and I'm his wife and no one has to know where me and

Johnny are really from. No one questions it. They think I'm like Harry, just the New York version, because he wouldn't be with me otherwise, would he. Would he? No one knows where I'm from except Harry. No one here knows *me* except Harry. Not even Johnny.

Sara/Kate/Katie is feisty, though. So although Harry doesn't say that since we left the hospital I haven't touched the baby; that he's done the feeding and changing round the clock; that when his paternity leave ends he's scared shitless of what's going to happen when he has to leave me here alone with two kids – she's picked it up, she knows.

She looks at me and says, "Gigi," so deliberately I want to scratch her eyes out, "you've done very well. C-section is very difficult. If you feel you need some extra support, then I'll leave a brochure here for the breastfeeding cafe around the corner and for the local borough's counselling services. They have excellent counsellors available if you'd like to talk to someone."

I'm about to say something but Harry cuts me off and says, "Katie, thank you so much, for everything."

Then she says, "Can I make you both a cup of tea before I go?" *These people with their fucking tea, yes, you know what, yes, tea is what I've been missing all along, you're so right, what I need right now is a goddam cup of motherfucking—*

Harry catches my eye. "Thank you, Katie, that would be lovely, but my wife prefers coffee. You know how Americans love a coffee," and he picks up the baby and ushers her out of the room.

She leaves and before he follows her out he stops at the door, holding Rocky close. "We all just want you to be OK. She just wanted to help," he says, with trepidation because he knows he's risked a flying rage or a wave of tears.

I swallow, hard, push my greasy hair behind my ears and meet his eyes. "I know. I'm sorry," I say. It comes out hoarse and monotone. He kisses my forehead and leaves the room to go smooth it over with Katie.

I put my head on the pillow and close my eyes but I feel like I'm rocking. Harry didn't tell her that. That to get through the worst part of the labor when I was pinned to the bed all I could do was rock back and forth. He didn't tell her that he's had to shake me awake every night when he finds me sitting up in bed, rocking back and forth in my sleep, sometimes cradling his bent knee and singing to it like it's a baby.

I'm lost, I'm scared, I'm hurt, I need you. I should have said all that too.

London, January 2016; Baby, 11 days old

The lights, the color of the walls. There's no windows. I don't know where the air comes from. When we got here Harry took Rocky and started running. He carried Johnny, took the baby and ran. Without me. *What if the baby dies before I get there? Don't look at the ceiling. Look at the floor. I don't know where the air comes from in here. I need air.* A flash of the oxygen mask they put on me when they took him out. A cage on my mouth.

I don't hold the baby much; I try, once a day, but he's so small. Like holding a feather with a boxing glove. But since we got home a few days ago I've started watching him. All night sometimes. I still can't sleep because it's chaos behind my eyes and it's easier … I mean, I'm not so scared if I keep them open. So I watch him through the mesh on the mini crib. Even though I can't pick him up when he wakes at night Harry still put it on my side of the bed. As if the baby is contagious and if I sleep next to him I'll catch it, the love I'm supposed to have for him.

He slept for three hours at a stretch but this time he kept sleeping. Parents always complain about the baby waking up but I don't. I'm in a state of constant alert while he's sleeping, waiting for him to wake up again. Because if he wakes up then he's alive. But this time, tonight, he slept for too long and his breathing was fast, then slow, then fast, then faster. Too fast. I woke Harry up. Turned on the lights. A drop in the pit of my stomach. Harry's eyes. *Shit, what do we do?* Little blue hands. Still breathing, he was still breathing.

Harry had Rocky and Johnny strapped in the car before I made it down the stairs. I'm so useless, I can't even get the kids in the car but at least maybe I got this right, maybe I did this right, the baby was in trouble and I knew. *Really, oh, congratulations, you're an amazing mother.*

There wasn't time for me to say to Harry that I should stay and he should go with the baby. Maybe this is better. What would he have said? *What the fuck is wrong with you? What mother doesn't take her sick baby to the hospital?* Harry wouldn't say fuck, though.

Harry says, "Sit in the back, between them."

"I can't, how?"

"Sit between them, watch the baby." He's scared. And since he's the only one here who's not crazy or a child that worries me.

I squeeze between the car seats but it hurts. Numb and painful at the same time in different places across my middle.

He doesn't park the car, just leaves it in front of the hospital and throws the doors open. He holds Johnny's hand on one side and carries the baby in the car seat on the other. He doesn't look to see if I'm following, just runs into the hospital with my kids.

By the time I get out of the car, close the doors and shuffle inside they've already checked in. I don't know where to go. An old man pulls his oxygen tank across the room like he's walking a puppy, chatting to it until he reaches a seat. A woman and a teenage boy, faces like stone, sit together in winter coats even though it's hot as shit in here. A skinny dude in a hoodie gets a Mars Bar out of the vending machine. I want to cry.

"Are you Mum?"

"What?"

"Are you Mum? Of the baby that just came in?"

"Yes."

"Come this way."

The nurse shows me how to get to the pediatric section, hit the buzzer, go through the door. *Follow the paw prints they put there for the kids. Buzz. Slam. Click. Locked in the hall. The lights pressing down. Don't look up. Eyes on the floor, follow the yellow line and count the paw prints until you get to the door. I'm locked in here. You're not locked in here, it's a hospital. Get to the next door, count the prints. What if he's dead before I get there? 13, 14, 15, 16, 17, 18. Hit the buzzer. Fuck. Hit the buzzer. Buzz. In. Slam. Click.* There's no windows here either but – *Where do you go, just find out where*

164

to go. I shuffle to the desk. "Hi, I'm the mother – um, the baby?"

The nurse is a chubby blond with her scrubs stretched tight across her hips, blue eyeliner smudged along with mascara in the craggy skin under her eyes. She's tired and getting older, but she's still fast in her white rubber Crocs. She starts to walk off to show me to the room but when she sees I can't keep up she slows down. She gives me her arm. "It's alright, love, take your time." She's got that East London way of talking, a punchline waiting under every sentence. Her voice matches her face – weathered, maternal. I've been a ghost since the day he was born but I feel like she's just seen me and I could cry because she called me "love." I say, "Thanks." I would totally hug her right now but Brits aren't huggers.

I get to the exam room. The doctor looks up. "Is this Mum?"

"Yes. Where were you?" Harry half-shouts, annoyed. It's not like him. It must be bad.

"Harry, I can't—"

"Jeej! Jeej! Rocky's sick." Johnny's wide-eyed, taking in the room.

"OK, buddy, I know, sit over here, here's my phone." I sit him down in a chair, find his game on my phone, turn down the volume. "We've got to talk to the doctor, OK? Be real quiet, OK?"

"Jeej, is he alright?"

"I'm trying to find out, sweetie, don't worry."

But I've missed everything. The doctor's been talking to Harry. I'm trying to focus on the words but I can't slow down my heart so if I keep my eyes on him at least he'll think I'm listening. Some kind of accent. What is he,

Greek? Turkish? Iranian? Somewhere hot with glossy, black-haired, olive-skinned people. The lights press down. I try to listen. I have to lean on something. *Don't look up, Gigi. Dehydration.* 14, 15, 16. *Special Care Unit, observation.* 17, 18. *Chest infection.* 19, 20, 21. *Questions, feeding, how much is he taking?* 25, 26. *Rapid breathing indicates.* 30, 31, 32, 33. *Something, something ...*

"Jeej, Jeej, how do you make this game go back? Go back to the beginning?"

"Johnny, baby, just wait." 37, 38, 39, 40. *Shit. Shit.*

"Jeej? Can you make this go back? The arrow won't go."

Doctor leaves, door slams. Shit, is it locked? Dammit, what's the doctor's name?

"I can't get the arrow to go back. *Please,* Jeej, can you make it go back? Jeej, I need to pee. When can we go? Jeej?"

Harry's voice like a thunderclap. "Johnny! That's enough! Dammit, Gigi, can't you make him shut up?"

50. 51. *What?* 52. *What?*

It's the way he says the T in "shut." When I say "shut up" it's full of d's and it's all one word. When Harry says it it's the T, razor sharp between the "shut" and the "up." The "shut" and the "up" cut deep.

Rocky's crying. Johnny's crying too. He's scared, it's the middle of the night in the hospital and Harry never yells. But Johnny also heard it: "Can't *you* make *him* shuT up." Like he's just my kid. Like we're strangers on line at the checkout and he's annoyed with my kid. He said Johnny would always be like his own. But now his actual own has come along and maybe he didn't know what that was going to mean. Now the ship's sinking and we've each chosen which one to save, Harry? Only thing is that I can't swim, so you have to save Johnny too, even if your arms are already full.

"I'm sorry, I'm sorry." Harry gets down on his knees, pulls Johnny into him.

Johnny says, "It's OK, Haribo."

Johnny calls me Jeej, just like my brother, Frankie, used to, and he calls Harry by his name, or Haribo sometimes, like the candy. He asked me the other day if Rocky would call us Mom and Dad, well, Mummy and Daddy because Johnny speaks British now, or if he would call us Jeej and Harry too. In his seven-year-old head they had to call us the same thing to be brothers. "Of course," I said, "of course he'll call me Jeej." When he says these things that's when the old worry rises up that I haven't done enough to make him believe he belongs to me. And here's Johnny thinking that he's not the same as this baby. He's right. He's not the same, but not why he thinks. It was never hard for me to love Johnny. I never had to fight to love him.

Rocky has to stay here so I have to stay here. *I have to stay here.* We're going to the post-natal ward where they can keep an eye on both of us. It's not special baby unit bad or anything, it's a chest infection, they have to watch his breathing and give him antibiotics. They're sending me the breastfeeding midwife because he's dehydrated and if I was *having trouble feeding I should have said so.* That's what the doctor said. My fault, I guess. Along with the panic and the baby getting stuck and the blood and the anesthesia overdose, all of it – sorry everybody, my bad.

"I can't do this. The doctor said it'll be five days for him to have the full course of medicine. I can't stay here for five days."

167

Harry puts his hand on mine. "It's OK, I'll be here, I'll do the days with you."

"What about Johnny? He has school."

"OK, I'll take him to school and spend the school day with you and pick him up and he can come and see you for a bit and then we'll go home. It's fine." Then a pause, a hesitation. "Maybe it's better for you to be here."

"What?"

"There's help here. The midwives, they can help you. Show you what to do. Help you be less scared." It's like he's punched me.

"You think I need to be in the hospital?" My fury is rising with the pitch in my voice, trying to drown out the fact that I know he's right.

"Please, that's not what I said." Harry reaches for my hand.

"You think I'm crazy and I need to be in the hospital. You can't handle how real this shit is so you want to put me in here where you don't have to be around me."

"That's not what I said." He pulls his hand away. Exhausted. Exasperated. His voice getting quieter while mine gets louder. He sits down, head in his hands. Rocky's in the little crib on wheels. A cannula taped to his hand for the antibiotics. Harry put a baby sock over it so he won't hit it or pull it out or poke himself in the eye. It looks like a cast, like he broke his tiny arm. Like his mother can't take care of him right.

She can't.

Harry raises his head to look at me but I look away. He speaks in upset whispers so he doesn't wake Johnny, sleeping curled in a ball in a chair in the corner.

"Something's wrong and I don't know how to help you. I haven't slept for ten days. What am I supposed to do? I'm meant to be back at work on Monday. Did you know that? Who's going to take care of them? Of you? You can't do it. What do I do?"

"Tell them I need you at home. Say the baby's sick. Take holiday." I start rifling through the baby bag to see if I brought anything useful. Of course I didn't. I dump everything out onto the bed.

"Johnny has to go to school. He needs his routine. He needs his parents." Harry tries to get in my line of vision but I focus on folding muslins and shoving them back inside the bag.

"You weren't too worried about being his fucking father an hour ago."

He leans his forehead on the wall. His patience has run out. I know I don't make it easy but I can't stop myself. Facing the wall, he says, shouting in hushed tones, "I'm sorry. I said I was sorry. It was a stressful moment. Did you not see that? You barely listened, you didn't hear a word the doctor said, you're not here, I have to do everything and I don't know where you've gone, but you have to come back."

"Come back? Come back? Did *you* not see what happened to *me*? Do *you* not see that I can't walk? Do *you* not see that I don't sleep? That I can't hold him? You know what? You know what, Harry? Go home. Take Johnny home. Take him to school tomorrow. Let all the mothers say what a great guy you are for raising someone else's son and taking care of your crazy American wife and making the big money and feeding the baby. You're a real hero. It's all you, you're the rock, you're the MVP, so you just take Johnny and go get your fucking medal." *Shit, he didn't deserve that.*

A midwife comes in the room. "We have a bed for you, Mum, if you'd like to come with me." *Don't call me 'Mum.'*

"I don't deserve this, Gigi." Harry's eyes have gone from brown to black.

"Neither do I," I say because it's easier than saying sorry.

Harry leans down to kiss Rocky goodbye. He picks Johnny up off the chair, still asleep, still young enough to be carried. I reach up to say, "Love you," in Johnny's ear. So he'll hear it in a dream.

Where's the window? Is there a window here just so I can see out? Me and Rocky and his bed on wheels are on the ward now, in another paper-curtain room. I hear a mother and baby through the curtain on the right, muffled, tired whispers and whimpers. I pull back the curtain on my left and there's the window, framing Big Ben across the Thames lit up against a black sky. 2:30 a.m. The Houses of Parliament dotted with yellow rectangles of light. Someone's in there working late. The Moon is full and white.

"Mrs. Harrison, Mrs. Harrison?" An authoritative whisper startles me awake.

"Yes. Sorry," I glance out the window. Ben says 3:15.

"Mrs. Harrison, I'm Mrs. Appiah, I'm a paediatric consultant, I'm here to examine your baby." Another face, another accent, another name. I have that moment of confusion I always get when the really important doctors say their names, because you don't call them Dr. here. They're always Mr. or Mrs. Like they're undercover. Her face is stern. Her hair is pulled back, smooth, perfect, nothing out of place. She's listening to his chest. She's worried about the baby. I feel like I'm in trouble. She's talking to me now. But I don't notice the words, just that she learned English somewhere else, somewhere in Africa maybe, the way all her t's are crystal clear, the breadth of her a's. She's not from here, neither am I. I wonder if she could take me home.

"What?" I say. She's in a rush and she's unimpressed, I get that but I can't help it, my eyes close and I fall back asleep for thirty seconds.

"Mrs. Harrison?"

Shit, wake up.

"Yes, yes."

"Mrs. Harrison, I am not happy with ..."

Fall asleep.

"Mrs. Harrison!" She doesn't whisper.

"What, yes." I haven't slept for so long and now I've crashed, I've gone down a hole and I can't wake up. I can't wake up.

"Mrs. Harrison, I do not believe you are currently competent to understand ... he needs ... to monitor ... every ... until ... understand? Mrs. Harrison?"

I've been sleeping sitting up. I open my eyes, startled. Ben says 4:10. Where's the baby? *You are not competent.* Where's the baby? Did the doctor take him? *You are not competent.* I roll onto my side, get my legs off the bed one at a time. The crib on wheels is gone. "Help!" I hit the call button. *Where's the baby?* I don't know if I've screamed out loud or in my head.

The midwife rushes over. "It's a'ight. It's a'ight, dear. He's at the station. He's with me. I'm watchin' 'im." She's got a West Indies accent. Her words go up and down. Like a song.

"C'mon, c'mon, let me 'elp you." She's warm. Her closely cropped hair keeps your focus on her open face, no lines in her skin. Her age is in her eyes, in the strength of her hands. You can feel she's held thousands of lives in them – and deaths.

She takes me over to the midwives' station in the hall. There's a desk with a tiny lamp, a low spotlight. Rocky sleeps in a swaddle in the crib on wheels next to a swivel chair, like just another piece of office furniture. "I could see you were sleepin' but little man needed his feedin', so I took 'im 'ere to be near me where I could keep an eye. He took ten mls but that was all. But we keep tryin'. He's so sleepy, poor dahlin'."

This is what it's come to, Rocky. A stranger feeding you while catching up on her paperwork. At least she's nice. She'll keep you alive. She can't love you, though. I can't love you the way I'm supposed to either.

"'Ere you go, try to give 'im some now." She hands me the mini bottle of formula.

"I don't, I don't know …" Before I can say no she picks him up and puts him in my arms. "'Ere."

His eyes are closed. I put the tiny bottle to the tiny mouth and once he feels a few drops he starts to drink.

"Ma'am, ma'am? Is this OK?" They don't say ma'am here but I'm not sure what to call her that sounds respectful.

"Yes, you're OK." She gets back to her files, writing her notes, shuffling her papers.

It's quiet. Echoes of a baby crying somewhere down the hall.

It's not natural but it's alright. "See, that's better, poor little one," she says.

"Ma'am, I'm not OK." It just comes out.

"I know. Was it a bad one?"

"Yes."

"A'ight. It will be a'ight. What's your name, dahlin'?" She looks at the file. "Gigi?" She puts the accent on the second "gi."

"Yeah and this is Rocky. My other boy is Johnny."

"Oh, just like an American TV show."

"About a bunch of mobsters?"

"Exactly. Didn't want to insult you just in case." She winks. "And you don't have to call me ma'am. We save 'dat one for Her Majesty. Call me Roxane. Now, would you like a cup of tea?"

Inevitable tea. "Thank you, Roxane. Just black, please."

"Black? Is that how the Sopranos drink it?" She winks at me again.

"Yep, just before they pop somebody." I smile. It's nice to say something and not have it lost in translation.

"Now look at your boy. Another twenty mls already. See? He just needed his mummy."

"Can I stay here next to you?"

"Of course, dahlin'. But there's nothing to be scared of." She puts a hand on my arm. Looks me in the eye.

"I'm scared of everything."

"Well, we just had a lady come in down 'dere, she got triplets. Let me tell you, then you would be propa' scared." She does it too, that British thing: make you laugh when you really want to cry.

She goes to get the tea and Rocky drinks his milk. I rub his downy hair, really gentle, like I used to with Johnny. Like I used to when Frankie was a baby. He opens his little eyes. "Hi. How you doin'?" I say. I brush my hand across his soft baby skin, but it doesn't feel like it did with the others. It doesn't feel like anything.

London, February 2016; Baby, 2 months old

What time is it? 2 a.m? 3? It doesn't matter because I've been awake for fucking forty-three hours. I've transcended time.

I do the nights because Harry has to work so he's got to sleep, even if he's better at the baby stuff than me. He's eight weeks old now. I know Rocky prefers Harry. With me he screams, but when it's Harry he stops crying right away. Harry says that's ridiculous, it's just that after being with me all day he needs the change of hands. But I don't think it's just anyone's hands that'll do; he needs the big, strong, capable, loving hands of his father. He takes comfort in the scent of Harry's skin; it's soap and confidence. He knows it's me because of the smell of my milk but given that he throws up everything I pump I guess he's not that eager when I come around.

The pumping makes me feel less guilty. If I can't breastfeed then at least I can say to the GP and the community midwife and the health visitor and the whole parade of people who ask me exceedingly personal questions every day that I'm pumping. When he was in the hospital I used their industrial pump which wasn't so bad and they kept saying that I had to keep going, it's the antibodies, he needs the antibodies. So ever since we got home, I just keep thinking, *Well, I did nothing else right; at least I can do this.* Only thing is I hate giving it to him. This should be the time of warm honey but all I have to give is bile. And he knows it. He prefers the chemical sweetness of formula.

I'm up because Johnny's been sick for two days and Rocky has reflux so if one's not screaming and shitting and puking then the other one is. And every morning I open the shutters downstairs and there's a new pile of fox shit on the windowsill saying, "Oh, good morning, Mrs. Harrison, have a shitty day!" Bastards. Nobody told me about the foxes until we moved here, and when I was like, "Um, why are there rabid dogs running the streets and should we call the police maybe?" everybody just said, "Oh, those are the *urban foxes*." As if that explained it. As if they're just a local breakdancing crew practising on the corner with a boom box.

There's pigeons the size of turkeys flying around here too. Wood pigeons, Harry said. One of them shit right on Johnny's face the other day on the way to school. I'm not kidding. I couldn't help myself, I was so tired from not sleeping, so tired of shit everywhere that I just yelled, "You motherfucker!" I felt bad, I thought I embarrassed Johnny. I've learned to suppress most of my New York reactions to things but then Johnny said, "Dammit, Jeej, can I get some help here?" with the bird shit stuck to his face. I almost cried because that was the New York still left in him. It has a British accent now, but it's still there.

Anyway, I'm flipping through the channels and feeding Rocky and there's these crazy Italian women with big hair walking in slow motion along the water right by the ferry terminal. The orange boats in the background, the skyline, the Verrazzano Bridge – it's all there. They're wearing fur coats and tight dresses with killer heels and I think I've really lost it now. I mean, that's definitely Staten Island on my TV in London in the middle of the night.

I text Stacy:
I can't believe they're here?
Stacy:
Who? What are you talking about?
Me:
Mob Wives!!!
Stacy:
They're showing that shit over there?
Me:
Me and Rocky are watching it right now
Stacy:
What season is it?
Me:
I don't know, 2 or 3? Early ones. It's amazing
Stacy:
Jesus you guys are so far behind. It's the last season over here now. I thought Europe was advanced and shit. What time is it there? Go to sleep
Me:
I don't know. Time has no meaning. I got to go, you're interrupting my show

I watch the women behind the men of the mob talk about their incarcerated husbands and fathers, meet for coffee, get their nails done and walk around the streets of New York City's underdog, the most underestimated borough, Staten Island. I pause the TV in the credits to see if I can spot my parents' house or my high school. I watch the orange ferry pull away from the dock.

Pieces of home. The blast of the ferry leaving the dock every half-hour, Little League games, hot dogs and pushing through the crowd on Bay Street to watch the Fourth of July fireworks over the City. The Thanksgiving Day Parade on TV. Pizza by the slice. Christenings and bar mitzvahs and sweet sixteens and getting caught buying liquor from the bodega with fake IDs. Hanging out in a used car that somebody's dad bought off one of their friends and listening to the radio turned up making too much noise in a parking lot in South Beach. Late-night coffee and cheese fries in the diner on Victory Boulevard. New York City heat in the summertime when you can see the air bounce off the sidewalk in waves. Handsome boys from shitty homes who carry their cigarette packs rolled up in their T-shirt sleeves. Sharon, Danielle and Stacy and people I love with hearts of gold who live in houses of sand fighting every day to keep it all from falling down around them. The goodness that comes with toughness. The grit it takes to make a pearl.

My boys won't know about the grind of fighting for a dollar that's only half your worth. They're going to have a different life. The lucky, privileged children of an average middle-class family, the product of a stable two-parent home. Someday they'll realize that they're not like me at all, the person they should be closest to. Or maybe they won't notice our lack of shared references and histories and people and they'll run off and be happy while I mourn the loss of our connection alone. Sad that we're so different, but also relieved. Lonely but grateful that their lives never resembled my own. And who I was before them, the place that made me, it won't matter.

But what do I know? Johnny's pissing the bed every night because I'm stressing him out. Rocky and I have a relationship of mutual tolerance. I feed him. I hold him when he cries and eventually he stops. There's not much more between us than that. It's not his fault. There's no one else to do this. I feel like he knows that so neither of us has a choice but to put up with the other one. I don't want to hurt him. I'm trying to love him.

Rocky finally falls asleep and I put him down on the sofa bed in slow motion, trying not to wake him. I put a cushion on one side of him so he doesn't roll off, not that he can, but that's what you're supposed to do. I lay down carefully and – *ah* – a sudden shot of pain across my middle. The ends of my wound pulling against each other, like one of those straw finger traps you get as a kid in Chinatown. I close my eyes though it will only be for half-sleep, my body on constant alert for Rocky's breathing, Johnny's cries, even though I don't answer them with love, only automatic instinct. Love will come back some other day.

I close my eyes. I feel the hospital bed under me with my arms wrapped in wires, the needle lodged in the top of my hand. I feel the rocking back and forth. But tonight the bed's floating in New York Harbor and seagulls fly past while I look at the Manhattan skyline, the way it used to be.

8

TEARS, TEA, RUBBER

A Wednesday in August 2016, 4:45 p.m.
London, Grand Euro Star Lodge Hotel,
Room 506

I hit reply to write back to Harry but I've spent fifteen minutes staring at the cursor waiting for my heart to slow down. This is one of the things that happens to me. My heart races at random moments when I don't think I'm panicking but my body decides that I am. Also the trouble swallowing. Not when I'm eating, but when I'm doing something ordinary, like waiting for the light to change so I can cross the street and suddenly I can't remember how to swallow. I try again and again and I can't and then suddenly I remember how and I'm flooded with relief. I wonder sometimes if my body does that just to get me the relief part. Also the claustrophobia. I don't want to talk about that, though, because just the thought of it makes me breathless.

He's waiting for me to answer. I expected him to understand me, to intuit this, to just know me and realize what was happening. But that was expecting too much; that he would do for me what I would have done for him. *Um, excuse me, Gigi, but you haven't asked him about work since the baby was born. You haven't asked him how he's doing for months. You haven't ...*

OK, don't do that. Don't start with the list of all the reasons that I'm a shitty wife. No, I haven't done any of those things. No. Because it's my turn, my turn to be the center and if he's not going to get it and he's not going to try then I'm going to ...

Leave? How's that working out?

OK, OK. Fuck.

Cursor's still blinking. I want to write to Harry that it's hard for me to think, the steady stream of alcohol, hormones and sleep deprivation make it hard for me to find the words to respond when people talk to me. I trip over phrases, forget the names of things. Thoughts come that I can feel but not articulate. My mind is always blank. No, not blank. That's not right. The opposite of blank.

My mind is flooded, overflowing with lists and needs and wants and musts. Dental appointments, school assemblies, vaccinations, birthday parties for children in the class that I don't know but that I must buy presents for and Johnny must attend. Shopping lists, dinners, electric meter readings, homework to finish, holes in school uniforms and outgrown shoes to replace. Parking permits, TV license renewal. Decisions, tiny micro decisions every minute of the day that must be made about food, sleep, clothes, morality, what laundry detergent to buy since the last one made Rocky break out in hives. The temperature of bath water; the moment to cross the street; the grams of sugar in snacks; the minutes of screen time; whether a knock on the head is bad enough to go to the emergency room again; whether he should take a vitamin; whether I call the doctor because I don't know what croup sounds like and he could die if I do the wrong thing – every decision requiring my thought and approval. Thousands of bucks stopping with me.

And worries. And questions. Has he moved up a reading level and if he hasn't then why not? How do I know if Rocky's allergic to eggs? Is Johnny's bike helmet the wrong size? How do I make them like books and vegetables? Does he need glasses? What's a cricket box and where do I get one? Will the baby die in his sleep if I turn the monitor off just this once so I don't have to listen to the crackle and hum of it all night? Did I explain homelessness right when we walked by the man under the railway bridge? Did I explain that girls and boys are equal but it's not OK to tackle girls on the playground no matter what the mothers of girls say about how they're "not girlie"? How do I explain to the mothers of girls that it's actually more important that he grows up knowing it's never OK to hit women? Ever. That raising a man is terrifying? Almost as scary as raising a woman.

People see me with my kids and I know that every choice I've made is posted on a living billboard. When Rocky cries or Johnny shouts in public or crawls on the floor under the table at the pizza place or gets into a fight at the playground, everyone looks and decides what percentage of blame to assign to me. And when they see me – overweight, tired, unshowered, in baggy clothes, quick-tempered, disorganized, bottle-feeding – that's not a difficult calculation.

At school, the teachers, young women who aren't mothers yet, who know everything about kids except for how to raise them, make helpful suggestions that carefully withhold judgment and barely conceal it. They tell me Johnny needs a math tutor, and to control his impulses better, and to use an inside voice, and a reading assessment because he's behind the other kids. And then they say to me – when I stand in front of them out of breath, rocking the baby, trying to keep him quiet while they're talking, sweat beading up on my upper lip – "Will you be signing up to the rota to read to the class? It seems that you're the only one who hasn't yet."

I see everyone's pity, disdain, relief that they aren't me and their absolute certainty that if they were me they would be doing everything differently. Better. I know no one looks at me and my kids and thinks, *Now there's a good mother.*

I look down at the phone again. Cursor still blinking. I type:

Johnny needs BigDog. Check the dryer because I washed it yesterday. If it's not there then he probably pushed it down to the bottom of the pillowcase again and forgot. Check his back for that patch of eczema. He gets itchy when he's upset. The Diprobase is in the medicine cabinet by the thermometer. Put that on him if he's scratching.

I press *send.*

No one sees this, though. How I'm barely breathing. How my skin is wrapped too tightly around me, my old self so far gone that I swear even my fingerprints have worn off my hands. And still, still I remember the

Diprobase. The stuffed dog in the pillowcase. Still they are at the top of every thought, still they are first, even when the rest of me has gone to dust.

Harry, do you see it? If no one else sees it do you, at least, even a little? What will you say if we sit down and have the conversation where I tell you that I'm crazy and that today is not just a day off? Will you remember that in the middle of it I thought about his eczema? Will you take into account – before you decide to leave and take them with you, before you decide to put me away some-where – that when his skin burns and peels I feel it too, and that on the lowest day of my life I still didn't forget my children? That the whole reason I'm here is that I can't forget, they're so embedded in my heart, their lives entwined to make a noose around who I was – I'm lost in the pain of loving them.

Tears again. God, I'm so tired of crying.

So stop crying.

Stop crying.

I feel a sudden rush of energy, a dam unleashed. I get up, put on my flip-flops, wash my face, gather my things, walk to the door. Johnny needs me. He's upset. I will open this door and leave this place and go to him. I walk unsteadily through the room, put my hand on the doorknob—

And that's where I stand still.

London, March 2016; Baby, 3 months old

7 a.m.

When I threw Johnny's truck against the window it cracked the glass. The front bumper split and the doors fell off.

One headlight kept blinking. On, off, on, off. A tire popped off in the crash and sailed into the kitchen under our status fridge: stainless steel, double door, "American."

Johnny loved that truck even though he's getting a little old for trucks now, but it was heavy die-cast metal, realistic, with a flatbed for carrying a helicopter. And I know that he loves it. But I picked it up and threw it anyway. Over the breakfast table, over Johnny's Cheerios, over Johnny's head, right at the window. Straight at the gray, gray, gray London morning.

I threw the truck because it was just the last thing in the long line of all the things. The shit-covered onesie in the corner on the kitchen floor. Harry's shoes left by the door. The garbage overflowing out of the can that Harry can't take out because he's a very important finance executive. The laundry basket reeking of urine and moldy towels. The dried food on my shirt. The letter on the table from Johnny's teacher. My hairy legs. The voicemail from my boss about my start date. The hole in the crotch of the only pair of jeans that fits.

Rocky was screaming for breakfast. There were no clean bottles and I couldn't wash the dirty bottle in my hand because the pile of dishes was too high in the sink. And I couldn't move the dirty dishes to the dishwasher because that was full of clean dishes that I hadn't unloaded from yesterday. I couldn't unload the clean dishes because there was no more counter space because of the dirty pots and pans from dinner two days ago and the sterilizer and some rocket made out of tin foil and a cardboard box that Johnny brought home from school that I'm not allowed to throw away. So on my way to the bathroom to wash out the dirty bottle I tripped. On the truck. Johnny left it in the doorway. Baby still screaming. Through the kitchen window just gray and more gray.

The truck was the last thing of all the things so I picked it up and threw it. Now the window has a nick in it, the bull's eye of a dartboard, cracks in the glass radiating like lightning bolts. And Johnny watched me do it.

"Jeej?" His hand is still holding his spoon mid-Cheerio, his dark eyes getting glassy. His brown, curly hair is matted on one side, sticking up on the other, tangled by sleep. He looks like he's outgrown his pajamas, not because he's getting bigger but because of what I've put him through.

"Jeej?" His voice is small and scared.

"Eat your breakfast."

"Jeej?"

"Be quiet, Johnny." I'm scared too.

There's a flicker in my brain. A silent home movie half a second long of "what if"? What if the baby had been the last thing of all the things this morning? A broken baby on the floor covered in glass.

I sit down across from Johnny. I drink a half-cup of coffee that I left on the table yesterday. I wonder how I'll explain this to Harry, what lie I'll tell, how I'll get Johnny to cover for me.

Because it's not an ordinary window. It's a pane in the wall of glass of the double-story extension that looks out onto the garden. This house. It took a long time for me to believe that we live here. Granite countertops. Four bathrooms with claw-foot tubs and stone tiling floor-to-ceiling. You could live in the closets. The breakfast table is next to the kitchen island. An actual kitchen island. Something I thought existed only in soap operas about rich people. Or in California. In the morning, light pours down from the skylights and through the wall of glass. Like church. Even a day like today, when it'll be gray outside, there'll still be light inside the house. Every morning Johnny eats breakfast looking through those windows at the hundred-year-old trees in the garden. He's never lived this close to a tree before. I wonder if he misses his old view of the fire escape and the bodega.

And now I've broken a window in this beautiful house. My anger has smashed the glass, scared my son, left my baby to cry. My anger permeates every room, sits heavily on every surface, blocks the doorways, thickens the air.

Is this how she felt? A flash of me and my brother hiding under the table while my mother threw dishes at my father. Me covering Frankie's ears so the crash-bang of the plates wouldn't scare him. Finding broken pieces everywhere for weeks. A ceramic sliver in my school shoes that cut my foot. We only ate off plastic after that.

I read the books, I watch the shows. I know that words come down on kids like fists and making them afraid all the time is as bad as bruising them. And I remember it, because Ma did it to us, and in the end I'm just like her, but I'm worse, because I know better. When Johnny brought that rocket home from school I tossed it on the counter and I didn't say, "That's amazing, darling, isn't that brilliant!" I didn't even manage, "That's real good, kid," like my dad used to say. Instead I threw it on the counter without a second look and said, "You want pasta for dinner?" And it crushed him. I know because that used to crush me too. I remember how that used to hurt but I did it to him anyway.

When it was just the two of us, when I wasn't broken, I used to read him a page of Shakespeare and a page of the Bible every night, like the mother in *A Tree Grows in Brooklyn*. I never raised my voice to him even though life was much harder then. Even though there was little money and no dad for him. It was simpler. We were happy.

Rocky's screaming is like torture but I'm paralyzed with yesterday's coffee in my hand. *Get up, Gigi. Get the baby.* How? *Step One, stand up.* Then what? What's Step Two? I look over and Johnny's left the table. I didn't even notice. I guess he knows how to do it too – what me and Frankie used to do – disappear, become invisible. His inheritance, rage and fear, our family jewels.

Cold morning air descends into the kitchen from the open skylight. The air here is always wet. So heavy you could pick it up and carry it. The baby's stopped crying. It's too quiet.

Shit.

Shit.

I start running through the house. *Suffocation, crib death, unconscious, dehydrated, drowning, smothered, SIDS, is he on the floor, did I leave him on his back or his front, what's the right way? Back or front? What if he threw up and he was choking? Where is he? Where is he?* "Johnny? Where's the baby?" I scream as I race upstairs. I turn into Rocky's room, breathless, panic crashing over me because I've done it now, I've actually hurt them. Now they're going to find out about me and take the kids away so I can't hurt them anymore.

But then, my battered heart cracks a little more. Johnny's standing on the toy box he pushed over to the side of the crib so he could reach over the top and get to the baby. He's leaning over holding the pacifier for Rocky.

"What're you doin', buddy?" I ask him from the doorway. His small voice answers me, "I couldn't find the milk but I found the dummy so I thought he might want it. He was really crying, Jeej. But he's alright now. I think he's hungry." Johnny uses the whole sleeve of his pajamas to wipe his nose. His voice is breaking; he's trying to be brave.

"I'm sorry I broke your truck. That was wrong. I'm sorry."

"I know, Jeej. I won't tell Harry. I have to get dressed." My loyal accomplice. He steps off the toy box after checking Rocky can hold the pacifier in his mouth and turns to go to his room. His bottom lip's shaking and his eyes are welling up.

"Can we hug it out, buddy?" My voice is breaking too.

"No, thank you, Jeej. I have to get ready for school." He said it British. Nothing that sounds like me in that sentence. He brushes past me, tears on his face.

I reach for Johnny's arm and he gets all stiff, struggling against me but not strong enough to pull away. He doesn't want me to hold him. I don't blame him. I let him go.

I pick up the baby and kneel down so Johnny can see my face. "I love you, I'm sorry. I'm trying."

He doesn't look me in the eye, but looks just to the left, at my ear. Raises his hand to play with my earring, like he always did when he was little. "I know," he says. He relaxes. He forgives me too easily, melts into my arms, curls into me, still my little boy. He holds his baby brother's hand.

I hold my boys and cry hot tears.

What-the-fuck-do-I-do-now tears.

Someone-help-me tears.

8:30 a.m.

Eventually I get up off the floor. There's no choice. Kids make you get up. I took off my holey-crotch jeans and put on my maternity leggings, found Johnny's knee socks and his PE kit and his goddam £1 coin for the goddam cake sale and put it in the envelope and got us to school.

Waiting for the school doors to open I stand with my back to a group of designer-athleisure mums and vaguely eavesdrop on a group of Whistles-wrap-dress-with-flats-going-to-work mums. I feel the elastic of my leggings slipping under Apron and settling on my scar as I watch the boyfriend-jeans-Breton-stripe-tee-metallic-sneaker mums agree on playdates and pick-ups. I pretend to be answering emails on my phone with one hand as I rock the pram with the other. I try to look busy; like I'm standing apart from the groups of chatting parents by choice and not because I don't know what to say. Probably best not to engage today anyway in case they can see this morning in my face.

It's not that I'm an outcast here. The other parents haven't tried to make me feel inadequate. They're too polite for that. There's no alpha-bitch moms, not like the movies. Mostly it's all types of working moms – power players with big jobs; small-business owners who work from home; part-timers doing jobs they're overqualified for; a chunk of stay-at-home mothers with a sub-set struggling with guilt and regret, and even a few work-at-home dads. Parents doing whatever they can the best way they know how. Juggling, balancing, plates spinning and balls in the air and other circus metaphors and everyone's trying to get through the day without getting fired or forgetting one of the kids somewhere.

Except – and this is a very big exception – that this is private school. In England. The country that invented elitism. So yes, they're doing their best, but that's a lot easier to do when you have money, education, a live-in nanny and a Range Rover. They work for that money, look at them – stressed, worried, anxious, wrinkled, exhausted, dehydrated, working every hour there is, working all night after the kids go to bed. But I think it must be easier to work that hard when power is part of your pay package. When holidays abroad and ski trips break up the months of long hours and work travel. It's easier when the money you earn is real, with real weight and depth; when you know that you're giving your kids the best there is and not just the best you can. I know they earn it because I know Harry earns it and I know what it costs, the toll that it takes. But I know lots of other people who work hard and earn their money too. It just doesn't get them that far. Sometimes it doesn't even get them dinner. And rich banker-type people forget that or don't think about it – that is, if they ever knew it in the first place.

I'm uneasy with how easy everything is here, in this world where people work hard, yes, but where they got that work because of privileges they aren't conscious of or don't admit too. I'm uneasy with iPads for each child in the family; kids who fly business to Barbados; second homes – the expectation of excess as part of the natural habitat. But I don't bring it up. We never talk about money in England. It's OK to drive it or have it on your wrist. OK for your kids to wear it as a school uniform. But you don't talk about it, or question it, because we earned this, after all.

Am I uneasy because I know it's unfair? Or am I uneasy because, now that I'm in it, I'm not willing to give it up? I'm doing what a mother does, right? Putting my kids first. This school's not for me; it's for my children. For them to do better than I did, that's the point. Isn't it? Is it? Is there a mother who would walk away if she had a choice? Who would send her kid to the struggling state school around the corner when the door's been held open to this place instead?

I'm a traitor to my old life and an imposter in my new life. Every day I play charades. And every day Johnny becomes more British, more 'middle class', which means something different in England than it means at home. He becomes more like these people and less like me. One day the last thread that connects us will finally break and he'll go with them. And any memory he has of those first years, of him and me in our tiny apartment, will fade away; a part of the story of his life that will be too small, too inconsequential to tell, even though it means everything to me.

Susannah, the class rep, makes eye contact with me and waves. *Shit.* On her way over to me she stops a couple times, makes a coffee date with this one for after drop-off, makes plans for tennis later with that one. I'm her last stop.

"Gigi, hello! Don't you look well? Oh, bless him, look at that gorgeous baby! Oh, well done you!" and she leans over for double-cheek kisses and coos at Rocky. Susannah's blond, not naturally of course, glossy and forty-something, slim and pretty. She's in distressed skinny jeans and furry gilet (possibly real) over a cashmere sweater that features a whimsical neon lightning bolt; dove-gray suede ankle boots with sassy Western fringe and a studded, cross-body bag, Valentino, in that perfect shade of powder pink. A long necklace with a star charm, tiny diamond shining in its center, is the finishing touch. Understated effervescence; she shimmers with careful control.

I want how she feels. I want to be slim and confident, perfumed with high self-esteem. I want to remember people's names, put mascara on in the morning, wear new shoes. What makes it worse is that Susannah is polite and warm and kind. She doesn't let me see her eyes see the hole in the seam of my maternity leggings. *Dammit, these have a hole too.*

Say something, Gigi. "Hi, how you doin'? Did you have a nice half-term?" I say after scanning my brain for what to ask her. Half-term was three weeks ago, no longer current for small talk, but it's all I got. I'm conscious that Johnny's clinging to my leg and hiding behind me instead of running around with his friends. Susannah cocks her head to one side. "Oh yes, lovely. Have I not seen you since then? Really, *really* lovely. We went to Morzine. It was fantastic. *Amazing* snow. And the *après ski*, well, turns out there were lots of families we knew who happened to be there too. So perhaps a few too many boozy late afternoons, but that's alright, isn't it? We brought our *au pair* with us, which is really *very cheeky*, I know, but so worth it because I just let her deal with the tired little darlings and I had an *actual break*. It was *heavenly*."

She looks at me for a response but I have no idea what she expects me to say. She thinks I know what she's talking about. I deduce that Morzine is a ski place, I don't know where and I don't know what *après ski* is but it must be something to do with alcohol because it always is. I've never had an *au pair*. All I can think is it must cost a lot of money to take a family of five plus an extra random girl skiing for a week. But that's not the right thing to say. So, instead I manage:

"Wow. Sounds real nice." I should say something like, *Yes, I heard the snow's been fantastic this year, aren't you lucky*, or, *Such a good idea, taking your au pair*, but I don't think of those things because they're not part of my lexicon.

Susannah continues, "And what about you? It's just that time when you're at home *all the time*, isn't it? When there's no difference between day and night? You *poor* thing. Is he letting you sleep at all?"

"Um, yeah, he's only twelve weeks, so you know …" *You know, Susannah, don't you? When it's so bad that you break a window first thing in the morning?*

"Well, you must come to Mums' Drinks this Thursday, will you?"

"Mums' Drinks?" I say things like that, *Mums' Drinks*. It helps move things along if I mirror what people say.

"Yes, did you see the WhatsApp?" *Oh God, Susannah, friggin' WhatsApp.* I ignore it. The only reason I haven't deleted the class one is because it would leave that message for everyone, *Gigi Harrison has left the group.* And even I can't do that. I say, "Oh, you know, I probably did but, baby brain. When is it?"

"Thursday evening, *please come*, everyone would *love* to see you and you deserve a night out, doesn't she, Johnny?" She bends down to address Johnny and rumples his hair. She's a gifted PTA rep who remembers all the kids' names. "Lovely to see you, I *must* be getting off, see you Thursday, I hope!" and Susannah floats off to join another group of moms. *Mums*. Well, I got through that. I must look normal.

Johnny's still clinging to me. I run my hand through his hair. What is it like for him, knowing what he knows and then watching me pretend in public? I take a deep breath and dig down to channel the kindness and understanding that's been in short supply lately. I owe it to him to try and love him more this morning.

"What's up, kiddo?" I say, bending down to be eye to eye.

"There's Jasper," he says in a quiet voice.

"What?" I ask.

"Over there, that boy." Jasper. That explains a lot already.

"He's the one who wouldn't let me play football yesterday at break." He points to one blond kid out of the hundred running around. A hundred blonds, two Black kids and an Indian girl. I'm looking for a white needle in an Anglo-Saxon haystack, but I've clocked him and now I know the one. The one I saw put his foot out and trip Johnny on purpose once when he ran to me at pick-up, Johnny splayed out flat on the ground in shock, sobbing. The one who took his candy last week on the field trip and Johnny was too afraid to tell the teacher. The one who made fun of the chubby kid on sports day. I feel a flare of the morning's earlier rage. It's surprising, the anger that other people's children can rile up in you. Few parents would ever admit it, but if you've ever felt it, if you've ever met a little shit like Jasper, then you know what I mean.

I get down on my knees, pull Johnny's forehead to mine. "You listen to me, the next time that kid says anything mean to you, you tell him to shut up, that he's not cool and call him a baby. Tell the other kids to call him a baby too. Because he doesn't decide what you do, you decide, you got me? If he ever hits you, you hit him back, twice as hard. And let everybody see you do it."

"But that's not kind, Jeej."

"No, it's not, it's fighting back. And I'm telling you that it's always OK with me if you fight back. You don't start the fight but you fight back." I hug him as tight as I can and keep my eyes locked on the back of Jasper's blond head until he turns around. When he looks back at me with his entitled freckles I mouth the words, "I'm watching you," and he turns away, pretending not to see.

9:30 a.m.

On the walk home from drop-off I stop for a coffee. An Americano. We lived here for a while before I figured out that that was the closest I could get to a coffee from home. They don't do filter coffee here. No glass coffee pots sitting on hot plates. I walk up to the counter. "Hi, how can I help you?" American. No, maybe Canadian, he's so nice, no, definitely Midwestern. Big, open, freckly face with a trendy beard. Probably doing his year abroad or whatever, exploring Europe, reading his poetry at open mics, picking up girls with accents. Optimistic and young. I'm angry that he exists and I'm sorry for him that he has to wait on me today.

"Can I have an Americano, please. Black with a little milk."

195

He puts the coffee in the machine. Nothing about me can possibly invite conversation but he says with a twang, "You have an accent, where you from?"

I say, "New York," in a way that means, *Please stop talking to me.*

"Cool. You know why it's called an Americano, right?"

I say, "No," in a way that means, *The fact that you are speaking is causing me physical pain.*

The young man, undeterred, continues, "Well, when the G.I.'s were in Italy in World War Two, they asked for all the espresso to be watered down because, like, it was too strong for them."

I say, "Oh," in a way that means, *I might actually die if you don't stop talking.*

He shrugs and shakes his head as he pulls the cup away from the machine. "Figures, so typically American, right? Now it's served all over Europe. Americans always expect to be catered to. Sorry, did you say you want milk in this?"

I try to keep a blank expression and pray, *Jesus Lord, help me not to hurt this young man* as I reply, "Listen, you Kansas-ass motherfucker, you would know what I said if you were doing your job instead of trying to teach me a history lesson. Now give me my coffee with milk in it and can I please have some shut-the-fuck-up with that?"

No, c'mon, I didn't say that. I'm depressed and angry but I'm not a total asshole. What I said was, "Whole milk, thank you." But I thought it and it made me smile.

I do the mother shuffle to leave the cafe: one hand on the stroller, one holding the coffee, back my ass into the door to open it. For a second I can hear Juvenile telling me to "Back that azz up" and a flash of me – the me before Johnny and Harry and Rocky – dancing with some guy in some club flickers in front of my eyes. That girl wouldn't believe it if she saw me now. I laugh out loud. I feel lighter.

But the feeling ends when I see my reflection in the cafe window outside. My hair's an awkward length, limp and frizzy. Harry's white button-down shirt, which I thought made me look casually classic and not still pregnant, clings to the curve of my stomach in this light, the buttons in the middle sticking out farther than the others. A patch of sweat spreads under my arm. The black maternity leggings are baggy around the knees. Did I show up at Johnny's school like this? Coffee drips stain the front of my shirt.

I watch a girl, maybe twenty years old, walk past my reflection and into the coffee shop. Asymmetric hot pink mini-dress under a cropped faux-fur jacket. Her white ankle boots – pointed, sculpted, architectural – have arrived from another galaxy. But her eye liner is smudged and her hair is swept up in a careless mess on top of her head with an ancient turquoise scrunchie, as though her hair doesn't know how incredible the rest of her looks. But London girls dress like that. Like a chipped manicure – smooth and pretty except for that jagged, edgy, gritty corner on the index finger where the polish came off. I watch her order coffee and I feel ridiculous and ugly and old, embarrassed to put my big, outdated sunglasses on, but desperate to hide behind something.

Ding. A text from Stacy breaks my stare.
    Hey G what's going on?
Me:
    Nothing. Wait, isn't it 4 in the morning there? You OK?

Stacy:

> *Yeah, baby's sick, been up all night. Now I can't sleep. Hey, you will not believe this*

Me:

> *What*

Stacy:

> *Tina caught Joey last night at Jesse's house. Finally*

Me:

> *That bastard*

Stacy:

> *I know. She's not giving back the ring. I told her not to*

Me:

> *Good. She shouldn't. How's the kids?*

Stacy:

> *They're good, look at this*

A picture of her son, Christopher, in his Tiny Tikes baseball uniform. Next, a picture comes through of her nails. A mint-green manicure with pastel yellow on the ring finger of each hand.

> *You like my nails?*

Me:

> *Love them*

Stacy:

> *Matches the baby's party theme. Bunnies and chicks. You know springtime shit*

Me:

> *Wish I could be there. I'm not doing so good today actually can you* delete, delete, delete, delete …

I delete *can you talk later* because a picture of baby Melissa comes through, in a lacy baby ball gown, stiff crinoline under the skirt. She's about to turn one. Stacy puts frilly headbands on her bald head so people know she's a girl. A tiny gold baby stud glitters in each ear. She's smiling. A living cupcake.

I type:
She's beautiful. I got to go. Have fun at her party
Stacy:
Send me some pics, I want to see this kid
Me:
OK

But there are no pics to send of Rocky from my phone. Harry takes all the pictures.

I have no pictures Stace because I don't really want to remember this time – delete, delete, delete, delete, delete
Me:
Love you
Stacy:
Love you

On the way into Sainsbury's I see the old man on the bench outside the pound shop. I've seen him on that bench every day since we moved here. Bloated. Pockmarked. The skin on his hands is taut, straining against the swollen alcoholic's flesh beneath. Sometimes he reads a newspaper cast off by some commuter. Sometimes he sits with a can – cider, lager, alco-pop. Sometimes he just sits, part of the ecosystem of the street, like the post box on the corner and the aging red phonebooth.

I was walking Johnny to school one day a couple months back when I saw him passed out on the sidewalk, surrounded by people calling 999 on their cell phones. A stroke or a heart attack, I didn't know, I just rushed Johnny past so he wouldn't see and said a prayer. But he's back on the bench today. So neither of us is dead. I guess that's something.

There's a lot of characters like him in this neighborhood. The Chinese lady who comes out of the corner store with a jug of milk strapped into a stroller like it's a baby. The Indian lady in her Technicolor saris who always wears socks with flip-flops, even in the rain, even in winter, and walks the streets picking up abandoned newspapers, refolding them and then packing them into her rolling shopping cart. The old dude with the long white beard on the mobility scooter who drives down the middle of the street daring the cars not to give way to him. The bald lady singing Polish folk songs and feeding the birds in the Waitrose parking lot. The people most people see and try not to look at with stories they don't want to know.

Once I'm in the store, I walk around noticing the displays that have changed since yesterday. Today there's samples for a new salted-caramel *Taste the Difference* cake. I grab some on my way to the wine aisle. There's another mother there with a toddler who's making her crazy and a baby sleeping in a pram. She's not one of the toned Pilates mums you see around here. Neither am I. We're both fat, exhausted and defeated, but we feel no solidarity. We just glance at each other to see which one of us is smaller, because if you're the smaller one, well, at least that's one person who's fatter than you.

I put two small 200ml bottles of wine in my basket for elevenses later. Elevenses in Britain is your mid-morning snack break. But at 11 a.m., instead of tea and cake, I have my first glass of wine. Just one. Just to stay calm. Same thing at 2 p.m., then at 4 and then one between 6 and 7 p.m. to get through the bedtime routine. Every few hours, like medicine. Wine wraps my feelings in gauze and then they don't feel so sharp. I don't yell so much. And I'm not the only one.

In America, unless she did it all in private, a mother couldn't drink this way all day. But here it's easy to do and there's lots of us who do it. You know us. We're the ones taking the kids to Pizza Express after school so we can get a glass of wine at 4:30 on a Monday. The ones at parents' evening who take the first polite glass and then grab a 'cheeky' second one on the way to the curriculum meeting because at private school your fees get you wine in a bucket at the door to the classroom. It's not hard to find wine during the day. It's right there in the supermarket, the corner shop, the gas station, the play date, the soft-play center, the kids' party, the children's museum cafe. Sanity, clarity, a healthy marriage, a therapist – those are all a lot harder to find.

I buy little bottles, two or three at a time, enough to have a glass every four hours. I take the empty ones with me when I leave the house so Harry doesn't see them. I don't throw them away; I faithfully recycle them in the glass bin outside Sainsbury's as penance. I know how ridiculous that is.

I step up to the cashier with my mini wine, formula, chocolate Hobnobs and toilet cleaner – a summary of my life laid out on the checkout conveyor belt. The teenage girl in her bright pink hijab at the register says, "Hello," smiles and makes eye contact. She recognizes me, I'm in here enough. She politely averts her gaze, as she always does, from judging my shopping, but she's too young to sell me alcohol so she has to raise her hand to get the floor manager to clear the purchase for her. How I must look to this girl, how feeble and pathetic I must seem in my daily pilgrimage for tiny bottles of wine to hide from my husband while she's in here working, probably saving money for school. I wonder how her mother raised her to be such a good kid.

She says, "Aren't they lovely when they're asleep," gesturing at Rocky in the stroller.

"Best part of the day," I say.

She smiles and she thinks I'm joking, but I'm not.

8 p.m.

Another end to another day which could have been yesterday or the day before and will be the same as tomorrow. The baby's asleep, Johnny's in his PJs watching David Attenborough. Harry's finally home. Johnny runs to him. They wrestle, read a story, and Harry puts him to bed. I kiss Johnny goodnight. He hugs me tight. He still loves me, but I can feel his relief that Harry's here and the day is over. Or, that the day with me is over.

I'm in the kitchen microwaving some frozen dinners. I wonder when Harry will notice the window. Right away, turns out.

"What happened here?" He points at it, loosening his tie and reaching for a bottle of wine in the fridge.

"Neighbor kid, hit a cricket ball over the fence."

"Well, have you spoken to them? Will they pay for it? Do they know what these cost?"

"Yeah, it's fine. It was an accident. They offered to pay right away. I talked to them. I called the company to get a quote." Lies. I realize too late that the glass is broken from the inside, pushing the glass out. It's not dented inward like it would be if a ball hit it the way I said it did. This is a major hole in my story. Harry must be tired because he hasn't noticed. Or maybe he has but he doesn't want to know the truth, because knowing the truth will mean that he will have caught me in a lie. Will mean that he knows something is wrong with me. Will mean that he'll have to do something about it.

He sits down at the table and I put a microwave curry in front of him, a lo-cal risotto for me.

"This looks great, Gigi, thank you." It's disgusting but he's too tired to care. "Anything else of note happen today?" He digs into the fluorescent-yellow rice.

How do I answer?

Actually, it was me. I cracked the window when I threw Johnny's truck at it.

Or:

I started drinking at eleven this morning because the sight of myself in the cafe window made me cry.

Or:

Johnny's teacher told me that he went to the head-master's office today because he punched that little shit who keeps bullying him because I told him to.

Or:

I'm so homesick my body aches.

Or:

Please help me. I'm in so deep I can't get out.

But I don't say any of those things. Instead I go with, "You know that old drunk on the bench who I thought was dead? Turns out he's not."

Harry says, looking at me, fork in mid-air, "Well, that *is* good news." We eat in silence. Forks clanging on plates.

After dinner we sit on opposite ends of the sofa. Harry says, "Oh, the new season of *Game of Thrones* is out," and he flips through the channels to find it. I say, dismissively, "Dragon porn," and I curl up thinking I'll catch a nap on the sofa for an hour before Rocky wakes up.

Harry is silent for a moment until he says, looking at the TV, "Newt rom-com."

I sit up and scramble until I think of, "Mouse thrillers." I smile, remembering when we played Last Letter Game that time we were stuck at JFK for six hours.

Then Harry says, "Scorpion drama," and I start to laugh; we both do.

I blurt out, "Armadillo horror!"

He yells, "Rat art house!"

I stammer, "Eel comedy!"

He shouts, "Yellow-billed loon ... yellow-billed loon ... uh ... um ... dammit, I'm out."

I say, "Get outta here, what's a yellow-billed loon?"

He says, "It's an Arctic bird."

I say, "Oh my God, you're an Arctic bird." We laugh. It's nice. It used to be easier.

I move down the sofa to be closer to him, because I think I want to say, I think I'll try to say— but then, Rocky's cries come over the monitor. Khaleesi, the mother of dragons, makes a breathless speech on screen. Harry watches her. Our moment is over. He doesn't move to go upstairs and I'm too tired to ask him to, knowing the argument it will start. I go give Rocky his bottle. And cry.

London, April 2016; Baby, 4 months old

How does she open that window? Can I ask her to open it, no, that's weird it's raining how does she open it if I really had to could I break it? Go to the bathroom until it's over. What do I do with the baby? No, don't go to the bathroom. You'll get trapped in there. Don't go anywhere just pretend nothing's happening.

Gigi? C'mon now. Get your shit together.

I can't, I can't. My hands are numb my hands are numb that means I'm not breathing.

Of course you're breathing, Gigi.

I'm not breathing there's no air.

Of course there's air, Gigi.

Don't drop the baby don't drop the baby.

Jesus Christ, Gigi.

Here it comes, rising lava climbing, climbing, back of knees, waist, spine, between the shoulder blades, back of neck, the heat, the heat, I can't ...

Gigi, count!

1, 2, 3, 4, 5, 6, 7, 8, 8, 8 and ...

"And you, Gigi? Cake?" Sukie asks me, breaking the trance of the panic. She can't tell I'm immersed in hot lava on her sofa.

Try to answer. If you can answer you can breathe.

I sputter, stutter, find words somewhere in the back of my throat. "Um, no, no, thanks, it looks great but I'm on a diet." I swallow, hard. Push the lava down. *Focus, look at them, listen, listen to every word, count ...* So I do. I try to focus even though my eyes feel like they're melting under the heat. We're in Sukie's big Victorian house. We're all holding our babies. Sitting on overstuffed sofas around a cream-colored coffee table. The table looks old, like it came from Sukie's great-aunt's barn. Its paint is distressed. Like me.

Fiona, a living stick figure in an outfit that highlights the flatness of her post-partum stomach, says, "Oh, I need to be on a diet too – I've never eaten so much cake!" All the ladies laugh. They nod and agree about how ravenous breastfeeding makes them, how they eat constantly, how they're going to keep breastfeeding as long as possible so they can keep eating cake. Ha, ha, ha, they laugh with that laugh they all got from their John Lewis wedding registries, along with the set of matching Le Creuset cookware.

I'm coming down from the wave now. It only lasts a few minutes but always feels like hours. It started in the hospital the night he was born. I thought that was probably all the drugs I was on. But it hasn't stopped. It gets me in confined spaces. Distraction helps. For instance, I'm keeping my mind busy wondering if Fiona made that diet joke because, even though I'm the fattest girl in the room, she doesn't think I'm *that* fat. So she doesn't think that joke will offend me because I'm one of them. But I know that, really, she's just sparked a skinny-girl conversation and they're all just ignoring me while they eat the cake that I don't. At least none of them noticed the wave. Most people are too self-absorbed to notice a woman drowning on land anyway.

Count.

Four blonds, two brunettes including me. Sometimes I forget which blond has which baby, they're all so similar, but one of them's Australian so that helps. There's a Geordie, Tracy, who I thought was Irish or Scottish at first, I knew it was a different accent, but then she said something about growing up in Newcastle. So I said, "Oh, do you have an ass tattoo like Cheryl?" But no one laughed. I thought it showed that I knew who Cheryl Cole was and that I could join in on British pop-culture conversations but it didn't come out right. It was the wrong thing to say. Tacky. Now they suspect I'm a chav. That's like white trash. They weren't sure before, me being American threw them off, but now they suspect I'm not middle class like them after all.

I'm only here with them because, by shitty coincidence, Sukie's married to Gareth who works with Harry and we ended up in the same local birth-prep class, held in the fluorescent lit, freezing basement of the Salvation Army, right after AA was done and next door to the weekly Slimming World meeting. That's like Weight Watchers. The surroundings for this magical time of our lives could not have been bleaker or more British. But I went with it, and every week me and Harry sat with the others and listened to the crazy hippy teacher predict dire futures for our babies if we used baby wipes and didn't breastfeed and had epidurals. One time, she did a half-hour on home births, because the NHS encourages them (yeah, I know) and my all-day, all-pregnancy morning sickness kicked in, right there, in the middle of the room. All I could think to say was, "Sorry, the baby just wanted to let me know that there's no way in hell we're having a home birth." Everyone laughed.

Once the classes were over and the due dates got nearer Sukie organized it so that we kept meeting during our mat leaves and now here we are – every week on Wednesday at each other's houses in rotation. I go most weeks because I know that if I don't show up then Sukie will say something to Gareth and at some point Harry will find out, in some casual conversation in the queue at Pret, and then he'll get suspicious about what I do with my days. And with the baby.

Queue. I never used that word before we came here. Impossible to spell.

My breathing slows. I look around the room to see what else I can count and I learn that we're sitting in 'Sukie's Tea Nook' according to the sign painted on a worn wooden board and hanging on the wall from a reproduction of a brass coat hook reclaimed from the waiting room of a fictional, but very old, steam railway station. Emma Bridgewater and Cath Kidston are having a turf war in here. A lot of polka-dots had to die to decorate this room. There are pheasants and strawberries on every plate and mug. And napkin. And pillow. Some fabric flowery bunting is draped with meticulous haphazardness over a distressed wooden china cabinet with glass doors. She doesn't keep dishes in there. Just her collection of new-but-vintage sugar bowls. I count. Nine out of twenty-two are labeled *sucre* because they are "French."

Parallel to Sukie's Tea Nook is Sukie's Extremely Expensive Retro British Kitchen complete with an Aga and new-but-old Smeg fridge. All the appliances are in matching cream and chrome. The floor-to-ceiling wooden cupboards are the perfect shade of lemony white with newly tarnished, battered brass drawer pulls and cabinet handles. A pastel blue KitchenAid mixer dominates the corner of the counter ready for when Sukie needs to really mix the shit out of something. And if you follow the gleaming creamy granite countertops along the wall to the entry of the corridor, you'll see hanging, to the right of the lemon-yellow doorway, above the vintage school chalkboard hung with twine displaying Sukie's shopping list (Chard, Agave, Beetroot, Tamarind, Mint, Gin – ha!) the ceramic casting of the baby's footprints. Framed in a very light blue, slightly distressed wooden frame. The little feet are perfect. Like everything else in this house.

I know I'm jealous. Because I feel inadequate. Because I can't even give the baby a bath every day, much less take him to a pottery shop to have his footprints recorded for eternity. Harry would say that it's "envious" not "jealous." A tip for anyone who needs/wants to piss off an American: correct our English. Works every time.

I reach for my glass of water on the coffee table, avoiding the cakes and homemade scones. I notice a jam jar covered with a red gingham cloth and tied with a piece of twine. It's labeled *Sukie's Sumptuous Strawberry*. Wow. That's an alpha move. It might as well be labeled *Eat My Jam, Bitches*.

I have a crystal-clear memory of me and Frankie sitting at our Formica kitchen table with a loaf of Wonder Bread and jar of Goober. Goober is peanut butter and jelly (or English people say jam because jelly is actually Jell-O to them: it gets complicated). Anyway, Goober is PB and J swirled together in one jar. It solves the problem of remembering to buy two products instead of one and also of needing to use two knives to make one sandwich. American ingenuity. Sukie wouldn't approve of Goober.

God, I want to go home so bad. New York home, I mean.

Rocky's asleep in my arms. The worst of the wave has passed now but my hands still tingle. I lower Rocky to my lap so that I don't drop him. So that they don't go home and tell their husbands about the fat American one who dropped her baby. I hold him closer and try to match his breathing.

Sukie says, "Well, I say, bring on the cake, ladies. The midwife said I need more carbs in my diet to fatten up the baby so I'm relaxing my usual standards."

"Oh, has being gluten free affected your milk? I hope you don't need to top up with formula." That's Georgina. Talking with one boob out, as usual, even though the baby stopped eating five minutes ago and he's asleep in his pram. But it's good to know she's prepared.

Sukie crosses her lean legs so that the long line defining her thigh muscle is clearly visible, camera ready. Her lovely, slim feet have been newly pedicured. She says to Georgina, "No, no, my milk production is fine, it just burns so many calories. We need those carbs! Humphrey's doing very well, no formula needed, thankfully."

Humphrey. Sharon would laugh her ass off if she heard that one.

"Well, that's lucky for you then, isn't it, Sukie. Isn't that fantastic," Tracy pipes up as she pointedly puts a cap on her baby's bottle. She's had a hard time with the feeding. I know she's also pissed that the two pounds Sukie gained in pregnancy have fallen off her. There's an extra nervy kind of edge in every word she says with that accent so you can't tell if she likes you or if she's about to kick your ass. She really forced herself into those jeans today. I can tell by the way she keeps pulling them up at the thighs. I saw her undo the button to sit down when she thought no one was looking. That's why I like her.

Sukie takes a sip of her herbal tea from a *Yummy Mummy* mug dotted with hearts in different shades of pink. "But ladies, I think the key was having the nighttime nurse for the first four weeks. I haven't told anyone aside from you about it for fear everyone will think me terribly spoilt, but I *do* think she saved us. She was absolutely worth the money."

"You were so clever to think of doing that! Charlie and I argued constantly about whose turn it was to get up. Luckily Sophie's slept through from twelve weeks, so at least we've got over that hurdle quickly," Fiona says. I admire that little bomb she just dropped about the sleeping through at three months. Artfully done.

Georgina sips her decaf with almond milk, and says, "Well, that's good for you and Charlie, I'm so glad Gina Ford worked for you, but I personally, and this is just me, I couldn't do it. I don't think I could put Rosamund through that just to get some sleep. The guilt! I mean, I can see that it works for your family, Fi, I *really* do, but I love feeding her when it's just the two of us and everyone's asleep. We're up a lot in the night, true, but she knows I'm *there*. I wouldn't give that up, d'you know what I mean? Not that you've given anything up, Fi, by regimenting your baby, it's not that, it's just – not for us, I suppose." Impressive. Even though Georgina would cut off her arm right now if it meant getting a full night's sleep, she still found the strength to make that little speech.

I leave Fi to reply because on the next sofa Tracy's giving an update about her stitches. "So I go for the six-week checkup and the midwife says, 'Well, how's it all feeling,' and I say, 'Great, never better,' *as if*, and she has a look at the war zone in my pants and she says, 'You can tell your husband it's safe to have sex now if you'd like to,' and I said, 'Of course it's safe for him, he hasn't had his vag stitched up to his arse!'"

Everybody laughs and Becky says, "Stop, I'm gonna wee on Sukie's lovely sofa!"

"I already did, sorry, love!" says Tracy, doubled over. And even Georgina and Fi have to loosen up and smile. We're all laughing, and for a minute I feel almost normal, like it's not just me, everybody's got something they're dealing with. I'm about to say something, something funny about sex or men or piss but then:

"Well, lucky for you, Gigi, you didn't have to go through any of this, did ya! Vag put through the shredder and pelvic floor dropped to your ankles!" Tracy says, and the ladies laugh again. Before I process what she means Georgina says, "Yes, Gigi, you certainly saved yourself, I'm sure Harry's grateful."

Oh. That's what they mean.

"Oh, but ladies, wouldn't you rather have your war stories?" Becky, the Australian one breaks in. "It was the toughest thing I ever did but choosing to just take the pain, well, I would do it again in a heartbeat."

"That's 'cause you're a nutter, Bex! No, I'm afraid I'd have to go Gigi's route next time, lots of drugs, too posh to push, that's the way forward. Not putting the va-jay-jay through this again," Tracy says, winking at me. But her face changes because I've started to cry; I didn't know I was going to but I am so I say, "I'm sorry, hormones I guess." But it isn't hormones. It's something much stronger than that.

Fi, who was always in the take-all-possible-drugs camp, comes over and puts a skinny arm around me. "We all have our babies, it doesn't matter how we got them, does it, Gigi. I think taking the easy route makes us smarter, don't you?" There are communal looks of concern and cups quickly put on tables and shuffling of maternal bodies on sofas to get closer to me and surround me with support.

"Sorry, I didn't mean to make you upset," Becky says. "I guess we're all just proud of ourselves for how we earned these babies. How stupid of me, the loss you must feel, that was really insensitive of me." I know she feels bad. But she doesn't feel bad about what happened to me. She feels bad for me that I'm not like her.

Sukie leans forward to put her thin, manicured hand with its diamond engagement ring stacked on diamond wedding band stacked on diamond push-present band on my rounded knee. "You poor thing."

They all look at me. I look down at Rocky. The lava wave is over but now the sweating has started. I stay focused on the miniature perfection of his face. Little eyebrows. He has Harry's beautiful long lashes. The tiny nose, just like mine. Well, not really, it's the space below his eyes, the curve of his cheek in that place before it becomes his cheek, the space we don't have a name for – that came from me.

"Well—" I start to say, to stammer out some kind of answer, but Georgina interrupts: "Are you upset about the breastfeeding? I mean, it must be upsetting for you. I would be devastated." The ladies nod in sympathetic agreement.

Fiona says, gently holding my elbow, "You know, there's something to be said about persevering. You can still do it if you want to. I had some trouble with Sophie. The latching on was a disaster in the beginning but we hired a lactation consultant and it made such a difference. I could give you the number."

"Hey, guys, why don't you let her speak. You're all on top of her," Tracy says. She's right. Sukie touching my knee. Fiona at my elbow, smiling supportively. Georgina staring at me, head tilted in concern. Becky turned toward me, attentively, even while she's feeding her baby. They're concerned, yes, but they're also proud of themselves, taking credit for something they don't know was never in their control. They think it was them – their strength, presence of mind, birth preparation, their life-sustaining breasts – that got them here. They don't know that birth and life and death are just chance. Who gets what has nothing to do with us.

Rocky stirs. In his sleep he raises a tiny fist in the air and stretches and yawns. His hand lands under his little chin and his head tilts to the side, dreaming. I look up at the well-meaning women around me. I didn't choose this. No one would choose this. Unless the choice was life or death, which it was. I survived and so did he. So I think that's a win, Becky, not a loss. I'm not devastated about the breastfeeding, Georgina. I'm devastated that I don't love this baby as much as I loved Johnny and Frankie and I don't know why. The last thing, Fiona, that I need, is another consultant or midwife or doctor to touch me and confirm that I'm inadequate, my motherly resources insufficient.

I could say all of that. I could give them the details and horrify them with my birth story. I could tell it in such a way so that they would understand that I endured more than anyone. I could shatter their illusions that they *earned* anything. But they're just women, doing what women do – seeking validation. Getting it by comparing themselves to other women. Supporting the ones they know are struggling but secretly satisfied that they are not.

I decide, instead, to let it go. Let me be the one who's done everything wrong. The one they can think of when they're scared and insecure so they can say to themselves, "Well, at least I know I'm better at this than her." I can be that one that helps them get through the day because no matter how hard things get, at least they're not fat, broken, bottle-feeding Gigi.

I break the silence. "Thanks, ladies, but I'm OK. I've done this before, remember, with Johnny, and anyway, I've got to go pick him up. Thanks for the tea, Sukie. Sorry, I've got to run." I get up carefully with Rocky and gather my stuff.

I put my phone down on the coffee table while I pack the baby bag and Sukie, Georgina and Fiona see the Oprah screen saver on my phone. I like to keep Oprah close to me for strength. It's a picture of her from the eighties that a non-American might not recognize at first glance. The Oprah I watched every day after school.

Fiona asks, "Who's that?" which really means, *Why do you have a picture of a Black woman on your phone instead of your newborn baby?*

"Oh—" I think for a second. "That's my mother," I say and pick the phone up before they can look again. I see them stop and quickly scan the afternoon's conversation to make sure they didn't say anything racist now that they think my mother's Black and that I might be too, or at least bi-racial. Georgina shifts in her seat and I can tell she's remembering that thing she said earlier about how Filipinos make great nannies as do Poles but one must be careful about the "others." I can see Fiona's face change, an internal cringe when she remembers what she said about the "extraordinarily imbalanced make-up" of the state high school by her house. Becky scans my face to look for signs of Blackness. There's an uncomfortable ripple through Sukie's Tea Nook.

I didn't say I'd let everything go.

Tracy gathers her stuff too and says, "I must be getting off as well." Then she turns to me and whispers, "It's too early for Johnny to get out of school, isn't it?"

"Yeah, it is." I look up for a moment and meet her eye.

"Do you want to come to mine then? I've got cake. Apparently, that's what keeps this lot so skinny." She wants to be my friend.

"That's real nice of you but I should be going, go to the supermarket to get dinner before I go to pick-up." I settle Rocky in his stroller and stuff a muslin in my bag when Tracy takes my hand.

"Hey, I'm sorry. Too soon to joke about it, yeah? Did you have a really bad time? I see you're not that same girl who used to vomit in our classes and then make us all laugh. I'm sorry, I shouldn't have made all those jokes, it's just my way, trying to make light of it all."

She gets that something happened to me on the sofa. Maybe I can try. "Yeah, I guess, I mean it was pretty bad, I'm still trying to—" but her phone rings and cuts me off. I push the words back down.

"Yes, I'll be right there, sorry, I'm so sorry," Tracy says into the phone. She turns to me. "I'm so shit, he's got his jabs today, I forgot, another time, eh? I need to run down to the clinic now, shit."

"It's OK, don't worry about it, you'd better rush," I say.

"We'll talk another time, yeah?"

"Yeah, sure," I turn away, but she steps in front of my stroller to catch my eye and says, "No really, promise?"

Whether we do or we don't doesn't matter; she asked. I'm grateful just for that. I almost smile. "Yeah. Thanks. See you next week," I say and push Rocky out the door, my scar pulsing with every step.

London, May 2016; Baby, 5 months old

"Hey, Jeej, how does the water in the sea stick to the Earth even when it's on the part that's upside down?" Johnny doesn't say hello when I pick him up from school. He unleashes a wave of questions from the minute I hug him hello. A day will come when he'll stop talking to me like this and I won't know about all the corners of his little world. I wish his energy would infect me, make me burst into a smile when I see him, but instead I feel drained, exhausted by the walk home before it starts. I'm so heavy but he's a little cloud of wonder. I try not to weigh him down.

"Jeej? How does it do it?" He looks at me with his big dark eyes. His buttons are askew after changing for gym, there's a blotch of ketchup on his shoe.

"Gravity," I say, taking his schoolbag and hooking it on the stroller, starting the slow walk home.

"What's gravity?"

"It's the force that keeps things on the ground."

"Where does it come from?"

"The Sun."

"How?" He holds the handle of the stroller like a surrogate hand.

"Radiation and magnetic waves or something, I don't know, ask Harry when he gets home."

"Did you know that Saturn is just gas and it's so light that if you put it on our ocean on Earth it would float?"

"What?"

"Do you know how?"

"No, do you?"

"No, I mean do you know how it does that, Jeej?"

"Listen, you're going way over my head here. I never heard that before in my life. Have a cookie." They don't say "cookie" here. They say "biscuits" which never sits right in my mouth. Biscuits are white fluffy things that people eat with gravy in movies about the Deep South.

"And also did you know that Pluto is a microplanet?"

"What? It's not a regular planet anymore?"

"Jeej, why isn't it a planet?"

"I don't know, you're the one who brought it up."

"Jeej, you don't know very much about space."

"Yeah, well, sue me. What else happened today?" And he goes on and on. Who chased who, who played spies, who wouldn't let go of the ball.

"What'd you have for lunch?"

"I don't know. Jeej, I got a sticker for perseverance!"

"Wow, that's cool. What'd you do to get that?"

"I dunno. Jeej, what's perseverance?" As I explain it to him and he thinks of another ten questions to ask me, Rocky, who's been sitting up, listening, gurgling his own answers to Johnny, drops his giraffe somewhere. Johnny stops mid-sentence and says, "Jeej, where's Jeffrey?"

It's one of those beige, rubber, French ones. Johnny named it Jeffrey. I don't really get it, some retro toy trend. It has brown oval spots for eyes and orangey dots for its giraffe skin. People kept giving them to us when Rocky was born. We got three of them. A prerequisite for babies in a certain tax bracket. I picked one up in a store to see how much it cost – £15. It's ugly, it doesn't do anything, it's not cuddly. They're supposed to chew on it but the only part that fits in a baby's mouth is the ear. I thought about sending one of the extra ones to Stacy for her baby, except I knew that she would open the box and the next text would be: *WTF? What is this thing?* I wouldn't have even kept this one, would've dropped it off at the charity shop with the others, but Johnny opened the box and showed it to Rocky. It's really more for Johnny that we kept it; something he could be in charge of for the baby.

I don't mind that Rocky lost it. It has no sentimental value. It's just another thing we have because there's a rule book somewhere about these things we're supposed to have so people don't think we're poor; not actual poor,

219

but rich-person poor: Bugaboo stroller; Range Rover/Land Rover and Fiat or Mini for zipping around town; Rolex for the man; Cartier for the woman; Chloé Marcie cross-body saddle bag for daytime or, if you work, Mulberry Bayswater; a cleaning lady; a Burberry trench; matching Boori nursery furniture with an ergonomic sliding feeding chair; Orla Kiely bedding, or at least the set of kitchen jars in three different sizes with matching tea towels and/ or oven mitts; Diptyque candles (£47 each, and that's not even for a big one); a skiing holiday; an au pair; Sophie Conran Portmeirion dinnerware; a Stokke high chair; Taittinger on standby in the fridge; tonic in the cabinet always ready for G and Ts, and preferably Fever-Tree, not some store brand; a regular window cleaning service; a Micro scooter for Johnny and an Islabike at £350 a pop; an Ocado grocery account; highlights touched up every six weeks; a regular gardener; wine that's £15 a bottle minimum on a rack or preferably in a mini wine fridge built into the newly renovated kitchen; a personal trainer; a cashmere beanie hat with a faux-fur pom-pom; and a weekly fresh flower delivery.

And this French, rubber giraffe.

I'm relieved that it's gone. I felt pressured by it, like I just couldn't live up to its English middle-class standards of clean, uncluttered homes and landscaped gardens and a knowledge of how to roast lamb. And Rocky doesn't care. But Johnny's here and to him, like any child, the loss of a toy is tragic and urgent. *God, please let it just be on the sidewalk somewhere so we can go home.*

Johnny runs back down the block to look for Jeffrey before I can stop him. The houses on this street are the same attached, narrow, three-story houses that line every street but so far this part of the block has resisted the finance power couples and their children – families like my family. These houses are skipped over by the daytime army of nannies and cleaners and window-washing guys. The retro milk truck doesn't stop here with its glass bottles at dawn. Instead there are lace curtains, ceramic menageries, garden gnomes, plastic conservatories added to the front thirty years ago and leaning at odd angles. There are no shades in the slim windows by the doors to hide the shelves of shoes kept there. Sometimes you might see an old reel for a washing line hanging from the corners of the outdoor/indoor foyers, with the boxers of the man of the house on display. The houses might be sided in cracked pebbledash, or aluminum siding from the eighties, or bricks painted a red-brick color.

The yummy mummies walk by pushing their babies and the professional couples say to each other, "Such a shame. That could be such a lovely house." Which is another way of saying that these people and their crappy stuff should just move somewhere else already, somewhere where they won't ruin the aesthetic and dampen the property values.

In front of one of those houses Johnny is talking to a sturdy bruiser of a boy and his grandma. The boy is holding the giraffe. "My baby brother dropped that, may I have it back, please?" Johnny says. But the boy and Grandma act like they haven't heard him. They mull around their front garden space with its carpet of astroturf. Not the expensive, middle-class, velvety kind. The kind that is obvious and unapologetic about being plastic grass.

The boy is eight or nine, tall and destined to be a big guy. Johnny's nearly the same height, but he's a twig next to him. The boy is sullen, in an Arsenal jersey and shorts that are too tight though he doesn't seem to mind. He's much too old for this toy and has no real interest in it. He knows it; Johnny knows it; Grandma knows it too.

Watching this scene is like reading a page pulled from the script of my childhood and the childhoods of everyone I grew up with. Mom is working her ass off somewhere in a dead-end job where they don't pay her enough for all the hours she does. Dad is working his ass off too, if he's around. Grandma doesn't want to be doing this but she has to. She's doing what she can but her swollen ankles and her diabetes and her blood pressure and just her fucking exhaustion from an entire lifetime of this shit don't make it easy for her to raise this boy. The boy takes care of her more than she does of him. He carries the groceries, washes the dishes, sits in the waiting room with her when she goes to the doctor. His hands already callused.

He sees how the skinny, rich families look at this street, at his house. At him. Like when the foxes get into the trash but Grandma can't bend down to clean up the mess in the morning. So he'll do it when he gets home from school. But the bankers in their suits on the way to the Tube who have to step over the scattered garbage don't know that, and they shake their heads in disapproval and disgust when they walk past his house. As if it was Grandma's fault, or his.

It's fucked up and unfair and upside down and this kid's been left behind before the race even got started. I know all this and I just want to walk away. But my boy's here too and he doesn't understand urban socio-economics in a class-based society. He doesn't know about structural inequality and capitalism. He just wants the toy back because for him there's only right and wrong.

I say, "Hi there, excuse me, my baby dropped that." Grandma's wearing a tank top tucked into the elastic waist of her skirt. She heaves herself into a folding chair in the pathway to her door and takes a slow drag of her cigarette. The elastic of her nude knee-highs is cutting into her calves below the knee. She says, "Well, 'ee found it. So I said 'ee could 'ave it." She takes another drag. The boy stands behind her squeezing the giraffe. It squeaks.

"C'mon now, you know that's a baby toy. He's too old for something like that. My baby dropped it. I'd like it back, please," I say, and I hold out my hand and Johnny's eyes get wider and wider.

"Well, 'ee found it. It were on the pavement. So it's 'is." I look at the front garden; broken concrete, plastic grass, the folding chair. Then I see her shoes and my heart catches, beats a double beat. She's wearing pink terrycloth slippers just like Ma's. Molded to her hammer toes. They're gray around the edges where the pink cloth scrapes the sidewalk because she probably wears them to the store and to pick her grandson up at school. I wasn't expecting to see Ma today.

I can feel Johnny's hot child's anxiety and disbelief at the unfairness of the crime he's watching this woman and her boy commit, disappointed in me for not fixing it and making it right. The past and present are burning up in front of me and falling off with the ash at the tip of Grandma's cigarette.

I drop my hand, drop my head. I look at her again and I know that with her silence she's challenging me to continue the confrontation. She's teaching her grandson to take what he can get, keep what he finds, give nothing away to people who've taken so much from this neighborhood, even if it's theirs. Keep the things they're stupid enough to lose and don't give anything back. For spite. In protest. If she teaches him to take what he wants from a world that's not ever going to give him anything then he'll survive and she'll have done right by him.

I don't know how to tell this woman that I have much more in common with her than the people on my street and it's not even about the fucking giraffe. I don't know how to tell Johnny that, yes, there's a difference between right and wrong but sometimes a small rightness doesn't matter because there's a much greater wrong happening. I'm not going to fight this boy and this old lady. But I can't let Johnny be bullied either.

"Johnny—" I turn to him, look him in the eyes, "we're going now. What this lady and her boy have done is wrong, and they know that, but this isn't worth it so we're going to let them keep it. OK? Rocky has lots of toys and he doesn't even like that one. So we can let them have it."

"But, Jeej, they took it, that's wrong. That's wrong!" He's so upset. He stamps his little foot; the tears are hot on his face. "It's a baby toy, he knows that!" And he points an indignant finger at the boy.

"I know, baby, I know, but it's not that important to us. It's more important to them which is why they're choosing to do the wrong thing." I try to take his hand to lead him away and to end this awful moment when he thinks I've failed him and Grandma thinks I'm just another rich bitch and none of us have won.

As I turn to take us home, thinking that it's over, Grandma says, "That's right. Walk away."

An old anger from long ago rises up. Ma did this to us too, pushed us down instead of lifting us up. I turn to the boy, his young poker-face already trained to give nothing away and I say, "It's wrong to steal from babies. She should have taught you that. You can be better than her."

I'm embarrassed as soon as I say it. He's just a kid. Just like my kid. Just like I was. And I'm standing here putting his grandmother down. What have I really said? I said that I'm ashamed of what I have now, of what they see that I have. Of Johnny's private-school uniform, emblazoned with the insignia of privilege. I'm upset that they don't recognize me anymore, that they can't see that I'm from a street just like this. That guilt and regret follow me everywhere. That the first time I went to the supermarket here and filled the cart with steak and fresh vegetables and chocolate and name-brand detergent I was exhilarated and then ashamed. By the abundance, the excess, the beauty of it, the fact my mother had never filled a cart with anything but white bread and pork-and-beans cans and store-brand dish soap that never got the dishes clean. And I remembered going to the store when it was still just me and Johnny, saying no to everything he pointed at, wiping away his tears and teaching him a hard lesson about the difference between want and need. So I watched other people fill their carts at Waitrose not even thinking about the prices of things, not counting up the cost of every item as they took it off the shelf, tomatoes on the vine and actual Heinz ketchup and brie and a pound of shrimp from the fresh fish counter. And I left my full cart at the end of an aisle and walked out of the store without buying anything, silently apologizing to whoever had to put it all back on the shelves.

Grandma says nothing, just stares into the distance like we're not there, smoking and pretending she didn't hear. I've failed. I was supposed to handle this but I didn't. I lead Johnny away; he's hanging his head, still crying, his footsteps heavy with disappointment in me. He's resigned to the injustice. But which injustice will he remember when he comes back to this memory decades from now? Will it be what the boy did to us? Or what we did to the boy? The only difference between him and the boy – my marriage to a rich guy.

And what's hurting me the most and making my cheeks burn? The fact that Grandma thinks I'm just another one of *them*, or the fact that I am?

I hear the giraffe squeak behind us as the boy throws it to the ground and it bounces off the plastic grass. Already forgotten and cast aside.

9

DETTOL, DIAZEPAM

A Wednesday in August 2016, 5:30 p.m.
London, Grand Euro Star Lodge Hotel,
Room 506

I stand at the door until my back aches. I let go of the doorknob and slide down to the floor. I sit, surveying the room from this angle. Red and white is the color scheme of the Grand Euro Star Lodge Hotel. Red carpeting, white linens with a red blanket and bedspread. The walls are painted red from the floor to the middle, then white to the ceiling. The wall above the bed is smeared with a dingy, gray accumulation of years of hair grease and styling products. There's a stain of unknown composition on the carpet.

It's filthy. An inch of dust on the baseboards. That bathroom – I can't even get into what's going on in there with the grout. Our house was never nice but it was always clean. Ma never said she loved me but she made sure my clothes were always ironed and spotless. Never new but clean. I crawl over to the card table and lean on the metal folding chair and push off of it to get to standing. Where they cut you for a C-section, it makes your legs work different. They don't have the same power. I kick off my flip-flops and pour some wine into a complimentary plastic cup that I'm pretty certain was used by the last guests of this room and not replaced.

I listen to the Housewives in the background. It's part one of the reunion episodes when they talk with Andy Cohen, their executive producer, about the events of the past season. They all wear glittering evening gowns. They're spray-tanned and highlighted to perfection. They sit on white sofas drenched in expensive jewellery as they recount hurt feelings and betrayals and watch back the most emotional clips of the show. Amber is questioned about her husband, Jim, and his Jekyll-and-Hyde personality. She says, "I don't piss him off at home, we don't hurt one another and he really is truly amazing as long as you don't fuck with him." Oh, Amber, sweetheart, that doesn't sound good. That sounds like something my husband would say about me.

Another email:

I've been looking for you. I thought I might find you walking somewhere on the common. Where are you? I'm so sorry. I didn't know things were this bad. I'm so worried. Please can we talk? We'll fix it, I promise, we'll fix all of it. We'll get you some more help for the house, give Stefka more hours, we'll get someone for the kids, we can even get someone to do the nights for a few weeks, a night nanny? Whatever help you need, I'll sort it, I promise ...

I breathe deeper than I have all day. I exhale slowly, my eyelids suddenly so heavy. This is why I haven't said it, why I haven't asked. *Help*. This is where I go left and he goes right. Because my skull is broken open and he offers me a roll of duct tape – gold-plated, finest quality, first-class duct tape, but duct tape nonetheless. I love him, I love him. But he doesn't know how to help. He doesn't know what help I need.

Ma was a cleaning lady. She cleaned offices at night for a few years when we were kids. Depending what shifts she got, if they clashed with Dad driving the bus at night, then after school me and Frankie would catch the ferry with Ma and go to work with her in the City. On the way to Manhattan we'd sit facing the Staten Island side, watching it get smaller and smaller, leaving the views of the City for the tourists who crowded the front of the boat. Within minutes we'd do something to annoy Ma, she'd yell at us and then we'd go out on deck and shout at the seagulls, barely able to hear ourselves over the roar of the engine and the water.

It sounds hard, going to work with your mother, but we liked it. There were always musicians busking, Jehovah's Witnesses walking around with the *Watchtower*. In the ladies' room someone always had a velvet display board with big, fabulous earrings for sale. There were clusters of Russian and Polish ladies commuting to their night cleaning shifts and tourists from everywhere. Deep South church groups in matching T-shirts or French high-school kids with cool Euro sneakers or groups of Korean and Japanese families. There were cops patrolling the boat, walking slow. Deckhands, tattooed and burly. The pigeons hitching a ride to Manhattan. On the old boats with the wooden benches there were hundreds of messages carved into the wood. *GM luvs KO. JJ gives good head*. Graffiti tags on the emergency fire hose. The ancient shoeshine men with their worn shining kits, their thick hands permanently stained with polish. Me and Frankie loved the ferry.

We'd bring sleeping bags and sleep under a desk while Ma worked a building through the night. We'd go in through the service entrance then hide in a bathroom until Ma checked that no office workers were working late, and when the coast was clear she'd set us up somewhere until her shift was over. Sometimes she'd have a key for some boss's office and then we'd get to sleep on a sofa or in some big executive armchair while she vacuumed and dusted and mopped.

Harry kept saying we needed to get someone to help with the house and he couldn't understand why I wouldn't hire a cleaning lady. He couldn't know what it meant to me. And then one night he came home late and found me sobbing in the kitchen, standing at the sink with the water running, overwhelmed by dirty plates and pots I had to put on the floor because the counters were too full of groceries to put away and laundry to fold. He sent me to the shower and cleaned the kitchen. Then he sat with me, pushed my hair behind my ear and said, "We can't go on like this, Pukes. Your mother isn't here, my mother isn't here, Stacy and Danielle and Sharon aren't here. You just cannot do everything on your own. You're not supposed to do this all alone."

I didn't answer him, I just listened to the echo of the names of all the people who weren't here but should've been. Like a bruise you forget about until you press it. I had a picture in my head of Ma, all the times she brought us into a fancy office at midnight to find they'd had a celebration lunch, leaving the catering boxes overturned; sticky soda spills still wet on the carpets; trash cans overflowing with half-eaten sandwiches; full coffee filters spilling grounds all over the floor. Or in the bathrooms, if a roll of toilet paper fell to the floor and unwound itself, they left it there, didn't even kick it to the corner of the bathroom; left it to soak up the water from the washing of hands and splatter from the sinks. When I got my first office job I always took my coffee cups to the kitchen and washed them instead of leaving them on my desk; just a small sign of respect for the person who cleaned in the middle of the night, whose kids might be sleeping in the office next door.

I didn't know how to explain to Harry that I didn't want a cleaning lady because the house was too much of a mess. That it was disrespectful to bring some hard-working woman into this chaos and pay her £10 an hour for back-breaking work that was worth much more than that. I didn't know how to make him understand that I couldn't hire a cleaning lady until I cleaned the house.

Help. Help is complicated, Harry. Help is hard to find. Help has to be trusted to see your inner workings, so why don't you take your help, Harry, and fuckin' shov— *Stop it, Gigi. Aren't you tired of your own voice yet?*

I shudder.

Yes.

I go to the bathroom, wet a corner of the small towel in the sink, get on my knees and start to scrub at the tiles. *He wants to help you. Tell him how. He loves you.* I need bleach for the mold so can't really help that, but I can work on the soap scum. *He was there once and he helped, remember?* The limescale really needs vinegar, but if I keep working on it, scrape it with a fingernail, it'll go. *Stop living like you're alone. Why did you do all this – the marriage, the baby – if inside you're just going to keep living alone?* I move to the edge of the bath to work on the hard water stains on the tap. If you don't have lime-scale spray you can use toothpaste and rub the metal with a cloth. Look, someone left a little travel one behind. Perfect. *Tell him to come get you. Tell him you're tired of living alone. He'll help you.* See? If you're just patient and keep at it, it shines up nice.

London, May 2016; Baby, 5½ months old

Harry sent me a text this morning: *Stefka, Cleaning Angels, 12 pm, 3 hours.* I put Rocky down for a nap and got to work. Two hours later and the upstairs bathroom was spotless. The taps polished, sparkling. The hair pulled out from the plugholes, the shower floor scrubbed, the tub shining. The toilet looked like a fucking diamond. You could eat soup from the sink. I used a grout brush for the floors and the tiles were like new. Cillit Bang and Dettol and Windolene – all these cleaners with their funny English names – they made my eyes water but the smell of chemical clean reassured me. I knew this woman would be appalled at the oven and disgusted by the carpets but she would know what I was about when she saw the bathroom.

I'm not sure how long Rocky's been crying when I finally hear him. But it was too long, I can tell from the volume, the red fury of his face clenched in baby rage, his little features squeezed like a fist. "I'm sorry, I'm sorry, I'm sorry," I repeat quickly and I pick him up out of the pool of vomit he's been rolling in, unable to get out of it, like quicksand. He's rubbed it in his eye and his hair, his cries rising from upset to distress. I hook my hands under his little arms and he vomits again as I lift him out of the crib, so I swiftly hold him like a football under one arm, tip his head downward so he can get it out. The baby bile and sour milk leave a small but violent stain on the light gray carpet. I get him to the bathroom and he gets one more shot at the tile.

I wonder if the orange stuff from that last little puddle – I guess it must be carrots – will come out of the grout that I just spent the last hour scrubbing.

The doorbell rings. He's stopped crying now that he knows he wasn't abandoned. But there's no time to change him. I open the door, half expecting it to be Social Services.

"Hello, Meesus Harreeson? I am Stefka." I wonder if I've forgotten that my house was supposed to be used as an ironic setting for a photo shoot for the Slavic super-model on my doorstep.

"Meesus Harreeson? Can I help you?" Stefka pulls her bleach blond hair with its black roots back into a ponytail, comes into the house, takes off her cool and tiny leather jacket and reaches for Rocky.

I snap out of it. "Sorry, I'm sorry, he was sick, I … come in, come in. I don't know what I'm supposed to do."

"Meesus Harreeson?" She looks at me sideways, talking to me like she might to an unconscious stranger who's just fainted in the street.

"You want give me baby and you change your clothes? I make the tea?" she says, smiling.

"Yes, thank you," I say. I don't remember handing her the baby but now she's holding him with her left arm, filling the kettle at the tap with her right. Rocky's whimpering but she's distracting him with the tap and the kettle, talking to him in a language I don't know. I look down at my shirt and now I see why she suggested I change. She doesn't know that this is what I always look like.

"Is beautiful house, Meesus Harreeson." She pops Rocky on the countertop and cleans his face with a dish towel. She starts to take off his wet onesie.

"He was vomiting, no? Where is his clothes, for change?" She keeps one arm on him, keeping him safe, while she stretches to the other counter, pours the hot water into a cup for me. *Where the fuck did she find the tea?*

"Tea for you. Baby is very hard work. Where his clothes, please?"

"His room is at the top of the stairs, first left. Thank you. Thank you so much," I say.

"Is OK, I love the babies," she says, and runs upstairs with him. Rocky is smitten. She could walk out of this house with him and never come back and that kid would be like, "Jeej who?" He would totally take the upgrade to this hot, young, nice, competent mom.

Can't let Harry meet her. He'll want the upgrade too.

I sip black tea in the kitchen and wonder what will happen next. I hate tea, we know this, but somehow, her tea is exactly what I need. Stefka puts Rocky in the high chair, gives him some water in a sippy cup. Where did she find that?

"Meesus Harreeson, house so clean! He was sick in bathroom, yes? I clean floor there, only a little. You like to change you clothes and I start laundry?" she asks, pointing at the piles on the floor. That's the second time she's mentioned me changing my clothes. I burst into tears.

"Meesus Harreeson? Is OK, is OK." She pats me on the back while Rocky bashes his cup on his tray. She smells nice.

"Call me Gigi, please," I say, completely at a loss for what to do next. This girl must think I'm crazy.

"Meesus Gigi, baby is hard work. I see you have big child too? Is boy also?" She points at Johnny's drawings on the fridge. "Yes," I say, "that's Johnny," and I point at his framed school photo from last year hanging on the kitchen wall. I remember buying the frame, putting the picture inside, hanging it. Last year. When Rocky was the size of an apple in my belly. I had a full-time job. I cooked dinner for Johnny every night and I put pictures in frames and I changed the sheets once a week. I ordered groceries online and kept a box of presents in the closet so that we never had to buy something overpriced at the last minute when Johnny was invited to a birthday party. I never forgot if he was invited to a party, not like I do now, showing up halfway through or almost at the end, saying we forgot the gift at home and we'll bring it to school but then we never do.

Stefka's voice cuts through my thoughts. "Is lovely boys. Beautiful house. Do not so worry. You very lucky."

She's right, I *am* lucky. But I don't want to be lucky. I want to take Johnny with me back to my apartment that was small enough to be cleaned in half an hour. Back where I knew how to do things, how to run my life, how to take care of a baby.

"I'm sorry, Stefka, I just met you like, five minutes ago, and look at me, I don't know what's happened to me."

"I am mother too. Two boys. Is OK. Some days is blizzard in house and some days is nice breeze." That must be a direct translation that hasn't gone right, but I get what she's saying. I probably don't sound that different to her when I talk to British people.

I watch Rocky play with a Tupperware box and a wooden spoon that Stefka also instinctively knew where to find. I watch her unload the dishwasher, which I don't think is part of the service, but I guess she can see I need all the help I can get.

I learn about her life. Her boys are five and seven.

"Where do they go to school?" I ask, expecting her to name somewhere local.

"Bulgaria. They live wis my parents." She says it matter-of-factly, but I feel a stab in my heart. There's a pause and I look at her to let her know I feel it.

"How often do you see them?" I ask.

"Once in summer for two weeks and two weeks in March."

"Twice a year?" I stop myself before I say, *That's all?* because that *is* all and I don't want to emphasize it. She knows.

"Yes, is hard. But they is happy boys. Very handsome." She smiles at me but as soon as she looks down to the dishes she's stacking the smile is gone.

I watch her quietly. This woman is standing in my house, working in my house and somehow still breathing. Even though the pain of being so far away from her boys must be killing her. She sparkles when she shows me the pictures on her phone, two tough little guys with buzz cuts, dark eyes like hers, in matching Nike tracksuits. Another one of them in Ralph Lauren polo shirts, one in navy and one in orange, crisply ironed, both buttons done up to the neck, the older boy with his arm around his little brother, smiling a tight-lipped smile.

"They're very cute. You dress them really nice," I say, noticing the aging communist wallpaper in the background.

"I buy the English clothes for them. They always handsome. If you know where to buy, is good price and my parents don't know what is style. I send package maybe every three month, for birsdays and Chreest-mus, of course. Chreest-mus is most expensive time to fly so I make package instead, beautiful clothes, toys, and I send card that this one is from Father Chreest-mus in UK."

She works in the kitchen, now and then going over to Rocky who gives her huge smiles. "Do you mind if I sit here? Am I bothering you?" I say. I'm pretty sure you're not supposed to hang out with the cleaner when she's working. I think the etiquette is to leave the house, or at least I overheard Fiona saying that's what she always does.

"Of course, Meesus Gigi. Is hard be alone all day. Cleaning is this way too, work alone all day."

She tells me about how her husband was working in the UK too but now he drives long-haul trucks around Europe so that's why he's not around and the kids have to stay with her parents. She talks while she works, telling me about how to get rid of the rest of Rocky's cradle cap but I don't really listen. I'm embarrassed at the state of my carpeting, the crust around the stovetop, ashamed that I can't find the energy to ever play with Rocky or be affectionate or do anything other than meet his most basic needs. I never coo at him or make him smile like this total stranger has been able to do within an hour of meeting him.

Ashamed that what I want – really, if you really went down deep into what I really think and feel – is to get away from this beautiful house and my beautiful boys. Get away from them. But this woman who is scrubbing the crusted mounds of old baby food off Rocky's high chair – disgusting dried mounds of it that I never noticed, that any good mother would've noticed, would've never let get to that point because she would've cleaned up after breakfast every morning – this young woman, prying old baby food off the designer high chair, only wants to be with her kids. And she can't be.

When Stefka leaves the kitchen I follow her. I carry Rocky on my hip and lean on the doorframe of whichever room she's in, sometimes talking, sometimes not. She tells me a lot about her boys. Her pain and pride are palpable. I show her my trick for using vinegar to get the hard water stains off the chrome in the bathrooms. She shows me how to change a duvet cover in one fluid motion, without struggling to make it fit. We do the pillowcases together. I gather up more laundry and start a new wash and I mop the kitchen while she vacuums the hall. The mess I've allowed to accumulate – it's not a one-woman job.

Then it's time for her to go. I'm relieved that the house is liveable again, but I panic when I see the stacks of papers and clutter and toys that remain. I can't face the rest of it without her. "Wait, um, so, what do I owe you for today?" and I prolong the conversation with questions that have obvious answers so that she doesn't leave. If she leaves I'll be in here alone again.

"Meesus Gigi," she says, holding both my hands in hers, "I come back next week. Please do not worry so much. And you do not have to clean before I come. Also, you do not have to clean wis me. Is my job, OK?" She winks at me. "You are good mother. Is happy boys. Baby is small, is hard time. Very soon you will do what they say in America – push your shits together. I see you next week."

I hug her. It's probably not very British to hug the cleaner on her first day but I do it anyway. She hugs me back. I pass Rocky over to give her a baby hug. He slaps his hand a little too hard on her face the way babies do. I close the door and put Rocky in a playpen in front of the TV. It's just him and the smell of Dettol to keep me company now. I admire the clean kitchen and pour some wine into a teacup.

London, June 2016; Baby, 6 months old

"I thought we should review your progress and set some goals for the coming weeks as today is our penultimate session," Lorraine says to me as if I was expecting this. As if I'm fixed now, post partum depression all cleared up.

Lorraine. The kind of older woman who looks like an ad for age-defying skin cream, one where they show three generations of women, and she's the last one, representing mature skin, except she thinks she should be the one in the middle. In her M & S wrap dress with her glasses on a string, I watch her check off the details of my post natal crisis on her little NHS form.

"What does that mean?" I say, as I push Rocky's stroller back and forth with my foot, trying to focus on the wall above her head in this windowless, dingy examination room in the community surgery which serves as her "office."

"It means that next week will be our last session." And she pulls out the anxiety/depression questionnaire that I have to fill out every week. The anxiety scale asks me on how many days have I felt nervous, anxious or worried; had trouble relaxing; been so restless that I can't sit still, and finally, felt afraid that something awful might happen. OK, all of those, every day, but that's because, hello, I'm a mother. So they should really just condense this shit down to: *Do you have children?* OK then, you have an anxiety disorder.

Then I do the depression scale. Do I feel tired; have little energy; overeat; feel bad about myself; or have trouble concentrating? Um, for answers see above. But my favorite question is: *Have you been moving or speaking so slowly that other people have noticed?* I feel like if that was my problem then I would be having a stroke and getting here to see Lorraine wouldn't be my first priority. And let's not forget the last question about suicide. Because if I was contemplating suicide, definitely one of the things I'd want to do is fill out this questionnaire.

"But I still need help, Lorraine, I'm not done." I keep my foot on the stroller, nudging it rhythmically while I circle the numbers on the scales.

"Yes, well, you've been allocated six sessions and unfortunately you missed two of those as you cancelled with very short notice. We cannot reallocate those sessions to you if you do not adhere—"

"Lorraine, the baby was sick. You're taking sessions away from me because my baby was sick?"

"Part of our work has been helping you to find people you can rely on."

"But I've explained that I don't have any family here."

"We've discussed that [audible sigh] at length," she says, trying not to roll her eyes. "We've also discussed that you need to look for support in other places."

"That's why I come here, Lorraine, for support."

Lorraine turns to face me, pulls her glasses down on the bridge of her nose so I can see her eyes, a gesture of her great understanding of the human condition.

"Gigi—" she leans in, elbows on both knees, "I see many women in this area who are just like you, they've had their first baby, sometimes traumatically, and that can be diffi—"

"He's not my first baby. Have you listened to me at all?" I close my eyes, foot still on the stroller, keeping it in motion like an extension of my leg. Then I turn down her volume. She's still talking, something about resilience, but it doesn't matter. There's some NHS trigger word I'm supposed to say that will make her keep me on but I don't know what it is, and even if I did, I don't know if it means they'll continue my counselling but also send Social Services to the house.

When they said I could get free therapy I thought it was so progressive, so not American. But it took three months to get the first appointment, weeks and weeks of distress piling on top of me. And then I ended up in a dirty doctor's office because no one listened to the part about the fluorescent lights and medical settings triggering my panic. I got Lorraine, watching the clock, checking boxes, deciding I'm better in four sessions that could have been six but that's my fault. Just like everything else.

I could find a private therapist, but that means I'd have to talk to Harry about it and I can't face that conversation. And it would have to be somewhere I could bring the baby, and I'd have to go during school hours, and I'd have to get on a train or a bus and go to Wimbledon or Mayfair. But these simple steps – a matter of a Google search and a phone call – are overwhelming and impossible in a world where a choice between doing the dishes or the laundry leaves my chest tight and my heart beating so fast that sometimes I sit on the front steps of the house with the baby so that, in case I pass out, someone walking down the street will find us and call for help.

Seeing Lorraine was supposed to be easy; close to home, I could walk, someone else did the admin. But Lorraine doesn't see me.

"… so, why don't we review the supports you have in place and talk about some ways that you can find other …"

Fuck this. "That sounds like fun, Lorraine, but I've got to go."

"Our session isn't finished."

"That's OK, I'm letting you know now, well in advance, that I won't be here next week."

I struggle with the door, my scar prickling every time I move the stroller. Lorraine doesn't help me. She just turns in her chair and says, "I'm sorry to hear that," not sorry at all.

The therapy was hard to get but not the diazepam. I told the GP that I was having a hard time and within my ten minute time slot, barely a question asked, she gave me the prescription and the number for the borough counselling service.

I said, "Can I drink on these? I can't be spaced out, I've got a baby and a kid."

She said, "It'll take the edge off. Bye now." And she smiled as she held the door open.

I've pushed Rocky to the high street. I can turn left, go home and take the pill, have a drink and let it all go. Or I can turn right, pick up food for dinner, get Johnny from school and be their mother.

"You alright, pet?" I'm startled by the voice. It's the white-haired checkout lady from Sainsbury's on her cigarette break. The nice one who loves babies. *Pet.* Such a sweet name to be called. She touches my elbow. "You been standing 'ere for a bit. You OK?"

I'm so tired. My bones are tired. Exhaustion is pulling them apart, stretching my veins in every direction like a spider's web, and I am just as impermanent. Transparent. I can hear the creaking hinge blink of my eyelids. I can't move from this spot, overwhelmed by the possibility of crossing the street. I want to lie down on this sidewalk, absorb the heat from the concrete. This morning I saw a black plastic bag stuck to the street. It was a shopping bag like you get from the corner shop, except I thought it was a dead bird and I started to cry. That's not the first time that's happened. Does this woman know how that feels?

"Lovey?" She touches my arm.

"Yes, sorry, I'm just so sleep deprived. You know how it is with these little terrors."

Somehow there's still the ability to speak, to be paralyzed on the inside but still moving on the outside.

"Oh, I know dear, but it goes by fast, too fast. Isn't he gorgeous? You give your mummy some peace, you 'ear?" she says to Rocky who turns to look at her with a dimply smile. Charm that he didn't inherit from me.

"You'll be OK, love, it don't last for ever."

"That's what they say. See you tomorrow. Always need milk and nappies, you know?" She pats my arm. I watch her put out her cigarette on top of a trash can before she goes back into the store. "Thank you," I whisper, and turn right.

WINE, FORMULA

A Wednesday in August 2016, 6:25 p.m.
London, Grand Euro Star Lodge Hotel,
Room 506

I've been crying for nine minutes. I know that because I've been holding the phone, watching the numbers change. The ladies are still bickering on TV but I've lost track of the plot. I check the phone again. Another new email. But this one's a sudden burst of hope – maybe we could talk and …

Gigi, babes, how are you??? Sorry I didn't get back to you last week. It's been mental. Have you seen my Guardian article? It's so huge for the firm. Anyway I just wanted to say don't worry about what happened in the office. It's OK, everyone understands. Remember when I came back I was a wreck too. So should we get the babies together? It's sooo crazy busy for me the next few weeks, but I've got the nanny now and I sent her your details so she'll coordinate a playdate at mine. I'll try to pop in if I can if it's my work

from home day. And let's do drinks next Thursday
night? Might have a Law Society thing but let me
check and get back to you. We all miss you here.
Got to run –
    Lots of love, Charlie xx

I'm still processing the fact that she's outsourced me to
the nanny when another email comes through.

Sorry hun, can't do Thursday and I'm in Manchester
on Friday. How about the third week of September?
xx

She doesn't mean to make me feel bad. She doesn't know
I'm in this room. She's offering the little time she has to
spend with me. But I feel bad anyway. It's not about me,
I know that. I know, I remember, that there's a kind of
ruthless self-centeredness that's crucial to survival when
you're a working mother, especially if you want to do
well.

She doesn't hear what a playdate with her nanny sounds
like to me. It just seems practical, efficient, because she's
only thinking about the list, how many things she can get
done on the list, who's watching her and how they're
keeping score. She doesn't know I'm barely surviving. She's
barely surviving herself but trying not to make it look
like she's trying, because this is a new stage; the part where
she becomes Superwoman.

She starts to succeed in her career and so she's expected
to hire someone to do the mothering. She has to tell this
story, where things are just 'crazy busy,' with a cheerful
eye roll because she's got to sell the myth or it crumbles.

If she doesn't make it look easy she doesn't get the important cases that put her in the *Guardian*. She also doesn't see her kids awake for five days out of seven but she's not allowed to tell anyone how much that hurts. Pain is not part of her story. She can't show us she misses them, but also she has to tell us that this career is for them. Everyone has to know that she's built all this herself but it's not for her, it's for them – their future, their education, their inheritance, their image of women – because she's a mother. Her achievements are never for herself.

Her success amplifies my failure. Highlights my mediocrity. I don't begrudge her except that I do. I'm proud of her. I'm jealous of her. I'm in awe of her. I think she can't really be happy like this, and I think she must be so happy, she's really making it. I say to myself I guess she's alright with another woman raising her children and I say to myself why don't I have her drive? I want her to succeed but I also want her success for myself, and if I can't have it, I want her to fail; fail at the mothering part at least so she can feel as bad as I do. So that I can justify why I'm in the house and she's out in the world. We all make choices, I say. We all make choices, she says. Each of us defending our choice, knowing that there are no real choices for either of us. There's just what you do because you have to do something, because they all need you, and they always come before you.

Another email flashes up:

Hello Gorgeous Mummies!
Reminder that tea and cake next week is at mine,
the usual time. It's Fiona's last meeting with us ☹

before she goes back to work! So come ready to have some afternoon Prosecco (pump and dump ladies LOL) and help us wish Fiona good luck!
You got this Fi!
Sukie and Humphrey xx

I hit reply:

Just because we happen to be at home with babies doesn't mean that it's OK to act like we're day-drinking moro—

I delete it before I say something that I'll regret – something valid, like I'm not an idiot, so please don't send me infantile-cheerleader-Prosecco-party-bullshit emails – but that I'll regret nonetheless. And anyway, where's my proof? My proof that I'm so smart, so accomplished and above this stay-at-home shit?

I pour more wine into my plastic cup, shut my eyes real tight; they're dry now from crying so much. And that's when I remember. I scroll through the phone till I find the picture. There's me and Charlie in the office, arms around each other's waists, wearing matching red patent-leather trench coats. I have to laugh.

Last year, Charlie had this terrible case of this mom who had got separated from her kids for years because of a series of visa rejections and mistakes. I helped Charlie with the appeal and when we won and her kids finally got here, she brought them all with her to the office and presented us with these two matching coats. She had tears in her eyes and she said, "Thank you. I'll never forget you. God bless you." And even though these coats looked like they

248

came from a sex shop, we had tears in our eyes too because we knew that she had gone and found the most fantastic, beautiful thing she could afford to say thank you. And these wildly inappropriate coats were it. We all hugged, and I said, "Well, no chance I'll ever forget you either, not with this coat in my house," and we all laughed and hugged again. And then me and Charlie wore them out to lunch, pretty sure that people thought we were hookers.

I keep that coat on the inside of the closet door. It peeks out from behind some robes and belts left on the hook there. Some days I don't even see it. But on days when it felt too hard to be a mom, and live in England, and have a job, and be pregnant, and wonder what the fuck I was doing all this for, I'd look at the coat, and I'd remember that I was good at something. I worked for me and I worked for Johnny but I also worked because my work meant something to people, maybe just to a few people, but it mattered. To them and to me.

We all make choices. But I feel like mine's being made for me. Like I'm going down a road I don't want to be on but if I choose the other one, I'll drive right off the edge. I write back to Sukie, because I know her email is bullshit:

Thanks. See you next week.
G x

I write back to Charlie, because I know her email is bullshit:

Wow, you're busy. OK, September. Proud to see you in the papers. You're on fire.
G x

I wonder if they know that my emails are bullshit too.

London, June 2016; Baby, 6 months old

"Really, Sukie, really? I'm surprised you've had this – change of heart, I suppose you call it. I guess it's just not my personality. I would never be able to cope with staying at home."

The speaker's voice carries across the cafe demanding the attention of strangers with its deep rasp, defying them not to hear her. She's used to being heard and taking up space. The voice of a woman who will stop in a crowded stairwell at school to have a private conversation about her holiday, blocking everyone's way upstairs and making them wait. The voice of a woman who throws open the doors of her Range Rover and claims the whole pavement with her children and dog and bags so that the general public is forced to move around her, as she expects them to, never saying sorry. A voluminous voice that doesn't know how to apologize but does know how to give orders.

I can only hear the conversation in between blasts of the espresso machine but I'm pretty sure she's talking to the Sukie I know. If I'd known she was in here I wouldn't have come in. Especially because I haven't gone to any of the group teas for a month. Now I'm stuck. I can't leave because I'd have to pass her table to get to the door. I can't go to the bathroom because I'd be right in her line of vision. So I have to keep my back to her table to avoid the awkwardness of her recognizing me. Because if she sees me I'll have to say hello, and she'll do that English thing where she won't introduce me to her friends. I'll have to introduce myself and then I'll feel fat and terrible because at her table they'll all be drinking skinny lattes and not eating and wearing identical size XS leather motorcycle jackets in shades of gray and navy blue.

After the espresso machine cuts off I hear Sukie's voice, hesitant and defensive. She says, "Well, it's the right thing to do for us, I suppose. It's just that at the moment—" Yeah, that's definitely her, but the big voice quickly cuts her off.

"I don't know how you won't just die of boredom, Sukie, but good on you, you're a much more devoted mother than me!" Ouch. Bitchy. Sarcastic. I'm intrigued so I take a sip of my coffee and lean back a little further to listen.

Another voice, softer than Bitchy, but still not on Sukie's side, comes through: "You should do whatever makes you happy, Sukie, of course, but have you thought about how you'll feel in six months' time? In a year? It might be best to keep a foot in, somehow, in case you change your mind."

Then Sukie, misunderstood, frustrated: "I didn't say it was forever, Imogen, just for now. I'm not ready yet. I'm not worried about me, I'm worried about Humphrey, leaving him, he's just a baby and I—"

Imogen again, concerned but unrelenting: "I just don't want you to regret it. Just think about Mum. Once you're on that road it can be hard to come back."

That hits a chord because I hear the tremble in Sukie's voice when she says, "But I'm happy. I'm very happy. We went through so much to have him, you both know that, I just can't leave him now."

"Oh, Sukie." Bitchy's exasperated. Sukie's tears are threatening but Bitchy won't let it go. "Going back to work doesn't mean you're leaving your child. It just means it's the twenty-first century and he'll be fine. More than fine. All of our children are fine."

Then Sukie, desperate to be heard: "That's not what I meant, I don't mean you, that you've left your children, I mean for me."

Sukie's losing this one, she can't convince them, and then Imogen says, "Well, it's not a choice for all of us, is it." Shit.

"Yes, I know. I know that we're lucky that Gareth … that's not what I …"

Sukie tries to backtrack, to start again, but then Bitchy comes in: "I don't think it even is a choice, really, not any more. I have Tillie and Sophie to think of, after all, and how they see me and how they'll see themselves."

"Yes, but the girls are in school, Tamsin," Sukie pleads. Oh, that's Bitchy's real name. Sukie goes on, "That's different to a baby. And I understand all of that, I do. I just … I just thought I would feel differently, but now he's here, and I don't know. It might be my last chance. I just want to be there, that's all, it doesn't mean that I think—"

Bitchy/Tamsin interjects, "But coffee mornings and cake baking and nappies? Really? What's happened to you?"

What's happened to any of us, though? I don't know why she never told us about her job. The house, the outfits, the shopping list on the chalkboard. I thought Sukie was a professional wife.

Sukie says, "So I'll never become partner in a firm and I'm fully aware of that and I'm doing it anyway. I want to be with my baby. Why is that so hard to understand?"

Imogen says, "Because we love you and we don't want to see you throw everything away. They do grow up, you know, and then what will you have? You're not just a mother, Sukie, there's more to you than that."

Just a mother.

Sukie says, "Well, maybe I don't want more. And what about you? Feeling guilty? Is that what this is about? Tillie still in floods of tears every morning, Tamsin? And does Sophie still call out for the nanny when she has a nightmare instead of you? If you're worried about your own children then work that out for yourselves, because what I do for my family is none of your concern."

Silence. Imogen and Bitchy/Tamsin have overstepped, but so has Sukie. That's always how this conversation goes. Each mother tears the other mother down, maximizing the other woman's guilt and minimizing her sacrifice. Bitchy/Tamsin brings an end to it. "You're right. It's not. I'm sure it will be wonderful for you, Sukie. Shall we get the bill? I have to get back to the office."

Imogen and Bitchy leave the table, but I look over my shoulder and see that Sukie didn't go with them. My choices are: a) keep my back turned until I know she's gone so that she never has to know that I just heard all of that; b) wait for her to go to the bathroom then make my escape; or c) get my stuff and get ready to leave in such a way that she sees my profile and then she has to be the one to say hello first. Then I pretend I didn't realize she was here even though Bitchy might as well have been screaming "Sukie!" through a bullhorn.

I decide on option b), until I hear her say to the waiter, "May I have a large glass of rosé, please?" Then I hear the muffled crying. She's crying. *Shit.*

I bite the bullet and turn around. "Hey, hey, Sukie?" She looks up, red eyes, tears she's trying to hide but can't.

"Oh, yes, hello. I didn't see you there. How are you?"

"I'm fine. You OK?" I ask, pulling Rocky out of the high chair and onto my lap, shifting over to sit at her table before she can object.

"Oh, yes, I'm fine."

Her wine arrives and I say, "Could I get the same, please? You don't mind if I join you, do you? Actually, even if you do mind, I have a policy about not leaving crying women to drink alone." She gives me a faint smile. She needs a friend, whether she wants one or not.

She says, "I'm sorry, it's my sisters. I've just had an upsetting conversation."

"Yeah, I know, uh, I was sitting right there, and, well, if you don't mind me saying, I think they were really hard on you."

There's a momentary silence and then she says, "They *were* really hard on me, weren't they?" She feels validated now. "They're my older sisters, Imogen and Tamsin. They're both very successful. They think I'm making a mistake leaving work."

"You're leaving your job for good?"

"Well, sort of. My plan was to go back at six months, which is now, and I've asked for a further three for the moment but I'm almost certain that I'm not going back at all. I know we have twelve months legally but I don't want to get caught up in having to repay any maternity pay or anything like that so Gareth and I have been talking. I'm pretty sure that's what I want. And they don't want me back anyway. I thought it would be straightforward. Have the baby. Go back to work. But, then ... it's not how you think it will be ..."

"Yeah, it's harder than it looks. It was really hard when I was working and I had Johnny on my own. It's not easy."

She looks off in the distance. I shouldn't have interrupted. There's a long pause, a silence I don't know how to interpret, space I don't know how to fill. This happens to me a lot. My speech has a different rhythm, a beat too fast but a thought behind, or sometimes ahead, but either way I get cues wrong for when it's my turn to talk. So I wait. I think she needs me to just sit here.

I have a little exchange with Rocky. A single tear makes a slow march down her face. She says, quietly, 'We couldn't conceive and then when we did, they didn't survive. One went early on and one at twenty-two weeks. And then one day I was thirty-seven, then thirty-eight and it had been years and no baby. We started IVF. It was brutal. I couldn't focus. I fumbled and made mistakes. Cost the firm money. I was signed off for a while and then came back again but then another round of treatments failed. I couldn't cope. When we finally were pregnant with Humphrey, I rebounded. Redeemed myself. But it was all a bit too late by then.' I lean forward to touch her hand but then pull back because that's not the right thing to do. That's not what she wants. She takes a long drink.

"I'm so sorry, I didn't know. You never said anything at tea when Becky talked about her fertility stuff." I bounce Rocky on my knee and pretend to fuss with his clothes while I wait for her to speak. I try not to look at her directly because she's skittish; like a bird that you want to see up close but if you move too quick she'll fly away. She doesn't like being so personal.

"Well, it's private, isn't it? I can't bear the way Becky goes on about it. It was painful and horrid for me. It brought me Humphrey but everything I went through …" She waves a hand like she can't bring herself to say the words. We both take another drink, contemplate our glasses. All these months I thought her life was a page in the Boden catalogue. A slim thirty-something woman leaping from the curb onto the street in coral heels swinging an azure, leather shoulder bag on her way to buy flowers at the market. She has that white British skin that thirty years from now will be thin as paper, but her wrinkles will be pleasant, symmetrical. She's pretty. But if you look at her long enough the sadness of losing her babies is there, in the faint lines at the edge of each eye. Poor Sukie. I thought she was one of those naturally thin people who never had to wrestle with her body, but her struggle was with injections and doctors' offices and lost children instead. They drained her body and left her like this: fragile bone and muscle with no reserves.

"I'm sorry. That must have been really hard. *Really* hard. I get why you want to stay home with him. And you should if that's what you want. Fuck everybody else and what they think."

Her eyes get wide. One corner of her mouth rises in a sad smile. I probably shouldn't have said "fuck everybody else" in reference to her sisters.

"Well, that's one way of putting it." She sniffles and dries her eyes, almost laughing.

"Sorry, I shouldn't have said that."

"No, you're right, Gigi. I'm doing what I think is best and they should all bloody well fuck off." We clink glasses. She's surprised that she likes me. So am I.

We talk to Rocky, chat about baby stuff, food and sleep schedules and baby classes to take the pressure off the moment, but I don't have much to say on any of those topics. Then she says, "Do you think I'm making a mistake?"

I don't say, *Sukie, no matter how much you love your job and how good you are at it, you'll cry every day when you leave for the office and kiss the baby goodbye. Then you'll cry in the bathroom before your first meeting. And sometimes on the train home. In the middle of the night too, when everyone's asleep and you walk into his room just to watch him breathe, feeling guilty about what you've missed.*

I don't say, *Sukie, if you stay home everyone will start to assume that you don't do anything. At parties, no one will talk to you after they ask, "What do you do?" and you say, "Oh, I'm home with the baby." They'll talk only to your husband and you'll slowly get drunk on your own in the corner while the employed people comment on the housing market. Your kid will literally shit on you for years. And a day will come when you would take any job – drive a garbage truck, call people about mis-sold PPI, work in a soft-play center – anything, if it means you could just get out of the goddam house and away from that fucking kid.*

What I say is, "I think you're a great mom and you're going to be OK," because what she will hear, all she needs to hear, is: *you're right, you're beautiful, you're a good mother.*

"Gigi," she whispers, and I see a wave of grief breaking over her again. She thought she was done crying and had pushed it all back down where it belongs in the bottom of her Gucci Soho Disco cross-body, but the tears come again. "He'll be our only one. He would have been the fourth and I would have had a house full of children. I don't want to be anywhere that he isn't. They don't understand, they think that's mad, do you think that's mad?"

"No, sweetie. That makes perfect sense to me." Poor girl. I pick up Rocky and pass him to her across the table. She talks to him and holds him like he's Humphrey. She's not what she seems – well, a lot of her is, but not all of her.

After a while she says, "I should be getting back now. I left him with Mum for a bit because Tamsin and Imogen said I needed a break – so they could chastise me more easily, I suppose. But I don't need a break, do I, Rocky?" And just like that, she starts her metamorphosis. She passes Rocky back, leaves half her wine undrunk, brushes down her blouse, shakes her hair, blots her tears. In an instant she's back. "Really, Gigi, you must come over again soon. It's always such a tonic having the ladies round for a natter. May I have the bill, please." She motions to the waiter, stands up to throw on her coatigan, the kind of sweater that would make me look like a queen-size bed but is flattering on her. I wonder what "tonic" and "natter" actually mean and infer they have something to do with tea at her house as she leaves a £20 note on the table.

I want to say, "Do you want to walk the babies on the common?" or "Could you order another glass of wine and listen for a while?" or "Could you stay for ten more minutes so that it's ten minutes less that I'm alone today?" But before I say anything she says, "Well, lovely to see you. I must be getting off now." She gives me double Euro cheek kisses and sashays out the door leaving a trace of Jo Malone Pomegranate Noir in her wake. I didn't even say bye.

Too bad, she could use a friend like me. I finish my wine and drink the rest of hers before I pay the check. Shit. I could use a friend like me.

London, July 2016; Baby, 7 months old

"So how's the GDL going, then?" Aneela looks at me from across her desk with bright eyes that don't mean to pressure me but are really pressuring me. Rocky's starting to fuss. *GDL, shit ... oh, shit!* It's the first law course I'm supposed to do, Graduate Diploma in Law, to convert my degree, the first fucking piece of the whole goddam puzzle, *oh, shit ...*

"Gigi, the GDL? How's it going?" There's a flash of concern across Aneela's face, and a hint of annoyance. I started it part-time last September, before I had the baby, and I said I was going to keep it up over maternity leave, and then I got fucked up, and didn't go to class, and after enough weeks of not going and not studying and not doing it, I stopped thinking about it, and I meant to call Aneela and tell her, but I kept not calling, and then I forgot, and now I'm sitting here, and the last time I thought about it was so long ago and my brain is so rattled and shaken that it actually didn't even occur to me that it would come up today and now what do I say, oh my God, oh my God ...

"Ah, Gigi, you're here, I presume this is the little one?" Lara, the big boss, the senior partner, appears at the door to Aneela's office. Black-frame glasses, white hair, Ferragamos, pencil skirt suit – an icicle in heels. The only one in the office who I could never make laugh. I didn't know I'd see her today. It's my "Keeping in Touch" day, the KIT. It's the law here. You get paid for two of them on your mat leave. I'm supposed to come back to work and touch base and pretend like nothing's happened and show them that I'm the same person who left here a few months ago – if not better – and I'm ready to get back to my desk and prove my worth and show that I can't wait to work twice as hard now to keep the same job.

I meant to get a new outfit for today. I also meant to cook Johnny a real dinner and get a haircut and stop drinking so much and have sex with Harry and deal with my new moustache. And I meant to keep at the GDL to show them, Aneela and Lara, that I was serious about what they said, that I was going to put in the work and I was going to do it and become a lawyer so my boys would be proud.

But I didn't do any of those things.

Aneela called a month ago to set up this meeting and she said then we could have lunch with the team. No KIT's in America. At home there's just your first day back after your six-to-eight weeks off and you better get back at it. But Keeping in Touch days here are supposed to help you *transition*. They're supposed to be friendly. Except that they're terrifying.

Aneela really wants me to make it. That's what she wrote on the inside cover of *Lean In. To get you to the finish line, Gigi, Love, A x.* And maybe I would and maybe I could if I was one of those women who was back in shape and reading the legal press to catch up on what I missed and saying things like, "Oh, I can't wait to go back to work!" and, "Of course I love the baby but work is so much easier than staying at home!" and, "You know, I love being a mother but I just really can't wait to use my brain again," and all those things working mothers are supposed to say about how much it sucks to be at home raising your kids. But I'm also one hundred per cent certain that when I walk out of this office today it'll be for the last time.

"Gigi?" Lara breaks me out of my trance.

"Sorry, I had a bad night, I'm a little out of it." *Wrong thing to say.*

"Yes, well, babies ruin all your plans, don't they?" Lara says, not in the joking way people say things like that, but in the way that makes me think she eats babies for breakfast.

"Yes, sorry, I'm still just getting used to things. It's really nice to see you, Lara. I'm looking forward to coming back." I pick Rocky up to do something with my hands. "Do you want to hold him?" I ask her. Of course she doesn't want to hold him. Lara is the last person on Earth who would ever want to hold my baby.

But Aneela, always good in awkward situations, breaks in, "Oh, please, me first, I want a go." She doesn't really want to hold him either, she wants to get back to talking about what the fuck I'm doing because they're paying for my GDL and I'm avoiding the question.

"Yes, well, I'm sure you have a lot to talk about," Lara says. "I'll see you at lunch. He's lovely, Gigi. Nice to see you."

When she leaves I turn to Aneela. "She's coming to lunch? Is it, like, a meeting?" I ask her as she hands Rocky back. He's fractious, thrashing around, doesn't want to be held so I start jostling him in my lap, waving my keys at him.

"There've been some changes to our structure, Gigi, she thought it would be a good idea to speak to the whole team, and since you were coming today ..."

I stammer, "But, but …"

"It's alright, it's all very relaxed, we all understand, we know you've been away." She's trying so hard to be good to me, she wants to be the good boss who does the right thing, who supports mothers going back to work, but there's a strain in her voice. "Of course, I didn't realise you were bringing the baby today. Do you think he'll manage?"

I didn't think I was bringing the baby today either. I wanted to have my head together, be presentable, actually see if I could come back here and I got Rebecca to babysit but she canceled on me this morning due to an art emergency or a crustless quiche crisis or some other rich-lady bullshit and I was left with a choice: cancel lunch and the meeting because I had no childcare and set that precedent before I even got back to work; or, bring him to show that I could handle it. And pray. Other women brought their babies to the office – it's Europe. They do shit like that.

"We'll do the best we can," I say. This is going to be awful. He's not one of those babies who just sits there and stares at stuff. He started crawling before six months, he pulls up on everything, tries to cruise and always falls down with a wail of frustration. He's thrown himself out of his crib twice. His arms are in constant motion. He doesn't want to be held – he wants to stand on you, to grab stuff, stuff that's lethal to babies, like hairdryers and computer cords and staplers. He's not the kind of baby who lets you eat at a restaurant or talk on the phone or who happily chews on a teether while you have a work meeting.

"Let's get over to the conference room but after that I'd like to talk about the GDL," Aneela says, as she pushes the stroller for me while I carry Rocky to the conference room.

I whisper to him, "OK Rock, c'mon, do this for Jeej, OK? It's just an hour, do it for Jeej." But he's ornery, impatient, over-stimulated by all the new faces and the bright office lighting. I try to get my brain to scan itself for what I could say to Aneela later, but Rocky has scrambled everything and I can only concentrate on keeping him quiet when we get into the conference room.

We walk into the room and I feel the spotlight. "Gigi, my God, how are you, darling? Lovely to see you. *Really* missing you around here, *really*. Now look, who's this? Can you believe it? Isn't he *gorgeous*?" Isla and Francisco, the other paralegals, give me double kisses and squeezes on the arm, Charlie takes Rocky from me and she coos over him. Francisco lets him clench his little fist around his finger. I relax for a minute.

A flash of a parallel me from another life. The strong me who used to put on a suit, strap baby Johnny on in the carrier, take the subway and drop him at the day care on the way to work. Work all day, pick him up, strap him on, take the subway home, bathe him in the kitchen sink, sing him to sleep, then read cases until midnight.

Lara enters the room; her turquoise eyes give Charlie a meaningful glance and she quickly hands Rocky back to me and grabs her notebook to rush to her seat at the front. People start taking sandwiches from the middle of the table and I decide to try to strap Rocky in the stroller and rock him to sleep but he's not having it. I pull him out and stay standing in the back of the room, swaying with him in my arms.

"Gigi, we're going to begin, are you alright there?" Lara says, and ten pairs of eyes look at me, some smiling, some supportive, some impassive, some questioning, some noticing that I'm still in the same maternity skirt I wore to the office three days a week toward the end. No one offers to make me a plate.

"Sure, please just ignore us, I'm listening," hoping they didn't hear the tremble in my voice. They're restructuring our division, new teams, but Rocky doesn't want to be swayed, he doesn't want to be rocked, he doesn't want to be here. Charlie gives me a quick glance to reassure me but I know I'm giving working mothers a bad name.

Lara keeps talking: "Due to the length of time it's currently taking for appeals to be heard, there seems to be an uneven distribution ..."

I keep swaying, put him over my shoulder, start pacing the back of the room, but it's not working. I try the pacifier. He spits it out and it tumbles to an unreachable place under the table. *OK, try a bottle, look competent, like this isn't stressing you, normal mom stuff. Get a bottle.* I spy the corner seat next to Francisco and sit down. *OK, just lean over, get the formula out of the bag, one step at a time.* I hold Rocky over my shoulder with one hand and try to steady him there while he squalls. I unscrew the cap of the formula with the other hand, then unscrew the cap of the bottle, put the two bottles next to each other ...

"Can I help you?" Francisco whispers, kindly, softly.

"Um, no, it's OK, I'll manage, thank you though," I whisper back as I watch the open bottle of formula slide out of my grip because I have to catch Rocky who's slipping from my shoulder with his head about to hit the – 5, 6, 7, 8 – table. Which it does. Loudly.

In the moment of silence before the huge intake of breath Rocky needs to prepare his scream, there's Francisco, wearing 200 mls of formula on his shirt and his size 32 pinstripe trousers, down to the tip of his pointy Paul Smith's. There's the room full of people who just saw me drop my baby on the conference table during my Keeping in Touch day. There's the turquoise eyes of Lara in black-frame glasses, her mouth taut, arms crossed, brow furrowed.

Rocky wails. A call to action. Aneela stands up, not knowing what to do first, saying, "What can I do, Gigi?" Charlie stands up, impotent arms outstretched, calling to me, "Gigi, are you alright? Should I get your bag?" Charlie, Aneela, Isla and all the others, passing napkins to Francisco, mopping up the table, I know they're looking at me but I stare at the floor, pick up Rocky, grab my bag and just say, "Sorry, I'm so sorry."

I run to the bathroom, holding my screaming son close to my chest, and get in a stall and sit on the floor with my back against the door. I hold him and rock, rub his fuzzy head and wonder what the fuck to do next.

"Rocky, baby, look what I have, look what I have." I try to keep an even tone, try not to let him feel my stress which is futile because he is my stress. And I'm his. His cries bounce off the stall walls and he's a hundred times louder in here. I have no back-up milk. I lost the pacifier under the conference table. I have a pouch of chicken, apple and parsnip puree and I try a bit of that on his lip. I still don't know what the hell a parsnip is. We don't have those in America. The taste interests him, he sucks on the pouch, the wail becomes more of a hiccup and a moan of protest between sucks. I realize that he's soaking wet. Urine or formula that ricocheted off Francisco's One Direction haircut. Could be either. But I have no spare clothes for him. They're sitting in a neat pile on top of the radiator by the door at home, along with the three clean diapers I was supposed to bring but didn't.

I get out of the stall and strip Rocky in the sink. I use a burp cloth and the scarf I'm wearing to improvize a toga diaper for him.

"Gigi." Aneela appears behind me in the mirror. I didn't notice her come in.

I can't help it. I say, "Oh, just fuck it. Fuck it. Fuck it. Fuck it."

"Is he wearing your scarf as a nappy?" she asks my reflection.

"Yes."

She takes the baby from me, holding him the way a mother with big kids does, surprised at how foreign it feels now even though she used to do this a thousand times a day. He grabs at her necklace.

She looks at me. "You're not alright, are you?"

I turn to face her. "No."

She jostles Rocky. "What happened? Was it a rough birth?"

"Yeah," I say. Rocky puts a hand on her face.

She says, "You're not ready then – to come back?"

"No, I'm not."

"It's OK. You take the time you need. Why don't you take him to the lifts and I'll get your buggy and bring it to the front?"

I look at her, thinking of the wreckage in the conference room. "But, can you tell everyone I'm so sorry."

"Of course I will. And we'll talk about everything else some other time when you're not so … stressed," she says, in that way where what she's really saying is she's surprised at how stressed I am. Surprised at how it's hit me. Concerned that she's invested a lot of time in me and she thought I'd do better than this. So did I.

"And Lara? I just don't …" I don't even know what to say.

"It's alright, Gigi, really. I'll explain."

"Thank you." I give her a half-hug and take the baby. She's being kind. Kind so I don't feel worse. But that sort of kindness always does the exact opposite.

I sneak past reception when no one's around and go wait by the elevator bank. I turn around to look for Aneela but it's Lara coming through the glass vestibule doors instead, pushing my stroller. "Oh, I didn't mean for you to do that Lara, Aneela said—"

She cuts me off. "I'm sorry this hasn't worked out today. But you're not the first person to have a baby at the firm."

"No, of course, I know that …"

"But perhaps you need more time than the others."

I say, "I'm sorry. I had a babysitter. She cancelled. I wasn't going to bring—"

She shakes her head. "No need to explain. This is how it is with children, isn't it?"

"Yeah, but when I come back, I'll be OK, I'll work it out." I sound desperate.

"I hope so. Bye now."

She turns on her heel, one manicured hand waving to me as she re-enters the office. Not a wave really, a hand in the air, like when you hail a cab, or get a waiter's attention. The hand she puts up for people to provide her with service.

When we're finally outside I buy some formula, diapers and a onesie and some baby sweatpants at Boots and give

Rocky a bottle in the stroller. He's calm and warm now, I watch his eyes fill up with sky and buildings and people until he falls asleep.

A text from Charlie:

Hey babes, sorry that was tough. Are you OK? I wanted to walk you out but Aneela said you'd already left. Let's get a drink soon and you can tell me all about it? Everything will be OK. Don't worry. xx

I'm too humiliated to respond, even to Charlie. I pass a shirt shop. So English with its stacks of shirts in neat wooden cubes. I buy a classic white one for Francisco and leave it with security downstairs when I pass by the office on the way home. I ask them to call him to pick it up. Kind of like when your mom brings something you left at home and leaves it for you in the office at school. Your gym shorts or your lunch.

If you have that kind of mom.

11

BUTTER, FROZEN DINNERS

A Wednesday in August 2016, 7:30 p.m. London, Grand Euro Star Lodge Hotel, Room 506

Twelve hours since I left the house. Soon my phone will be dead. Soon I'll have finished the second bottle of red. Oh. No, the first bottle still has some in there. Either way, either bottle, I've had too much to drink. And also not enough. I sink into the bed. I've barely moved today but everything aches. I feel my bones grinding against each other trying to find the grooves they fit in before the baby grew in the space between. Feel the new length of my feet, the new thickness of my wrists, the new width of my ribcage. The curve of my lower back, the arc of an S where it used to be straight. I put my hands on my belly – misshapen and puckered, like an old balloon, dimpled latex, forgotten and slowly deflating behind the sofa now that the party's over.

Even my hands. You expect your stomach to stretch and for your breasts to drop but your hands, how they change – the cracked skin, the ragged nails, burns from the oven, burns from the iron, red from the constant washing. The skin on the back of my hands is dry and loose, no longer elastic. There was a time when he kissed the back of my hand. When his burdens fit perfectly in the hollow of my palm and mine in his. We carried our burdens for each other, in each other's hands. I loved him and he loved me; yes. But it was more than that.

Teresa knows. Not long now and she'll be headed to prison to start her sentence. On the TV they're doing a montage of clips from the past season, her voice heard over the footage of her bouncing, playing daughters: "I had a normal life and now I'm in this nightmare." Prison is just weeks away but she sits there on the sofa with quiet dignity in a gold, floor-length, fish-tail gown, shimmering like a mermaid on the Jersey Shore.

The gold eye shadow above her long, fake lashes brings out a bronzy green in her eyes I've never noticed before. Joe, her husband, sits on a stool behind her, stoic, burly, uncomfortable in his suit, the shape of his arms visible through the expensive gabardine. He is not a man who can be contained in a suit. He is a man who made grave mistakes. It's unclear how much Teresa understood about the fraud but it's clear that she trusted him. She signed whatever he said to sign, and now she'll pay for it. She'll pay, for loving him and trusting him blindly and being a loyal wife, with a year of her life. A year of her children's lives that she won't see. But she shows no bitterness and betrays no anger. She stands by her man.

They're two people on the precipice and it's hard to know if they'll be holding hands when they make the jump. Who knows what it's like between them when the camera isn't rolling. What I know for sure, though, is that she will at least reach for him as they fall even when he tries to pull away. She will reach for him until the very end when he lets her go. The camera closes in on her face and she says, "Oh my God," in a low voice, to no one and to the whole world and to herself. The conversation goes on around her but the camera catches her exhaustion, her disbelief at what is about to happen. Her gold dress, an expensive, flashy, empty shell. "Oh my God," she says, and the pain is so real, so intimate. I have to look away.

We're falling now, Harry. And you think you're reaching for me but I think you're letting me go. And I'm reaching for you too, but our hands don't fit together like they used to.

London, May 2014

I'm at this party dressed as a nun and drinking a glass of wine. I'm a nun because Harry is the Pope and he got me this outfit so that I'd match him. Of all the things we could have worn he went hardcore Catholic. I think he just wanted to wear the big hat.

The guy next to me is a giant French baguette and he's standing with a woman in a suit and a messy blond toupee. Boris Johnson. "I like your costume," I say to the bread, trying to be sociable.

"Oh, thanks. I'm English, you see, and my wife is French," he says before Boris breaks in.

"Yes, and so I am dressed as English and he is dressed as France!" she says with her pretty accent.

I nod and smile, thinking that, *What the fuck are you talking about?* is probably not the right thing to say to these nice people.

It doesn't matter because I'm quickly saved by Livvie, the hostess, dressed in a skin-tight matador outfit, standing on her coffee table and yelling, "Shots! Shots! Drink!" Two girls wearing different versions of Bjork's swan dress, you know, for Iceland, walk around with trays giving everyone shots in little plastic cups. We're supposed to drink whenever the people on TV sing in their native language.

Everyone turns to the huge screen and the volume goes up on the pretty blond rapping in Polish wearing a sexy version of her national dress – an embroidered blouse, short, floral mini, corset belt, red beads, high boots, hair in braids wrapped around her head. The name of her song is 'We Are Slavic.' As she yelps away two barefoot, buxom peasant versions of her perform household chores at the front of the stage – one suggestively rubs clothes on a washboard while the other pornographically churns butter. Then she breaks into the English part of her song: "Cream and butter taste so good, we will prepare for you delicious food." The crowd goes wild on screen and in this living room. I take my shot.

I'm not drunk enough for this.

We're at a Eurovision Song Contest party. Eurovision is an annual singing competition where every European country sends an entry. It's like a combination of the Olympic opening ceremony and the Miss Universe pageant and *RuPaul's Drag Race* and *American Idol* and SexyDanceTimeNight in the basement of that Russian nightclub I went to once in Brighton Beach. There's pyrotechnics and flashing lights, thousands of people in the audience waving every flag of Europe. And randomly Australia and Israel who are also contestants. They sing every genre of music, most of it in bad English. Then all the countries vote. And I guess people all over Europe have parties and get wasted and watch it. Which is why I'm here like an asshole in this nun outfit next to this loaf of bread drinking a glass of wine.

A text from Sharon:

Jeej, you OK? You going out tonight? How's it going?

She's checking on me. We've only lived here for four weeks so she's just making sure we're alright. And we are. I am. I mean, I will be. This party, for example. Not really my scene but Livvie is one of Harry's really old friends and she was so happy to see him. Everyone is glad he's back in London. So I just nod and smile and take everything as a learning experience. Like tonight, now I know what people mean when they say something is *Euro*.

I walk over to the Pope who's talking to Kurt, a massive man with startling blue eyes and platinum blond lashes that clash with his black, braided wig. He's wearing a women's flamenco dress, chest shaved for the occasion. He's Dutch and he's married to Livvie.

"Cheers," I say. "Nice dress."

"Ah, hello, a sister of the faith, with the Pope. I get it, man! You are well?" Kurt smiles and says this in his almost perfect English without an accent except for the sequence of the words that's just slightly off.

"Um, yeah, this is sort of an out-of-body experience, but yeah," I say. Harry puts his arm around my waist, which feels wrong in our outfits, but actually, is probably realistic.

"Yes, I told Kurt you've never seen Eurovision," Harry says.

"No, I never heard of it," I say and Kurt looks astonished. "Oh, no? It is great. Greatest music party ever."

"Sure is," I say, because I can't tell if he's being sarcastic or European.

Livvie, already very drunk, bounds over to us and puts her arms around me. I like her. I know we'll be friends. "Oh, darling, I'm just so, so, *so* very happy for you and Harry. *So happy*. He's such a good one. Aren't you, darling?" she says, pulling Harry into a group hug. "I just am *so* thrilled for you both. Quite annoyed that we didn't know about the wedding, mind you, but I'll forgive you because it's the most romantic story I've ever heard. Oh, wait, SHOTS!"

Harry and I laugh and grab our next round of shots from one of the Bjorks.

"What's this one for?" I ask. "Big facial hair," she says, and we look at the screen.

"Wow," Harry says, adjusting his conical hat. And I can see why. I do my shot and text Sharon:

We're good lady, thanks. I'm dressed like a nun, Harry's the Pope, we're doing shots and watching this Austrian drag queen with a beard sing her ass off

Conchita, with her tiny waist in her gold gown and huge beard, belts away like Céline Dion on screen. Harry pulls me closer toward him. I look around the room, the alcohol sets in, Conchita sings something about being a phoenix, and America – home – suddenly feels very far away.

"If she shaved she'd look just like Danielle," Harry says in my ear, making me laugh and push back the tears.

274

"Oh my God, you're right," I say, my voice cracking, "it's her drag double. Friggin' beautiful. Don't ever let Danielle sing, though."

But he knows. He takes me by the hand and leads us through the crowd and we find a spot off to the side away from the noise. We stand together, not talking, just watching the contest and the party for a while, his arms around my waist. I lean my head back into his chest. We stay like that. My breathing slows to his rhythm. He kisses the top of my head. A moment of just being. He's good at that; at catching me right before I fall; at giving me a break from being strong.

"It will get easier," he says.

"I know."

Soon the French entry bounds onto the stage. A band called Twin Twin singing their song, 'Moustache.' It's an eighties electro-pop band and they sing in French except for the refrain, "I wanna have a moustache!" The huge screens behind them show massive, flashing, handlebar moustache graphics and their background dancers do a move which you can only describe as, well, the moustache.

My phone buzzes. Sharon answers my text.

England sounds weird. Have fun

I take a deep breath, feel the weight of Harry behind me, and then Livvie screams, "Shots! Shots!" in the background. It's double shots now for the French singing *and* the facial hair.

I turn to face Harry, straightening my habit. He says, "Have you had enough? Do you want to go?"

"No, I'm good. Get those shots in, John Paul, let's do this."

Then we drink and jump around with his friends and yell, "Moustache!" with the crowd. I shout, "Shots!" with Livvie on her coffee table while on the TV Russian identical twins connected at the head by their ponytails start swaying on a giant seesaw. I trade outfits with Kurt. I lead a conga line with Harry's papal staff. I throw myself in. He watches me, and loves me, and throws himself in too. And someday when I tell him that I need to go home, my first home, I know that he'll be here when I get back.

London, July 2016; Baby, 7½ months old

The key turns in the lock. Harry's home. He opens the door and steps over the pile of mail on the floor under the slot. He doesn't pick it up. He's been away for a few days for work. How many days has it been? Two? Three?

The boys have been asleep for a couple hours. I must have been sitting here, on the floor by the kitchen table, for at least as long. Asleep maybe, or just staring at the wall.

I think of a hundred things to tell him. About Johnny's report card and how bad it is and Rocky flipping off the changing table and how I managed to renew the parking permit for the car, he'll be impressed by that, and then I could tell him about Lorraine because I never told him about her and that I spent a half hour with Johnny tonight working on his reading so that maybe he can catch up by the end of the summer, and how it's not fair because it's just his focus is off because his mother is depressed and anxious, and then Harry will hug me and tell me that it's OK, that Johnny will be OK, that I'm a good mother, I'm a good mother, I'm a good …

"Hello," Harry says, taking off his tie, throwing his bag down. He steps over a pile of clothes and goes into the kitchen.

"Hi," I say. There's a long silence while he roots around looking for a dinner that doesn't exist. "I, I mean there's a lot—" I start to say but he interrupts.

"Any food knocking around?" he asks.

I say, over my shoulder, "Sorry, there's nothing ready. I didn't have a chance. I didn't know you were coming back today, I mean, I guess I forgot. I haven't eaten either. You want to order something?" *We'll just figure out dinner and I can tell him, tell him about … that I'm …*

"What are these?" He holds up some frozen dinners. Ready meals, that's the English word for them. "Can I have one of these?" He's sharp, testy.

"Sure," I say. He chooses spaghetti carbonara for himself and puts the other boxes back in the freezer. He doesn't offer to heat one up for me. I didn't even realize I had bought that – frozen pasta. I've betrayed every Italian grandmother on Staten Island.

"How do I do this? Microwave or oven?" Harry asks me, annoyed, tired.

"I don't know, read the instructions. Those are oven ones, I guess."

"What temperature?" he shoots back at me.

"I don't know, Harry. Read the box." *I can't tell him anything.*

"It's been a long day."

"OK, so now you can't read?" *Why is he doing this?*

"Not now, Gigi." It comes out sterner than he meant it to. Or not.

Another long silence while he tries to figure out how to feed himself. Sliding off the cardboard sleeve, poking holes in the plastic film, saying without words that he's annoyed that, once again, nothing was prepared for his arrival. That he's worked all day and travelled and what is it that I do all day? I can hear him thinking it, *What does she do all day?* as he flips over the cardboard sleeve to check the temperatures again.

I pretend not to notice. Change the subject. I need therapy, I'm struggling, the doctor gave me a prescription for drugs weeks ago and maybe I should take them but I say, "I have to pay for Johnny's cricket membership."

"Fine." Harry holds the cardboard sleeve close to his face to decode the instructions.

"Also the bill for the dentist," I say, finding it hard to stay composed. I can't stand this. He's a fucking grown man and he has to make a show of how he's "making dinner."

"OK, I'll transfer some money to the house account."

"There's the card for your aunt on the table to sign."

"OK." Because I do that too now. Remember his fucking shit for his fucking family. Even though that aunt calls me Georgina because Gigi isn't a "proper name."

He flounders around the kitchen looking for a, "Baking tray? What's a baking tray? Do we have one? It says put on a baking tray."

He wants me to do it. Find the baking tray, make the food, be the wife. Let him focus on his one very important task, his one thing, his *work*. He's too important to heat up this ready meal because he *works*. He's forgotten I have a job, that I know what it means to work. That when I did my work I came home and did all the home stuff too. I didn't make anywhere near the same money as him but dammit if I didn't work as hard at *both* my jobs.

"There's a baking tray in the bottom drawer. Johnny has a game, I mean a cricket match, on Saturday. Can you take him?" *Because I can't. Can you take the baby too? Can someone take the baby because maybe if you took the baby for a day—*

"OK, where is it?" He's half shouting.

"Surbiton."

"No, the baking tray."

"The bottom drawer." *Please, just for that one day, because if I can get to Saturday and he just takes the—*

"I'm in the bottom drawer, I can't find it."

"It's there."

"Where?"

"Well, ordinarily, if something's not right on top you might find that using your hands to move other things out of the way may help you to find it. That's called 'looking for something.' You live here, you should find out where we keep shit."

It goes on and I let it. The fruitless search for the hidden pot holders, the camouflaged serving spoon, the missing condiments that are visible only to women. There's an implicit meaning in every clang of a pan, pans that should not even be clanging because he's making a fucking frozen dinner.

Twenty minutes of silence while I sort the laundry mindlessly and he checks the window of the oven compulsively so he doesn't burn his food. He finally sits down to eat. Alone. He opens his laptop to read the news. Then, "I'm out tomorrow night and the night after."

"But you just got home."

"It's part of my job, you know that."

"Lucky you." I leave him to his pasta and load the washer and try to figure out how this went wrong. How I went from needing him to hating him so fast. How I went from wanting to tell him everything to saying nothing.

"I'm going to bed. I'll be in the guestroom."

"I just got home, as you said, but of course you will," he says to his screen, winding spaghetti absent-mindedly on the fork.

I stop in my tracks and say, with my back to him, my head bowed, "Why should I go up and down stairs all night when I can just sleep near them?"

"It's fine, I understand, you just haven't slept in our room for I don't know how long."

"And you haven't gotten up in the night for I don't know how long either."

"I have a deal on. I have work. It'd be nice if you would acknowledge me and what I do for this family. It would be nice to have some support sometimes." *It'd be nice, Gigi, if you could just have sex with me when I want it and make fucking dinner and not be mentally ill or make me dread coming home every night to listen to you complain about the life I've made for us.* There's a silence and then he says it again, "It would be nice."

"Yeah, it would." *Yeah, it would.*

"I'm under a lot of stress."

"Of course you are. I can't imagine."

"That's not what I'm saying. You know that's not what I'm saying. I'm not competing with you. Have you ever asked, even once, how I'm doing? God, you're so self-absorbed." And he pushes back from the table, takes his tie off. He can't stand the sight of me. "Do you think nothing has changed for me?"

He's been waiting to say this for months. *What about me? What about me?* I've been feeling him not say it, I've actually felt it cross his mind when I've interrupted him watching rugby or asked him to give Johnny a bath after work. He's said it finally. But I don't care.

I stand in the doorway of the kitchen, pull at my T-shirt so it doesn't cling to my belly, my breasts. I feel exposed under this light so I bend down to start picking up toys, throwing them at a basket, each toss punctuating my fury.

"What's changed, Harry? You leave the house, go to work, talk to adults, eat whatever you want whenever you want to, your clothes fit, you don't pee sideways, you go to drinks at the end of the day with other men who have wives at home taking care of their lives too. Oh, and you get paid!" I'm screaming now, throwing toys like grenades.

"Have you ever once – ever once – thought about packing Johnny's bag for school? Washing his uniform socks? Labeling his shoes? And now there's a baby. Do you know what formula we use? What size diapers? You never once thought about it, you've never had to because I'm here – I AM HERE – I am here washing your boxer shorts, feeding your children, trying not to disappear. All you have to do is go to work, just like you did before. So what's changed *so drastically* for you? What's so different about your new life?"

Harry exhales. He speaks quietly. "You. You're gone." He unclenches the sides of the table he was holding onto before, no longer needing the support.

I stop short. If I speak now I'll break down and I don't want to give him the satisfaction of being right so that he can comfort me when I cry. I don't want to be comforted. I say, "So you've noticed."

Sarcasm is a weak defence. Of course he's noticed, he loves me. I know that. I know that I make things worse when I get angry and defensive and refuse to acknowledge him and refuse to acknowledge him acknowledging me. But I don't want to share this space.

This is mine – this pain, this anger. I just want him to say – anyone to say – *yes, it was terrible, Gigi. What happened to you was the worst. You have a right to be mad and sad. No one has been through as much as you.* I gave up my body, my work, my friends, my home – all of it for this man and these kids. They can't have my trauma too. I pull out a chair and sit down at the opposite side of the table because I'm too tired to stand or leave the room. Just too tired.

Harry looks at me across the table. The light above him shows the patch on the top of his head where his hair is thinning. His stubble is flecked with gray. That's new, I haven't seen that before. The collar of his work shirt is frayed at the corners from too many dry cleans. That's not like him. He's so meticulous about his work clothes; even now, at this late hour, in this argument, he's still wearing his cufflinks. He looks at me with his velvet framed eyes. I haven't seen his face for months.

He says, "What you did, how he was born – I'll never discount that, I'll never say it doesn't matter or that you should get over it. I thank God you survived it. But it happened to me too. I was there. You're not the only one struggling. I lose my place in my presentations. I lost three clients in the space of two weeks. My last review was a warning. I haven't hit my numbers for the third month in a row. While you're sleeping in a separate room I'm working on our finances into the night to make sure we can still pay for Johnny's school in case I get fired. Yes, you sleep less than me, no, I don't get up with the baby, but do you know that Johnny crawls into bed with me at three every morning? And whispers to me for an hour about all his worries? That he won't go to back to sleep unless his arm is around my neck and he's holding my hand? You don't see any of that either."

Any goodwill he built up with his frayed collar and his flecks of gray evaporates. "No, I don't. So what, you want credit? I'm sorry you can't keep your head together at work. I'm sorry I never considered the impact on *you* of everything that happened to *me*. And Johnny's gotten into bed with you about three times, but you know what, your efforts with him are heroic. I don't know how you're managing."

"Gigi, I ..." Harry says as I leave the table. But then he gives up. He's thinking it's not worth it. He's right, it's not.

He stays in the kitchen with his laptop open to the sports pages, luxury car websites, triathlon videos. His world that has nothing to do with me. Or that hasn't for a long time.

As I get into the guest bed on the floor above I hear a dish break against the stainless steel when he throws it in the sink. An accident, of course. He's not hot-tempered or volatile, he doesn't throw things. But maybe that would be better. Preferable to what I know he'll do in the aftermath of this dish breaking. He may leave it there, another mess for me to clean up, claiming ignorance of how to handle this chore, claiming that he didn't bother because I would just tell him he did it wrong anyway. The mess will be my fault, the consequence of my Crazy. And if I get angry about being framed this way it'll only prove that what he says is true.

Or maybe he'll wrap up the shards in old newspaper and leave the package on the counter by the sink so that I'll have to ask in the morning, "What's this?" and he'll explain, secretly satisfied to have evidence that he does actually help around the house. He won't admit that's why he left it there although we both will know that it is but I'll seem irrational for making the assumption. This will infuriate me. He'll say that I'm unreasonable for getting angry about the fact that he cleaned up the mess. I won't be able to articulate that the fact he had to leave the evidence on the counter is worse than doing nothing at all. And he will be damned if he does and damned if he doesn't. This will also be my fault.

I turn on my side. I could fix this if I just go downstairs, hug him, tell him that I do acknowledge what he does. Say that I know it's been hard for him too, that of course it was scary for him to have to see his wife cut open and his baby torn out. That I love him, that I'm sorry I haven't asked him how his day was for eight months, and that we'll be OK, we just have to get through this time. This is the hardest time, I should say, but it won't last forever and we're going to make it. That's what I should say.

That's what I should say.

12

SOUP

A Wednesday in August 2016, 8:30 p.m.
London, Grand Euro Star Lodge Hotel,
Room 506

The TV's still on with the sound off. I listen to the bathroom faucet drip and watch the ladies laugh and yell at each other silently. I've kept the phone to my ear for a while, unsure whether this is a good idea. The receiver smells like someone's breath. Finally, I dial the numbers on the ancient international calling card I keep in my wallet.

"Yeah." Dad picks up.

"Hi, Dad, how you doin'?" I say, trying to sound normal.

"Hey," he rasps and grunts as he shifts his weight. I hear the effort it takes for him to sit up and talk from his usual position, lying down in front of the TV.

"You guys OK? What's going on?" I ask, casually, wondering if he can hear in my voice that I've left my family.

"Same old, same old, you know, same shit, different day."

"How's Ma?" I ask as his TV gets louder in the background. He's turned up the volume during this call so he doesn't miss anything they're saying, instead of turning it down so he can hear me.

"She came out of the room to eat lunch today, so, you know, that's better, I guess."

I say, "It's getting close to Frankie's time." That's what we call it because that's the easiest way to say it.

"Yeah, it is. She did this on his birthday too."

"How long's she been in the room?" I ask, surprised at the steadiness of my voice.

"A few days, I don't know, since Saturday."

"Is she saying anything?"

"Nah. What's she gonna say?" We don't speak for a while. I listen to the voices change on his TV while he flips through the channels.

I say, "OK, you need money? You need anything?"

"Nah, sweetheart, we're fine. We're saving on food now that your mother's stopped eating."

"Dad …"

"What? It's true. She eats too much anyway. We're fine, don't worry."

"Wait, Dad, did you try the soup? The cream of chicken? She likes that one."

"Yeah, I forgot about that, your trick. OK, I'll get some later. Anyway, you OK?"

"Yeah, you know, busy, the kids. I'm thinking about Frankie too. I got a lot to—"

He cuts me off: "OK, so take care, tell Harry I said hi. Oh, the baby, how's the baby?"

"He's, he's fine. He's good. So's Johnny."

"Yeah, OK, I gotta go. They got the old *Columbo* on."

"OK …" but he hangs up before I can say bye.

Ma and I are both sitting in rooms drinking alone, silent in our parallel pain. There are a thousand ways that she hurt me but I forgive her every time because there are a thousand ways that I'm like her. There are things I do because she did them. Because I saw her do them. I did them with her. She did them to me. I don't know how not to do them to my kids.

I thought it would end with me. I thought if I left her behind then it ended with me and my kids would never have to know. That they would grow up without knowing this feeling that's put me in this room alone, the same room she sits in alone across the ocean. But trying to leave Ma is like trying to leave my own skin. So maybe I should go before they learn any of this from me, before they get too old to forget it. Maybe if I go while they're young they'll unlearn me and undo everything that me being their mother has done to them already. I'll melt away from their little lives, like frost in spring, before they can remember what I've done.

Staten Island, March 2002

I could barely open the door and I thought it was because they hadn't been picking up their mail and it was built up behind the slot, but it was Ma, slumped in the corner between the door and the shoe rack.

"Ma." I slide in through as much of the door as I can open. "Ma," I say gently, so I don't startle her. She snorts in her sleep. I get down on the floor, pick up her hand to stroke the back of her palm. "Ma, you gotta get up, you can't sleep here." Alcohol fumes and cigarette smoke emanate from her crumpled body. The grief and toxins like a vapor almost visible in the air. She's awake enough that I can get her to her feet, lift her up by putting her arms over my shoulders. She doesn't weigh as much as she did when Frankie was alive.

"Eugenia, my head, my head," she slurs, her head rolling back on her shoulders. The living room is dark ever since Dad covered the windows with black garbage bags so that they wouldn't have to look at the hole in Manhattan. But a ray of sunlight comes through the kitchen window and I can see the dust thick in the air. I put Ma in her chair. "Eugenia!" She shouts my name, then mumbles, just before her head hits the headrest of the La-Z-Boy and she falls asleep. She snores. I cover her with a fleece blanket. The one with the three white kittens in a basket on the front.

I pick up the beer cans and half empty boxes of chicken wings, Chinese food containers thick with mold. Dad is doing the best he can but he can't keep up with driving the bus and taking care of Ma. So it's the housework that he's let go. He says the driving is therapeutic. By which he means it gets him out of the house so he doesn't have to be with her all day. I can't blame him, for not wanting to be here, for not being able to carry her grief when he's got so much of his own. He drives his around all day. She drinks hers. I cry on public transportation, sometimes without noticing until I catch my reflection in the glass of the subway doors as they close.

I clean the house like Ma taught me. I do things how she likes them, vinegar and baking soda to get the crap off the stovetop, the cheap vodka she keeps under the bathroom sink to make the faucet shiny and to disinfect the bottom of the tub. I wash the dishes, remember why they're all melamine and not ceramic. Her rage has mellowed. She doesn't throw things anymore.

I dust the frame of Frankie's high school graduation picture. She was never one for keeping our childhood things, but since he died she's been combing through the house, finding any artefact he once handled and taping it around his picture in the kitchen. A forgotten half pack of cigarettes he kept under his mattress. A Domino's menu where he wrote down a phone number without a name. A letter to Santa, God knows where she found that, asking for a bike that he never got. An expired MetroCard she found in one of his jacket pockets.

When everything is clean I make soup. Her favorite, Campbell's Cream of Chicken. I open the can, turn it upside down, add water, heat, stir. The solid block of soup indented with the ridges of the tin can eventually melts into liquid.

I hear Ma behind me, shuffling into the kitchen. "When did you get here, Eugenia?"

"A few hours ago, you want some soup?"

"Aspirin, where's the aspirin?" She sits down at the kitchen table and lights a cigarette. I give her two aspirin and a cup of water.

"You want some coffee?" I ask. "I just made a pot. I found you by the door again, Ma, were you trying to go somewhere? Do you remember?"

"Yeah, coffee, is there Coffee mate? If there's no Coffee mate I want the half-and-half, did he buy the fuckin' half-and-half?" She ignores my question. Keeps smoking. Dad and I have found her all over the house like that, passed out, seemingly in the middle of doing something before giving up and laying down on the spot.

I open the fridge. "Your lucky day, Ma, Coffee mate and half-and-half. Take your pick." I pour the coffee and put both containers on the table. I turn around to stir the soup.

"You don't need to take care of me now, you can go," she says. I don't let her see that I notice her hand shaking when she pours the Coffee mate.

"I came to see you, Ma, I don't have to be anywhere. I'll just hang out for a while."

"I don't need a babysitter."

"Have some soup, you'll feel better." As I bring it to her at the kitchen table she knocks the bowl out of my hands to the floor. The soup scalds the back of my hand as the bowl hits the ground.

"Get out! No more fucking soup!" she screams, but with her voice so hoarse from all the drinking and smoking it doesn't make the impact she wants it to. On automatic pilot I bend down to start cleaning up the mess but then I catch myself. I stop.

"OK, Ma, OK. I'll go." I say it calmly. I say it this way every time she yells at me to get out. Once a week.

I pick up my coat, put my bag over my shoulder and say, "Bye, Ma." I close the door behind me and sit down on the front steps. I'll wait outside until Dad gets home. At least it's springtime now and it's warmer out. This routine was much worse in the winter when I had to stand outside the house in the cold. I give it about fifteen minutes, then I walk around to the back and stand by the kitchen window. I left a small gap between the kitchen curtains while I was cooking so that I'd be able to see in from outside without her noticing. I look in to see her sobbing. The smoking and drinking makes her crying sound like coughing – raw, wheezy, she can't get any air. Her cigarette has burned down to the filter. When she stops crying she stares at Frankie's shrine, bites her nails, rubs her eyes, finishes her coffee.

Then my eyes well up with tears and I try to swallow the lump in my throat. I'm flooded with relief. I watch her pick up a roll of paper towels and start mopping up the floor. Once a week for six months – since we lost Frankie – I've come here, cleaned up, made soup and Ma has screamed at me to get out. Sometimes she leaves the soup on the table, untouched. I know because it's still there when I come back, dried up and cracked like a model of a scorched-earth desert inside a bowl. Dad leaves it there too. He doesn't clean the kitchen because I don't think he can stand walking in there, face-to-face with Frankie surrounded by the minutiae of his life. Ma stopped cleaning because just waking up and breathing were all she could manage.

So for the past few weeks, out of my own exhaustion and desperation for something to change, I've left the mess. Left the soup slowly dripping down the wall, left a puddle of it on the floor, plastic bowl overturned in the middle. I've left it to see what she would do. To see if she even saw it. We all lost Frankie, but for Ma, every day has just been a continuation of the minute that we knew he was gone. No sunrise, no nightfall. No living after that minute. Just alcohol and scraps of paper from the pockets of his old clothes.

But today I'm watching her kneel on the kitchen floor and clean. Something she always knew how to do. Something she was good at. She's doing one small thing that isn't drinking, or yelling and passing out. One normal, small thing. Today she's not leaving the soup on the floor.

13

SUDOCREM

A Wednesday in August 2016, 9:35 p.m. London, Grand Euro Star Lodge Hotel, Room 506

I fell asleep again but the phone vibrating woke me up. Disoriented, I got out of bed and reach for the baby but he's not here. Because I'm not home. I take a minute to remember where I am. Another buzz. A text from Sharon:

> *Jeej, WTF. What is happening. Harry called me. Tell me where you are*

Before I can process what she's saying, *buzz*. A text from Danielle:

> *Are you OK? What are you doing? Harry called me. Give me the number where you are and stop acting crazy*

Buzz. Sharon again:

> *I'm going to keep texting you every minute until you answer me*

Buzz. Now it's Stacy's turn:

*Sweetheart everybody's worried. We can't help if
we don't know where you are*

Buzz. Sharon:

*I'm not fucking around. I'm like a dog with a
bone Bitch. Give me your number. You're in some
hotel right?*

How could she know that? Oh my God, another
one. *Buzz.* Danielle:

*I just talked to Shar. Are you in a hotel? Are you
having an affair? I don't know what's going on
with you but you need to call us*

Buzz. Stacy:

*G I just talked to the girls listen if you're having
an affair it's OK we've all been there we'll help
you thru. Just call us*

Buzz. Buzz. Buzz. They're relentless. Suddenly there's a
shwoop sound from WhatsApp. I open it on my phone.
They've created a group and called it WTF GIGI. Harry
called in the big guns.

Sharon:

*OK Harry said you've been gone all day he doesn't
know where you are. You need to tell us. We're
just going to call you. That's all. We won't tell
Harry until you say it's OK, we'll just let him
know that you're safe? Alright? Just like that time
we covered for Stacy and what's his name, Jose,
that Puerto Rican kid she liked back in the day
when she was going out with Jimmy. OK? Listen
hun everyone makes mistakes*

293

Stacy's bubble pops up:

Excuse me, Jimmy cheated on me first, remember?

Then Danielle:

Marriage isn't easy. Is this new guy hot? Anyway
if you're struggling we're here for you

Back to Stacy:

Gigi sweetheart it's us. Let us in

Now Sharon, taking no prisoners:

Fucking tell us where you are already!

They keep going. It's like the Housewives have jumped out of the TV and into my phone. Maybe it's the wine. Or the sleep, hours of sleep today. Or the fury with which my friends are firing their love at me, or my husband, who I've obviously scared the shit out of and who's finally found a way to get to me.

I put the phone down for a minute, unsure how to answer them. The show moved on to the next season while I slept. I watch Teresa get out of her lawyer's car and walk into her house for the first time after her year-long stay in prison. She puts both hands up to her face in disbelief that she's finally home. Her and Joe hug and cry in the kitchen. Of course, no woman has ever looked more amazing on release from prison than Teresa. She's in skin-tight skinny jeans, knee-high boots and a black leather jacket with a peplum waist, hair straightened, full makeup done, because she is, and always will be, a Real Housewife.

And then there is the moment when they run to her, her four girls, throwing their whole selves at the mother who's been gone for so long, piling on top of her, clinging to her knees and arms, grabbing any part of her they can get – they sob and cry. The real tears of little girls, their agony and love pulsing through the screen. By the time the Pampers commercial comes on, with the baby boy crawling to his mother, mother embracing child, inhaling the sweetness at the nape of his baby neck, the cup of blue water poured on the diaper, I'm crying so hard I can't breathe.

I sit up in bed too quickly and my scar pulls against itself in the bed of nails that lies between my hips, where they took him out of me. He survived. And so did I. Maybe I'm already old, like Barbara says, because I know that I survived.

I pour the last drop of wine into a plastic cup. The phone battery's at two per cent. I type:

Girls. Grand Euro Star Lodge Hotel Balham High Street Room 506 Google it. Tell Harry I'm fine. I'm not having an affair. You bitches are crazy

The phone by the bed rings. All three of them are on the line through some kind of conferencing Danielle set up. It's like trying to have a conversation with a flock of chickens.

Sharon:	"Gigi, what the hell, where are you? Are you OK? You got everybody frantic over here."
Danielle:	"Can you hear me, CAN YOU HEAR ME?" She screams down the line.
Stacy:	"Shut up, first, Jeej, are you safe? Are you hurt?"

Me:	"I'm fine, I'm in a hotel room and I'm fine."
Stacy:	"Have you taken pills? Are you trying to kill yourself?"
Me:	"What? No, what are you talking about?"
Danielle:	"DO I NEED TO CALL THE AUTHORITIES IN YOUR COUNTRY?" Danielle screams as though she's called a war zone where no one speaks English.
Me:	"It's England, Dan, and no you don't need to get the US embassy involved."
Stacy:	"Danielle, I swear to God … Gigi, sweetie, what's happening, why did you do this, did you walk out?"
Me:	"I don't really want to talk about it."
Sharon:	"Well, you better start talking before I come over there and make you talk."
Me:	"OK, I'll wait for you to get the next flight over, Shar."
Sharon:	"Did Harry hurt you, did he do something to you? If he did something to you I will fucking track him down."
Me:	"Jesus Christ, no, I'm fine, I just – I don't want to talk about it."

They all start talking over each other, relieved that I'm OK but furious that I won't say anything. Then Danielle says, "Oh, you know what, this is just like a hostage situation and we're the handlers, so we have to talk to her and like, ask her her demands and shit and then relay that to Harry, you know?"

Sharon half-shouts, "Great plan, Danielle, thanks. Jesus Christ, this girl, ignore her. Tell us what's happening, Jeej."

I take a deep breath and say, "No, you tell me, tell me what's happening at home."

That's what they do. For an hour they catch me up on their kids and their men. Sharon's looking for a house, Stacy's getting promoted, Danielle's experimenting with new nail colors. They meet up every Thursday in that bar on Bay Street after work. Ladies' night. The guys stay home with the kids. It sounds nice. I say I wish I could be there. I say I wish I could be there every Thursday.

I say other things too. How I thought I was dying when they were cutting Rocky out of me, how he got sick, how I couldn't hold him. How Harry's rich and I'm not and we love each other but there's things that neither of us get about the other one. And it's always going to be that way. Sukie and Tracy. The scar. Apron. Fucking up at work before I've even gone back. Lorraine and sleep deprivation and how I'm so worried about Johnny. Also that it's August. Almost September. My body still remembers the grief even when the pictures in my head are starting to fade. And all I have left is Frankie's voice on the phone. And that Ma is sitting alone in her room too.

Me:	"It all went sideways after the baby. Nothing's where I left it, you know? Nothing looks the same."
Stacy:	"That happens to everybody, Jeej. Everybody goes through that."
Me:	"But what do I do now? What do you do after you fuckin' fall apart like this?"

Danielle:	"It's like a rubber band, Jeej. You can stretch it till it don't go no more, but it goes back to the same size once you let go. It ends up across the room but it's still the same rubber band."
Sharon:	"What? Dan, what the fuck are you talking about …"
Me:	"No, no, I know what she means, I know what she means."

We keep talking, or I keep talking and they listen. Even though I hear Stacy's kids screaming in the background, the beeps of the supermarket checkout line where Danielle is standing, Sharon still at her desk at work, distant office phones ringing. They have work emails and families to get home to and lunches to pack for tomorrow and dinner to make – still they listen to me.

Danielle:	"OK, honey, first things first. Did you eat today?"
Me:	"No. Just wine, but I got the pizza, it's cold."
Stacy:	"You can order wine with takeout? That's awesome. Anyway, Danielle's right, eat something, you drank too much on an empty stomach, that's why you feel so crappy."

I follow her instructions. It's a relief to be told what to do. I pull over the pizza box and grab a slice.

Sharon: "OK, now, next thing, I'm gonna text
            Harry and tell him where you are. Is
            that OK? I'll tell him not to go there but
            I can't guarantee it."

I think for a minute; it may not be OK, but it's
inevitable.

Me: "Yeah, OK."
Sharon: "OK, good, you need to get out of there,
            sweetie, I just looked at that place online
            and, oh my God, no wonder you're so
            depressed, what a shithole."

She makes me laugh. I'm surprised at the sound.

Sharon: "You got a cigarette and some coffee?
            You need to sober up and make a plan.
            Step by step, write it down."
Me: "You and your lists, always with the lists."
Sharon: "That's right, and I'm making one now
            that says number one, get Gigi the fuck
            out of the hotel."

She keeps talking but that stops me. *Out of the hotel*. Retrace
my steps, rewind, leave the hotel, walk back into my house,
step over Harry's shoes, pick up the baby. Go back.

Stacy: "G, are you there?"
Me: "Yeah."

Am I here?

Sharon: "OK, so Harry wrote back on the group text, 'Thank God, please ask her if I can come and see her.' What should I say? G? Gigi? You still there?"

London, a Wednesday in August 2016; Baby, 8 months old

I walk into the bedroom and Harry says, "Good morning, darling." It's 7 a.m. but I've been up since 3, never falling back asleep before there was another cry, another bad dream, another feed, another bed to be stripped in the night. The baby was always up twice a night. But tonight it was Johnny too. When Johnny has a bad night, growing pains in his legs or nightmares, it's like my heart being torn out of my body, because in his semi-consciousness he calls for Mama. He only ever calls for Mama at night. Never Jeej. I think it's me he's calling out for, but sometimes I know it's her.

I'm fragile, brittle. Like the crack in the window downstairs we haven't fixed that hasn't shattered yet but could at any moment. In my peripheral vision there's Harry in the doorway of the en suite wearing an Italian cycling cap, fluorescent base layer, one high-tech cycling sock and nothing else.

"Don't talk to me until you've put that thing away." I'm not joking, the way I used to about his midlife Lycra crisis. I'm blunt, unamused. Before Rocky I used to think Harry's middle-aged cyclist costume was funny, with the weird bib shorts and the tight tops, but now I feel like if I had known that Harry puts his socks on before his underwear every day I don't think I would've married him. I scrounge around the bedroom floor for diaper rash cream.

"Gigi, you've caught me in the middle of getting ready, is that allowed? This is still my bedroom, isn't it?" Harry says, half-smiling, trying to diffuse the bomb.

"What's that supposed to mean? What kind of comment is that?" I say, noticing that he put on the other sock. But still nothing on his piece.

"It means that this is where I sleep and change my clothes because it's my bedroom."

"Really, you *sleep* in here? That's interesting." I'm so raw. I feel like raw red meat being shredded on a cheese grater. And I can't find the goddam ... what's it called, the fucking, what is it called, Desitin, no, that's America, what is that shit called here ...

To keep myself from screaming I start pulling apart piles of clothes on the floor. I know they're not hiding it, but if I don't keep moving, if I don't find it, if I don't stay focused on this one thing ...

"Why are you having a go at me first thing in the morning? What's happened?" Harry asks.

"Oh, sorry, you must have missed it because of all the sleeping you were doing."

He sighs, "If it was a bad night that's all you have to say, you don't have to bludgeon me like this."

Through gritted teeth, hardly above a whisper, I say, "I was up with the baby every hour and Johnny had that nightmare again."

"Ah, yes, I heard him."

"You heard him?"

"Yes, at about four, was it? He called for Mama." *Snap.*

"You heard him at about four?"

"Yes. I heard you too." *Crackle.*

"You heard me? And you thought, *Well, she's on it so I'll just fucking go back to my forty winks*?"

"What did you want me to do?" *Pop.*

"GET-THE-FUCK-OUT-OF-BED!"

I don't know how I got here but I find myself with my hands clutching Harry's fluorescent shoulders, his back against the wall, his dick, unbelievably, still roaming free.

"Gigi? Are you alright?" He leans his head down to find my eyes, loosening my grip, gently detaching me from his shirt to help me sit on the bed. I'm afraid, ashamed. Insane. I run my hand through my hair and a clump of gray and brown strands comes out from the back of my head somewhere.

Harry's staring at me, unsure what to do.

All I can say is, "What did you do with the fucking Sudocrem?" *That's what it's called, motherfucking Sudocrem.*

"It's in the bathroom. I used it because I ran out of chafing cream for cycling. I'll get it. Then we need to talk about how to help you get through today."

He goes into the bathroom and I think about that word, "help," how gentle that sounds, how nice. If someone helped me. A moment of hope and then Harry, finally fully clothed, hands me the tub. It's nearly weightless in my palm which can only mean one thing. I take off the lid. Empty.

"I'm sorry, I ..." Harry says, but doesn't finish.

I let it fall out of my hand to the floor. I watch it roll toward the windows. "I told you these floors were uneven," I say in a calm, clear voice.

I leave the room, walk downstairs, grab my keys, wallet and phone. In the background the baby's crying. Johnny's grabbing my sleeve but I can't hear what he's saying. Harry runs down the stairs and I think he's calling my name, yelling it. A stack of mail on the floor. A series of plastic bottles lined up next to the recycling bin. A pile of laundry festering in a corner. A carpet of Weetabix crumbs under the table.

Rocky needs something and so does Johnny. So does Harry. So do I. I put on my flip-flops, pull my robe close around me, and then I trip over Harry's shoes. He left them by the door again. I pick them up, open the door, and hurl them into street. A car alarm goes off.

I start walking.

14

STEEL

A Wednesday in August 2016, 10:30 p.m. London, Grand Euro Star Lodge Hotel, Room 506

I hear Sharon's voice asking me what to tell Harry. I say, "Thanks, girls, I gotta go. Don't worry, I'll be OK." I hear their worry as I hang up. I'll explain tomorrow.

I get my calling card and dial my parents again.

My father picks up. "Yeah."

"It's me again."

He says, "What's up, you OK?"

"Yeah, just checking on Ma. Did you make her the soup?"

My father yells, "What?" He's turned up the TV again.

"Did you make her the soup, Dad, cream of chicken?"

"Oh, yeah, yeah." I can see him, eyes glazed over, barbeque sauce on his undershirt. His face lit up in the dark by the blue light of the screen.

"Well, Dad? Dad?" Trying to get his attention. "Dad! Did she eat it?"

"What, the soup?"

"Yeah," I say.

"Yeah, she came out the room and she had some soup. She's cleaning the kitchen now."

"Really?" I feel a sliver of relief, not sure whether it's for her or me, or both of us.

"Yeah, Jeej, you know the routine. She'll be OK. Listen I gotta go, they're doing *Murder She Wrote*."

"What?"

My dad says, "You know, the lady detective, your mother likes Angela Lansbury. Talk to ya' later."

"OK, Dad." I hang up. I turn off the Housewives. Thanks, ladies, you were good company today. I crack the window to have another cigarette. Something's glinting on the window ledge. A metal ashtray. It would be bad if that fell on someone's head below. Overcome with an urge to be a good citizen, I reach out and just barely grasp it with two fingertips. It slips out of my hand onto the carpet, scattering soggy cigarette butts. Pink lipstick still stains most of them. Some other woman in here before me. In the low lighting of the hotel room the writing on the back of the ashtray glints up at me. PRODUCT OF GREAT BRITAIN STAINLESS STEEL.

I put out my cigarette, slide into my flip-flops, grab my wallet and keys, leave the pack of smokes for whoever has to clean this place. Probably a woman with kids. I pick up all the cigarette butts. I take out my ten pound note for emergency taxis and leave it under the ashtray. I hope she gets it. I walk to the door and look at the fire escape plan again. An 'x' marks Room 506. I open the door.

In the hallway I walk slowly, running my hand along the peeling textured wallpaper, feeling its grit under my fingers. Downstairs there's a new bored Slavic girl at reception. Blue eye shadow and false lashes. "I'm checking out," I say.

"You have room tonight and one more night and day," she says, taking my credit card suspiciously.

"I know, but I need to go home."

She slides my credit card into the reader. "No discount for not stay tonight," she grumbles.

"I'm not asking for one. I just need to go home."

Outside, the sky is purple and the air is misty. It's not rain and not drizzle, just water making its presence felt. The not-rain beads up on the fleece sleeves of my robe. The walk home is chilled and damp. August in London.

I open the front door afraid that everything will look different. "Hello?" I say quietly, as though talking to spirits in a haunted house. As though I'm unfamiliar with what lies behind each doorway.

"Meesus Gigi?" Stefka appears and startles me. "Meesus Gigi! I am so happy! So worry. Come, come." She leads me by the arm into the living room like an invalid, scanning my outfit with concern.

"Where's Harry?" I ask, confused, uncomfortable that Stefka has been in my house in my absence, taking my place, although I know that's ridiculous.

"Meester Harry call me about five, he says he's going to look for you, I stay wis boys." As an afterthought she adds, "Boys is fine," because I haven't asked. "I call him now. Say you home?"

I say, "No, it's alright. My friends told him where I was. I'll call him. You don't have to stay, let me give you some money for a cab." I'm glad he called her. What an angel she is. I feel grateful but also vulnerable and overexposed.

"No, I stay? Keep you company? Is no problem."

Rocky's cries blast through the monitor and Stefka turns to go to him but I stand up from the sofa with noticeable effort, hold her wrist and say, "Thank you, sweetheart, for today. I'll be OK. You go home. See you next week." I smile, hoping that I convinced her.

Stefka grabs both my arms. "Meesus Gigi, mother is like soldier in war. She train, she fight and kill. And then – she die."

"Wow, Stefka, that's, uh … thank you." She hugs me tight. "Is OK, is OK," she says. And it is. Or, it will be.

She leaves and I hurry upstairs to Rocky. His tears are wild with anger and relief when he sees me. He clings to me tightly, buries his head under my neck. My phone rings. Harry. I answer, in a whisper, "I'm home."

A long pause. "I was at the hotel. I was trying to find … it doesn't matter, I'll be there soon," Harry says.

"I'm sorry," I say.

"So am I."

I pace the living room floor to lull Rocky back to sleep and through a narrow space between the curtains I see Stefka sitting outside on the front steps. Making sure I'll be OK until Harry gets here. She doesn't know I used to do that for Ma. Or maybe, somehow, she does.

I put Rocky back in his cot and check on Johnny, fast asleep. Harry's key finally turns in the lock. I meet him in the kitchen and he holds me tighter than he has in a long, long time. We say a lot without words. We did this easily, once. It's more work now. There's more to say, more to hold.

When we finally pull away he says, "I called Sharon, she sent me to the hotel, they were worried when you hung up, I told her—"

I interrupt him. "I broke that window." I look at him. The past few months have made him older.

"I know," he says. He's looking at me too but I don't know what he thinks of what he sees.

"I drink wine out of tiny bottles during the day when I'm alone. I don't get drunk. It's to stay calm. But I need to stop," I say to the floor.

"OK." He strokes my hair.

Confessions fly out of me like angry crows beating their wings against my chest to get free. "I miss home. I'm lonely. I fucked up at work and I dropped the baby in the office in front of everyone. I don't know if I can go back. Not because of that, just because I'm … everything's so …"

"OK. We'll deal with it. One by one. Let's take the boys to New York, see your friends. Let's talk about work tomorrow. I'm sure it's not as bad as you think. I'm just glad you're home." Harry rests his chin on the top of my head and I can feel him close his eyes.

If I were more generous, more gracious and humble I'd say thank you now. But I'm not ready. I let the silence sit between us for a moment.

"Harry, it's August. It's almost Frankie's time."

"I know. I haven't forgotten. I know it is." He looks down into my eyes. "I should have asked you about it, I'm sorry, I didn't pay enough attention."

"It's hard when there's no one to remember but me. You know?"

"I know, I'm sorry." We're both tired of standing but before we move from here there's one more thing to say.

"I'm sorry today was so bad." It's hard for me to say because part of me thinks I shouldn't apologize for my rebellion. I had my reasons. Part of me is stunned by how my pain took over. The edge it pushed me to. Part of me *is* sorry. But not for what I did today. I'm sorry for all of us. Sorry for what happened to my body and my brain. Sorry for Rocky's terrible introduction to life. Sorry for what Johnny has witnessed and how I've frightened him. Sorry for the helplessness that Harry's felt all along. It didn't just happen to me. I'm sorry that it happened to all of us.

I tighten my grasp on Harry's hand. He looks at me. "It's OK," he says. "You're home. Let's get some sleep."

"OK."

"Gigi?"

"Yeah?"

"Just please don't leave again."

"I won't."

Rocky cries at 3:30 in the morning. I pick him up, hold him to my chest, whisper to him, sit in the old rocking chair. It's a moment I usually dread, the nightly semi-conscious moment of fury that he still doesn't sleep through the night. But tonight I'm relieved that he needs me. I may not feel that way by bath time tomorrow, but for now, I sit in the rocker and tell him that I've always loved him. It was buried very deep and I had to move every rock, one by one, and dig through mounds of pain with my bare hands. But I've found it now. It was always there. Even when I couldn't feel it.

"Jeej?" A tired little voice behind me in the doorway to Rocky's room. Johnny, hair sticking straight up, rubbing his eyes.

"Hey, buddy, it's the middle of the night, go back to bed," I whisper.

"Were you poorly?" He stands at the foot of the chair, his shadow cast across the room by the night light. Just like another little boy I used to know. The meaning of my life, stretched out there in his shadow. The last time I ran away. This time I came back.

"Come here." I gather him up onto my lap. He's so big now. All knees and elbows. Soon he'll be too big to curl up on me like this. Rocky pats his brother's face to say hello.

"Jeej, are you happy now? Harry said you were poorly. Are you better now?"

"When I'm with you I'm happy," I say into the top of his head. I'll keep saying it until the day it's true again.

In the window I see our faint reflection, the three of us in the rocker. All of us breathing in the same rhythm. They're content, half asleep. In this moment I'm home and that's all they need. Through the curtains I can see the Moon. She's a tiny sliver tonight. She's got a long way to go. So do I.

EPILOGUE

My phone rings. I know who it is. I put Rocky in his jumpy saucer thing and leave him in front of Food Network. It's been a Food-Network-all-day kind of day for us, well, for me, but I did take a shower and I bought groceries. They're still in the bags on the floor. But I bought them.

I find my phone on the kitchen table, still ringing. I have to answer because she'll call back in fifteen minutes if I don't. That was their deal with me. Every day, in rotation, one of them calls once and texts twice, and if I don't answer, they'll badger me every fifteen minutes until I do. Their own brand of harassment therapy.

Me: "Hey, what's up?"
Sharon: "What's up with you? How you feelin' today?"
Me: "I don't know. I went food shopping."
Sharon: "That's good. What else?"

Me: "That's it, I guess. Johnny has a soccer game later. I'm going to try to go. I showered already so I wouldn't have that excuse. If I just don't talk to any of the other parents I think I'll be OK."

Sharon: "Yeah, because other people love it when you're really unfriendly. It's one of the things you're good at."

Me: "Anyway, the counsellor is today at five."

Sharon: "OK, that's good. Listen, you're doing everything, you know that, right? You're doing all the right things."

Me: "It doesn't feel like it. It feels shitty."

Sharon: "I know, I know it does, but this is just the shit from before the storm."

Me: "You mean the calm?"

Sharon: "No, like, how everything is darker before the storm."

Me: "OK, listen, it's either darker before the dawn or calm before the storm, which one?"

Sharon: "You know what I'm saying, like when the clouds are swirling and it's dark and the shit happens and then there's the storm."

Me: "That's beautiful, Shar. But I'm good on storms, I had a storm ..."

Sharon: "That's what I'm saying, you already did the storm. And now – this is the shit."

Me: "Have you thought about doing this professionally? Maybe a career change?"

Sharon: "OK, fine, your sarcasm is intact so you must be fine, just call me if you need me and answer my text later, alright?"

Me:	"Love you."
Sharon:	"Love you."

I put the phone down. I'm about to go back to the sofa but I see the groceries on the floor and I make myself put them away. Not every call is like that. Sometimes I'm sobbing, sometimes I'm yelling, sometimes I don't say anything at all and they worry about me. But today is OK. Today has been mostly Food Network but there were the groceries, the shower and, maybe later, the soccer game. That's not a bad day. That's a day of tiny victories.

Some days are panic-attack-in-the-playground days; paralyzed-and-sweating-in-the-pharmacy-because-I-can't-find-the-baby-shampoo days; Stefka-sitting-with-me-all-afternoon-because-I'm-crying days. Terror-that-I've-thrown-my-life-away-and-will-never-get-it-back days. Brittle days of shame and sleep deprivation. Days when Johnny eats leftover pizza for breakfast and dinner. Days when nothing changes and nothing will ever change again. Days when the steel gray sky of London is the color of my heart and I just want to go home.

But there are other days too. And I start to count them, and they are not every day, and they are not most days, but they do happen. The day I take Rocky to playgroup. The day I call Tracy and we go for a walk. The day I meet Charlie for lunch after the third time she asked and Rebecca babysits and I'm grateful to her and I don't say anything passive aggressive. And neither does she. The day I write my résumé. The day Harry calls a sitter without me asking or telling and he just does it and we go out and it's awkward because we forgot how to talk to each other but then he does it the next week and the next and we start to remember. The day we sleep in the same bed. The day I take the medication. The day I don't have time to reach for wine because I've been busy taking care of my kids and looking for jobs online and I start to feel better.

One day I open the closet and try on clothes that aren't leggings and oversized sweaters. Most of them don't fit. Fuck it. I throw them on the floor. I fold up the old jeans and tops, the suits and pencil skirts, and put them in garbage bags for donating. I'll drop them off on the way to Sainsbury's to get dinner and then I'll go pick up the boys. As I turn away to take the bags downstairs, a sleeve of the red patent leather coat hanging on the back of the closet door catches my eye. I pull it on, tie the belt and pop the collar. I go downstairs, step over Harry's shoes and take a last look in the mirror. I smile at my reflection, with my eyes, just like Tyra and Stacy taught me. Then I open the door, one bag in each hand and lock it behind me. I take a deep breath. And I start walking.

ACKNOWLEDGEMENTS

There are many people whose support, time, and energy made this novel possible and to whom I will always be indebted.

I am beyond grateful to have had the honour and privilege to work with two extraordinary editors, Jocasta Hamilton and Jenny Jackson. Jocasta, whenever we spoke about Gigi it felt less like editing and more like a concerned conversation about a real person, our girlfriend going through a rough time who we were both worried about. She came alive on these pages because of you. Jenny, thank you for your big-picture thinking and positivity, and for caring about Gigi as much as I did. You have both made this an infinitely better book, but I thank you most of all for how you have made me a better writer.

I am very grateful to have the support and guidance of two stellar agents. Thank you to Alice Lutyens at Curtis Brown for reading my words, for getting Gigi, for understanding me, and taking a chance on us both. Thank you for your vision, your belief, and your tenacity. I am so lucky to have you in my corner. My thanks also to Zoe Sandler at ICM Partners. Thank you for believing in this book before you even met me, for knowing exactly what to do with it, and for always being the reassuring voice of reason on the other end of the phone.

My gratitude to Tom Bromley, my tutor at Faber Academy, for your encouragement, expertise, and insights when this book was in its infancy. Thank you also to the lovely group of writers whom I met on Faber's Work in Progress course where this book was born. Without your honest critiques, Gigi would not be the woman she is in these pages. Special thanks to Su Lynch for all your advice early on.

Thanks and love to Elaine Davenport for reading my manuscript multiple times, for your feedback, and for allowing me to borrow from our shared memory of 9/11. My loving gratitude to Lesley Bourns for your insights, advice, and calm reassurance at many stages of this process. Huge thanks and love to Lesha Merley Hill, for your thoughtfulness, honesty, perspective, and for sharing all your knowledge about books.

Thank you, Addie Haler Burke, for your time in answering my questions and helping me with my research into the technical aspects of adoption in New York State.

Thank you, Barry O'Leary, for fact checking the legal and immigration aspects of this story and for your encouragement.

Many thanks to those who gave me their valuable time to answer questions and provide critiques, feedback, notes, and suggestions at various stages of writing: Jessica Alexander, Diana Baxter, Deborah Bial, Nicolle Brooks, Carlos Carela, Amy Denton-Clark, Sarah Rose Gregory, Jessica Jones, Maleeha Kirmani, Julian Lewyckyj, Tia O'Flaherty, Mariah Pizzano, Jen Rachman, Alexandra Rella, Justine Schettino, Nicola Waskett Bannister, and Emily Williams.

Thank you to the casts of *Real Housewives of New Jersey*, *New York City*, *Atlanta*, and *Beverly Hills* as well as to the cast of *Mob Wives*. I have never met any of you but I, like millions of other women, feel as if I know you. You have been a light during some of my darkest times.

Much of this book was inspired by my observations and experiences during the births of my sons in London and the many women and mothers I crossed paths with during my early years of motherhood. Thank you to them. Some are my friends to this day. Some are women I may have only met in passing, but with whom I shared a glance of mutual understanding. Some had a courage I have never seen, before or since, and their strength and their mothering in times of adversity is something I will never forget. Some were strangers, encountered in supermarkets and playgrounds, who showed me and my children great kindness, and sometimes, great disapproval. All are woven into my memory. All have stayed in my heart.

To my little boys, Leo and Rex, thank you for giving me so much material to work with. I hope one day you read this book and feel in its pages that you are the heartbeat of my life and that you always have been; that there are no words I could ever write to explain my love for you or for my gratitude that I am your mother.

Finally, to my husband Tim, my partner in all things. Thank you for your love; for making me laugh every day; for leaving your shoes by the door where they are right at this moment as I write this; for believing that I could write a book and making sure that I did. This book, our life – they are possible because of you.